The living hairs prickling. No one appeared at the top of the stairs to her right, yelling at her to get out, so she kept going.

She hoped Quincy was in the kitchen, where the food was. If not, she would have to think about exploring further. Quincy could be crouched inside an empty room, scared. For all his fierce bravado, he was a small animal, and vulnerable in so many ways. What if this household owned a pit bull? Or a mastiff? She almost whimpered aloud thinking about it.

Chase braced herself with a deep breath, inhaling another whiff of the delicious aroma, and peeked around the corner into the kitchen. Sure enough, Quincy sat on the counter, devouring the meatloaf. But what caught Chase's attention was the man, lying on his side on the floor beside some scraps of paper, his back to her. She knew him.

She breathed his name. "Gabe? Gabe?"

Quincy turned his head toward her and blinked his gorgeous amber eyes, then returned to his task.

Gabe must be injured, she thought. She knelt and shook his stiff shoulder. No response. She rolled him onto his back. Gasped. A steak knife was stuck in his chest. That couldn't be good! She reached toward the handle to pull out the knife, touched it, then hesitated, and started to draw her hand back.

A soft voice from the doorway said, "What have you done?"

The wooden floor planks creaked as she tiptoed across the living room. Chase flinched with each footfall, her hand on the railing. No one appeared at the top of the stairs.

FAT CAT
AT LARGE

Janet Cantrell

BERKLEY PRIME CRIME, NEW YORK

THE BERKLEY PUBLISHING GROUP
Published by the Penguin Group
Penguin Group (USA) LLC
375 Hudson Street, New York, New York 10014

USA • Canada • UK • Ireland • Australia • New Zealand • India • South Africa • China

penguin.com

A Penguin Random House Company

FAT CAT AT LARGE

A Berkley Prime Crime Book / published by arrangement with the author

Berkley Prime Crime Books are published by The Berkley Publishing Group.
BERKLEY® PRIME CRIME and the PRIME CRIME logo are trademarks of
Penguin Group (USA) LLC.

For information, address: The Berkley Publishing Group,
a division of Penguin Group (USA) LLC,
375 Hudson Street, New York, New York 10014.

ISBN: 978-0-425-26742-4

PUBLISHING HISTORY
Berkley Prime Crime mass-market edition / September 2014

PRINTED IN THE UNITED STATES OF AMERICA

10 9 8 7 6 5 4 3 2 1

Cover illustration by Dan Craig.
Interior text design by Kelly Lipovich.

*Dedicated to the late, great, mighty Agamemnon,
my inspiration for Quincy*

ACKNOWLEDGMENTS

I've had a great team of people reading and catching errors for me. Thanks to Barbara Moye, Gale Albright, and Kathy "Eagle Eye" Waller for helping out. Also, to early readers Daryl Wood Gerber, Janet Bolin, and Marilyn Levinson. Krista Davis, Janet Koch, and Peg Cochran are always in my corner. To Paula Benson and Kinli Bare Abee for reading and assistance. For information on bruxing, to Andrew MacCrae, who was the first to give me this guidance. To my wonderful agent, Kim Lionetti. To my editor, Danielle Stockley, whose ideas generated the Fat Cat Mysteries. To my family for putting up with my long hours, days, weeks, and months of writing. Hubby has done a LOT of dishes and laundry. To Jessica Busen for encouragement and assistance. To all of the Austin Mystery Writers for support and encouragement. My department in charge of cat food, KB Inglee and Bodge, has my sincere thanks, also my dessert bar tasters, the choir at Concord United Methodist Church, Knoxville, Tennessee. And to all the wonderful Guppies, without which I would never stick to it or have the courage to submit a thing.

I'll mention that I rearranged Dinkeytown a bit and

probably mentioned some businesses that aren't there any-more (and some that never were), so it's slightly made-up, but every single person is entirely made-up.

If I've fluffed anything, it's because I didn't heed advice, or just wrote it wrong.

ONE

The butterscotch tabby cat crouched in his soft-sided carrier in the strange room. His nose twitched. This place was full of the smell of fear. He hadn't eaten for two hours. Time for a decent meal. At least a snack. He clawed at the inside of the zipper. The top flap budged a bit. After he silently worked at it for a few more minutes, the flap opened far enough. Purring, he sprang out.

Charity Oliver jumped up from the plastic chair in the examining room and caught her cat. "Quincy! How did you escape?" She stroked him and he twisted his head to lick her hand.

"Here, let me, Ms. Oliver." Nice deep, rumbly voice, she thought. The veterinarian took the cat from her. His strong hands were warm. He cuddled Quincy, who began a steady purr.

"Please call me Chase, Dr. Ramos." Only Anna called

her Charity, after all, and hardly anyone called her Ms. Oliver.

Dr. Ramos set Quincy on the stainless steel examining table and fished his stethoscope out of his lab coat pocket. After sticking the earpieces into his ears, he bent his dark curls close to the cat to listen to his insides, then palpated Quincy's stomach.

Chase felt bad about the poking and prodding her little darling was enduring, but Quincy didn't seem to mind it. In fact, he licked the vet's hand.

This guy was no ancient fuddy-duddy vet, like the one in Chicago, she thought. The pictures on the pale blue walls were of angelic children and fluffy pets, not clinical diagrams. Her heart rate sped up a little as she twirled a strand of her straight, honey-blonde hair. He couldn't be much older than her own thirty-two. And not bad looking at all.

After the vet had taken Quincy's temperature and peeked into his ears and mouth, he lifted the cat onto the scale and frowned.

"Is he healthy?" she asked. "I wanted to get him checked, since we just moved here. I adopted him from a shelter. He was the smallest of the litter. Little stick legs, and that sweet tail—it stuck straight up. Someone had dropped them off on the beach." She shook her head. "I can't believe he's gotten this big. Isn't he handsome?" She was chattering. Like a ninny. She needed to stop chattering.

"You say he was found on a beach? Lake Calhoun?"

"Oh no, Lake Michigan. I got him when I was living in Chicago."

When the vet looked at her, she noticed his deep-set, coffee-brown eyes for the first time. They matched the little chocolate labs on his white coat. Except the little dogs couldn't give her that flutter inside.

"Where do you live now?" he asked.

"Here. Minneapolis. Dinkytown." There, that wasn't chattering.

Dr. Ramos straightened and stuck his stethoscope into his pocket. He rubbed his palms together with a papery sound. "He's a nice-looking shorthair, healthy for now. You need to make some changes, though. I'm afraid Quincy is far too fat for his small frame. Fifteen pounds is more than he should be carrying."

Okay, the vet wasn't *that* good looking. Quincy wasn't "far too fat." Was he?

Quincy meowed and batted at Dr. Ramos's elbow. Chase thought the cat was disagreeing, too.

"We'll have to put him on a diet," the vet continued, catching Quincy's paw and stroking it. "Is he an inside or outside cat?"

"Um, inside." Mostly inside. Except when he got out. Quincy was a clever escape artist.

"Good." He whipped out a prescription pad. "Here's what we'll need to feed him."

We?

"See that he doesn't eat anything else, other than a few treats. Is he used to eating twice a day or once?"

"Well, I leave his food out."

"Twice a day, to begin with. One-third cup per serving. I'll write the amount here. We take his bowl up when he's finished. Treats only once a day. That's written down, too."

"But he usually munches all day long. He doesn't eat that much."

"He'll get used to it."

Definitely not that good looking. Poor Quincy! "He won't like that."

Dr. Ramos gave her a stern frown. His eyes were more of a hardwood-brown than coffee. "Do you want a diabetic cat?"

Who did he think he was? Her sixth-grade teacher?

She raised her chin in defiance. "I'll see what *we* can do."

The vet turned to go. "Bring him back in two weeks. I want to see his weight down by at least a pound."

Chase pulled her little Ford Fusion into the slot behind the Bar None and carried Quincy up the wooden steps to her second-floor apartment. She set him, in his carrier, on her kitchen counter and returned down the inside staircase to fetch the bags of cat food she'd bought on the way home.

She stopped beside her car and closed her eyes, turning her face up to soak in the late summer warmth. This last week of August, the temperatures were already dropping a bit, but the sun still put out heat. The leaves of the small trees at the edge of the alley parking area riffled in the slight breeze. The trees were green, but the autumn blaze of color would begin soon. A few marshmallow-fluff clouds drifted in the impossibly blue Minnesota sky.

Chase brought the bags in through the back door of the Bar None, where Quincy spent his days, plumped them down on the granite counter, scooped out enough food for tonight, then hurried upstairs. She was expecting her business partner, Anna, and her best friend, Julie, for dinner, and to sample a new recipe Anna was trying out.

After releasing Quincy, she mixed up a salad and put sandwiches together. The women would eat the minimal meal in haste, then start sampling dessert bars.

Anna Larson, Chase's business partner and so much more, arrived first, tripping lightly up the stairs.

"You amaze me, Anna," said Chase as Anna hung her brilliant blue sweater on the hook by the door. "My stairs don't bother you a bit, do they?"

Anna gave a short laugh. She was the age to be Chase's grandmother, early seventies, yet she ran up the stairs as easily as Chase, or more so. She wore blue jeans, sneakers, and plain T-shirts, but loved topping her outfits off with sweaters in various shades of blue. Today's was adorned with yellow chrysanthemums.

"I thought we should try these. Pineapple Walnut Dream Bars." Anna spread a printout on the counter. "I cobbled this recipe together from a couple of others we've done in the past."

Quincy came into the kitchen to greet Anna. He rubbed against her blue jeans until she picked him up and rubbed his round tummy. "Who's a good boy?" she asked. "Who's a cuddlekins?"

Quincy purred that, obviously, *he* was the good boy and the cuddlekins.

Chase picked up his empty ceramic bowl from the floor and rinsed it out, then filled it with precisely one-third of a cup of mixed cat food, half new and half old. The woman at the pet store had told her to mix the two for a few days.

After Anna set him down, he cautiously approached his bowl and sniffed. He gave his mistress a baleful stare with his amber eyes, then picked at the food.

"It'll be okay, Quince," said Chase, softly. "You'll get used to it."

Was that a doubtful expression she got from him? He let out a howl.

"What's wrong with Quincy?" Anna snatched him up.

"He's on a diet. He doesn't like it."

"That's right, you went to the vet today. Shall I give him a treat?"

"Only once a day, the doc said."

Anna widened her eyes in horror. "Once a day? I give him num nums all day long."

"That may be our problem."

Anna grabbed a handful of his usual treats and fed them to the cat. "He's starving."

"He's not starving. We're supposed to use—" She looked for the new treat box, but she'd left it downstairs. And now she was saying *we*. "He has special treats now. Dr. Ramos says he's too fat."

"Quincy is large-boned. You tell that to this Dr. Ramos."

Julie, Anna's granddaughter and Chase's best friend since childhood, arrived and the three women sat down to their meal.

The dessert trial went well. All three agreed that Pineapple Walnut Dream Bars should be sold at the dessert bar shop co-owned by Chase and Anna.

"But the name is cumbersome," Chase said. "Besides, we have several called Dream Bars already."

"How about Hula Bars?" Julie asked. "The pineapple and the coconut taste like something Hawaiian."

Anna snapped her fingers. "Yes! That's it. I'll call them Hula Bars."

The shop and Chase's snug apartment above it were located on the fringes of the University of Minnesota, in an area of Minneapolis called Dinkytown. It was a small neighborhood with wide sidewalks and its own distinct, comfy, homey aura. Chase and Anna wouldn't have thought of locating anywhere else. Not only because of the location, but because the property had been in Anna's family for three generations, first as a jewelry store, then as a sandwich restaurant, and now as the Bar None.

"These are every bit as good as the raspberry ones." Julie finished her last bite and dusted powdered sugar from her fingers.

"Take the rest home, Julie," said Chase. The sweetness, offset by the dusky walnut taste, lingered in her mouth. "They're in a plastic box on the counter inside."

The women sat sipping lemongrass tea on Chase's balcony. The temperature had dropped with the sun and they were wrapped in sweaters.

"We won't be able to sit out here in another month or so," Julie said. Chase's best friend bore a family resemblance to Anna, her grandmother. Both women were shorter than Chase's five six and they had the same periwinkle-blue eyes. Anna's short bob was gray, while Julie's was still dark brown, since she was exactly Chase's age.

Chase warmed her fingers on her mug as a gust of brisk air hurtled down the street. "We almost can't sit here tonight. I wonder if we're getting a cold snap."

"I'll stop by the grocery store on my way in tomorrow morning," Anna said, "to pick up coconut extract and some dried pineapple. I think we have everything else in the shop for the new recipe."

The plastic bin of Hula Bars lay on the counter, unguarded. The kitchen, indeed the whole apartment, smelled like goodness. The sweet scent tickled the nose of the hungry cat. He wondered why the food and the snacks were so poor lately. Following the enticing odor, he jumped up and explored the countertop. It was no problem to bat the container to the floor, where the lid popped off and the contents were strewed across the tiles.

"I'm going to have another half cup," Chase said, rising. "Anybody want more?"

She saw them both shake their bobbed heads in the dark, lit only by the light spilling from the living room French doors. They were two warm, wonderful friends and she loved them both.

When she got to the kitchen, she spied the remains of Anna's creation on the floor and let out a squeal. Quincy had polished off at least two of the cookie bars. The cat glanced up, blinked, and sauntered away to clean his whiskers.

"What am I going to do with you, Fat Cat?" She picked up the mangled treats and dumped them in the trash. "Sorry, Julie," she called. "Quincy ruined them. You can pick some up at the shop tomorrow." She cuddled her cat for a moment. She didn't want him to feel bad. He was bound to be ravenous until his weight went down.

After Anna and Julie departed, Chase poured a glass of pinot noir and rested her feet on the hassock in front of her favorite stuffed chair. She loved her living room every bit as much as her shop. It was decorated in mocha and cinnamon tones, with the soft leather couch being her big splurge. Framed Impressionist prints she'd picked up at the Art Institute of Chicago—the one place in Chicago she missed—graced the walls. She braced as Quincy pounced into her lap, his purr motor on high. Had he gained a pound already?

Laci Carlson, one of the two sales counter helpers at the Bar None, stared at the bags on Quincy's shelf in the shop kitchen. "Quincy isn't out of cat food. Why did you buy so much more?" Laci, who had recently graduated from high school, was petite and delicate, with huge sky-blue eyes, and insisted on curling her long, naturally straight hair every night. By now, early afternoon, it was beginning to lose the curl.

The cat being discussed was safely latched in the office, where he spent his days during business hours. "He's on a diet," Chase said. "Do you think he's all that fat?"

The other salesgirl burst into the kitchen from the front. "There you are." She stabbed a long, thin finger at Laci. "Have I not told you a dozen times to put the checks *under* the twenties? And to write down the driver's license and phone number?"

Laci wilted a bit before the taller woman. "I forgot,

Violet." She fingered the edge of her Bar None smock. The identical smocks, mulberry-colored and edged with pink rickrack, had been embroidered with the Bar None name and logo by a friend of Anna's named Willow Vanderling, who lived in Pennsylvania. On the two women, they seemed like completely different garments. Vi's looked sleek on her taller, more elegant frame, and the first thing you noticed about Laci's was the trim, the color picked up by her pink blouse with frothy white lace edging. She favored frilly pastel tops with pearl buttons at the cuffs.

"I'll handle this, Vi," Chase said to the tall, self-assured woman.

Violet huffed and turned toward the salesroom.

"You really do have to—" began Chase.

"I know, I know. Violet just makes me so nervous. I'd rather work when she's not here. It's so nice and peaceful when she goes on break."

"We'll go back to the old schedule next week, but I need both of you now. You know how many dessert bars we sell to the parents when students are moving onto campus."

Laci slunk through the swinging double doors to the front, the salesroom. Chase, alone now in her kitchen, reached for one of her large stainless mixing bowls and got down bins of brown sugar, flour, and baking powder from the open shelves that lined one wall of the no-nonsense kitchen. She stuck the conglomeration under her commercial mixer, set it whirring, and opened the refrigerator to pull out the shortbread base she had baked yesterday for Cherry Cheesecake Dream Bars, one of their specialties.

Anna Larson came through the back door while Chase was breaking eggs into a smaller bowl.

"Is that Doris Naughtly's Beemer I saw out front?" asked Anna.

"If it is, I won't stop her from shopping with us, Anna."

"I know she spends plenty of money here," said Anna,

"but I still wish she'd take her business elsewhere." Her frown made it clear that Doris's car being in front didn't make her happy.

Chase knew a little about their old feud, but would like to get the whole story. She made a mental note to work on that one day soon, then started mixing in the eggs. "Can I help you carry anything?"

"Could you bring the sodas in from my car? I'll take over your mixing. What is it?"

"Cherry Cheesecake Dream Bars. I'll get one of the girls to help me carry them."

Anna bought several cases of soda every week. The college kids liked carbonated drinks with their sweet treats.

Chase pushed through the swinging doors. She loved the front of the shop. The décor had been left up to her and she was pleased with the way it had turned out. The walls, striped with the colors of raspberry and vanilla, stood behind low shelves painted cotton candy–pink. The glass display case glowed from the lights within, illuminating trays of Lemon Bars, gooey Oatmeal Raspberry Jam Bars, and a colorful array of other flavors, from pink lemonade to margarita cheesecake.

There were several customers in the shop, but only one was ready to buy. Doris Naughtly stood before the glass case, one hand on her hip, the other waving her diamonds at the tray of Lemon Bars. Violet was waiting on her, so Chase looked around for Laci to come help her unload. She found her behind a tall display of boxed treats on a table near the front talking to Ted Naughtly, their heads close together.

That romance seemed to be heating up. Ted, Doris's son, seemed like a nice enough kid, but had been sent home from Purdue in December, the middle of his sophomore year. His father, the owner of the second-floor donut shop a few doors away on Fourteenth Street, railed to all who would listen that the grading was probably unfair, the professors must have had it in for his kid. Flunking out didn't seem to bother Ted nearly as much as it did his father.

"Don't you want some Peanut Butter Fudge Bars for your husband, Mrs. Naughtly?" Violet asked.

That girl was a crack saleswoman. Chase was so glad she worked in the Bar None.

Chase turned to look at Doris before she followed Laci into the kitchen. Doris hadn't answered. The woman had a sour expression on her perfectly made-up face. She pursed her lined lips for a moment. "We are no longer together."

"Oh," Violet breathed. Chase raised her eyebrows, startled. When did that happen? she wondered. She wanted to stay and hear the whole story, but it would seem odd—and nosy—since she was mostly through the doorway. She'd get the scoop from Violet later.

Or . . . maybe she could get it from Laci now. They went to the parking place behind the store and each lifted a case of soda from the trunk of Anna's robin's-egg-blue Volvo.

"What's going on with the Naughtlys?" Chase tried to sound casual.

"Why? What did you hear?" Laci's blue eyes grew even larger than usual.

"I just heard Doris say that she and Gabe are no longer together."

"Oooh!" The young woman wailed. She gripped the case of cans, squeezed her eyes shut, and let her sudden tears splash onto the cardboard, leaving damp splotches.

"Oh dear." Chase set her case down and took Laci's. "What is it?"

Laci sniffled. "It's been so hard on Teddy. He's so heartbroken."

He hadn't looked heartbroken to Chase. He had looked very interested in what was inside Laci's frilly blouse.

Chase was sorry she'd asked. The girl was so overly emotional.

"Maybe they'll get back together. They've been married an awfully long time."

Laci shook her head, mutely, taking the cardboard case from her, still weeping. "They're getting a di-divorce."

"Let's go in. You can go to my office for a bit to compose yourself if you need to."

She nodded. "I suppose Ted's gone by now anyway."

Chase counted to three. "If you'd rather talk to Ted, go do that instead." Chase shifted her case and took a tissue from her pocket. "Here, dry your face."

Laci stared at the crumpled tissue.

"I haven't used it. I stuffed it in my pocket this morning." Chase thrust it at her.

"I have some," Laci said, and proceeded into the shop.

Chase counted to twenty this time. Laci and Violet were by far the best candidates she and Anna had interviewed six months ago when they opened up. Maybe someone new needed a job by now. Who was she kidding? She knew she wouldn't fire the girl. After the humiliation of being let go from not one, not two, but four jobs in Chicago, she'd never do that to anyone else. Either Anna would have to fire her or Laci would have to quit.

Chase came in the door, left open by Laci. Quincy padded in behind her.

Anna let out a stifled scream and pointed at the cat. "A mouse," she whispered, so the customers wouldn't hear her.

"Oh, Quince. He must have run out when we opened the door."

"But how did he get out of the office?" rasped Anna.

"How does he ever get out? I wish I knew."

She chased the cat around the prep island and succeeded in cornering him. The mouse was, luckily, dead. After she persuaded Quincy to drop it, Chase picked it up with about thirty paper towels and took it out to the industrial-size trash bin, being careful to keep the cat inside the kitchen.

When Chase reentered, Anna had redeposited Quincy in the office. Chase wondered what she'd given him to eat. Anna was adding the coconut extract and nuts to the eggs and brown sugar for the batch of Hula Bars she had just started.

"You want me to finish them up and you can go out front?" asked Chase, scrubbing her hands with a stiff brush at the deep sink against the outside wall.

"Absolutely not. I have no desire to come into contact with—"

The tinkle of the chimes on the front door was followed by a booming voice. "Well, well, well. Here's the happy family."

Anna groaned. "Not Gabe!"

He didn't come in often, mostly because his wife brought him his favorites, the Peanut Butter Fudge Bars Violet had suggested. Maybe, thought Chase, he's come to buy them for himself since they're splitting up.

She rushed out front. Gabe Naughtly blocked the way of his wife and son as they were trying to get out the door.

"What's your hurry?" His rotund body produced a lot of sound. His gravelly voice filled the little room.

"Mr. Naughtly, can I help you?" Chase hurried to the trio.

The man swiveled his mostly bald head in her direction. "Hold your horses. I just got here."

Chase saw that Violet was packaging six of Gabe Naughtly's favorites.

"Gabe, leave me alone." Doris looked distressed. Ted tried to look bored, but concern showed on his face, through the three-day stubble he'd cultivated. He was much taller than his little round father but, even at his young age, was tending toward beefiness.

To Chase's surprise, Gabe stepped aside to let his wife leave. Doris lifted her head and managed an air of aplomb as she swept past him. Ted threw his father an intense stare that Chase thought looked hostile.

Gabe stood frowning after them for a few seconds. Then he stumped across the wooden floor to the counter. "I'll have a half dozen of those." He poked his finger at his usual, leaving a smudge on the glass.

"All set," said Violet, hoisting the white paper bag printed with the Bar None name and logo, a cookie bar beside a fat ring striped in dark red and pink.

"Has the health inspector been here?" he asked Chase.

Health inspector? Again? "No. He was completely satisfied last time you sicced him on us. Why would he be back?"

"I told him about the rats behind your store."

"What rats? The ones you put there? The white ones you bought from the pet store like last time?"

"Ha. Very funny. You won't be laughing when they close you down. The rats might be indoors next time."

"I'm not laughing now." Chase felt her face turning bright red, her heart racing. She clenched her fists to keep from punching him. The man was an absolute pig. "Vi, don't sell those to this man. Gabe Naughtly, leave my shop. Don't come here again."

"Over my dead body."

"If that's what it takes."

She felt Vi and Laci's amazed expressions at her implied threat. Gabe's glare was just plain mean.

"You'll see," he said as he stomped out.

Vi silently set the paper bag below the counter. Laci got busy rearranging the prepackaged treat boxes. Chase stalked toward the kitchen, but Anna stood with one of the swinging doors open.

"I heard everything," she said. "Don't worry, the health department won't close us."

Chase collapsed onto a stool, starting to shake as her adrenaline rush let up. "What if he puts rats inside, instead of in the alley?"

"Quincy would catch them," said Anna.

"But what if a customer saw one? He might do it, you know. That would be the end of us."

Anna stroked her hair. "He can't do anything to us, sweetheart. The business is going well, we're making a profit already, months ahead of our schedule. I even heard two women talking about our Toffee Bars in the drugstore yesterday."

"I don't know why he wants this location so bad." Chase leaned her head into Anna's body.

"Probably because we're doing so well, Charity. He's probably picking on us because we're the newest business in the area and he figures we'd be the easiest for him to dislodge. He's wanted to relocate from the second story for a long time. I know he's approached other business owners about buying their properties. Trouble is, he doesn't have the money to do it."

Anna's hand on her head soothed Chase. She started to relax.

"But he sounded serious. I'm afraid he'll do something awful to close us down."

"How could he? Why don't you take a walk to work off some of your negative energy."

Anna was right, Chase told herself. He couldn't shut them down. Could he?

TWO

Laci and Violet had just left and Anna pulled down the front shade with the words "Bar None—Closed" on the other side. It had been a busy, profitable day.

Chase gave Anna a high five as she turned. "We did it again."

Anna's smile gave Chase a needed lift. She loved how the skin around her eyes crinkled, kind of like the way butter topping will crisp up on the top of a cookie bar. Anna was the sweetest person she knew. After her parents had died in a small plane crash, Anna Larson had taken her in, per her parents' will. After all, Anna had raised Chase's mother.

A knock sounded on the closed and shuttered front door.

"That's Julie," said Anna, moving the shade aside to check.

"I came for my Hula Bars," Julie said. "Did you make some today?"

"I did," Anna said, "and we sold most of them. Let me

see if there are any more." They both followed Anna into the kitchen, where Chase needed to finish the cleanup.

"Laci and Violet are outside arguing," said Julie. "Did you know that?"

Chase and Anna sighed in unison. Chase freed Quincy from the office. He jumped up with all the grace of an Olympic gymnast and patrolled the counters for leftover crumbs, pointedly ignoring his mistress. It was his nightly routine. Chase had her own routine, as a result, disinfecting the countertops last thing every day.

"Those two," said Anna. She rummaged through the refrigerator for the leftover Hula Bars.

"They were at it today," said Chase.

"I hope you realize that we can't continue to have them working here together," Anna said. "I'd like to replace Laci, but then we'd have to go through the whole hiring process again."

"That was torture, wasn't it?" Chase said. "There were so many unsuitable applicants. You really think we should let Laci go?"

"I'd like to see that," said Julie. "You can't stand to fire anyone. You told me so yourself."

It was true that Chase was a natural born peacemaker. She disliked confrontation immensely. But Chase also didn't want Anna making all the decisions, since they were partners. After all, Anna was the one who had picked Laci and Vi to hire. Chase just knew that she couldn't fire either of them.

Chase shook her head. "Yah, you're right." Then she brightened. "Hey, I have some dirt on the Naughtlys. They're splitting."

"Wow," said Julie. "What's he going to do without all her money?"

Anna, who had been bending low, straightened up. "They were both in here today and—"

"Anna," shouted Chase. "What were you doing?"

Anna's eyes widened in innocence. "I wasn't doing anything."

"You slipped a cookie bar to Quincy."

"Only one. Here are some of the new bars." Anna put them in a bag and gave them to Julie. Then she hefted the garbage sack out of the wastebasket and headed to the back door.

"What's going on?" asked Julie. She climbed onto one of the stools at the work counter and Chase sat beside her. After Julie had graduated from law school, she'd taken a job in the district attorney's office. Chase was so proud of her for getting through law school and landing a good job.

"I did something awful today." Chase studied her lap.

"It couldn't be that bad." Julie ducked to see her friend's face.

Chase raised her head. "I got into an argument with Gabe in front of my staff and some customers."

"It's not the first time, is it?" Julie grinned. "He's not your best friend."

"No, he's not." Chase smiled at Julie and gave her friend a fake punch in the arm.

"I made her walk around the parking lot a few times to cool off afterward," Anna said, returning from taking out the trash.

"It did make me feel . . . a little better."

"But I meant, what's the big deal with Quincy?" Julie said.

Chase told her all about the visit to the vet and Quincy's new regimen, since they hadn't discussed it last night.

"I hear Dr. Ramos is kinda hot," Julie said.

"I thought so at first, Jules. But he's mean, putting Quince on such a tiny amount of food. Look at him. See how hungry he is?"

Julie swiveled her head left, then right. "Where is he?"

"Oh brother." Chase ran out of the shop to the alley. All she caught was a glimpse of his fluffy tail, disappearing around the corner at the end of the block.

She pounded down the alley, her heart racing, but couldn't see him when she reached the corner.

"He's gone!" she shouted. "I can't find him!"

Julie and Anna both came running.

"He's never gone beyond the alley," Chase said. "That's a little worrisome."

"We'll get him," Anna said. "Julie, you go left. Chase, you go right. I'll cross the street."

Chase rounded the corner and circled the block, peering into every doorway and nook and cranny, inspecting the branches of the small trees that grew in the round sidewalk cutouts, eventually coming to the front of her own shop. Laci and Violet were still there, glaring at each other.

Violet noticed her first. "What are you doing? Did you lose something?"

"Yes." Chase fought to keep her voice from quavering. "Quincy got out. I don't know where he went."

"He'll come home, won't he?" Vi asked.

"I'm not sure. He's mad at me about the diet."

"We'll help," said Laci. "I'll search across this street."

"Vi, could you watch the back entrance in case he returns? I don't want to leave it standing open." She pictured Gabe crouched in the alley waiting for his chance.

"Sure thing."

The two young women bustled off, calling Quincy's name and peering into window wells and doorways, as Chase had been doing.

She continued up the block, coming to the next corner. Quincy had gotten out many times in the past, but had never gone beyond the end of the alley. He usually hung around the

large trash bin, hoping to snag a warm rodent. That cat's
tummy was never full. Where would he go? Would he get lost?

The cat strode along the tree-lined street. Cooking smells
wafted out of the houses and condos. The strong odor of
meatloaf drew him to one of the buildings. The smell was
stronger here because the front door was slightly ajar. That
was no problem for the butterscotch cat. He hooked a claw
around the bottom edge of the door and inched it open wide
enough to admit him. The smell of meat intensified here. He
rolled in some paper scraps on the floor, but that wasn't it.
Up there, on the counter. That was his goal. There was
another smell, but he ignored that one and jumped over the
object sprawled on the floor to get onto the counter.

At the end of the block, Chase looked across the street
to see Laci canvassing the stores and businesses, her huge
tote bag slung over her slender shoulder. Vi carried one
similar, but it had a different shape to it. Violet's was more
square, so Chase was sure she was seeing Laci. Chase
decided to continue into the next block. Everyone else had
this one covered. All the buildings on this block were businesses, some with living quarters above like hers, with stair-
ways in the rear.

A block away, the shops ended and condos sprang up
with a few nice houses sprinkled in among them. Chase
made her way slowly down the street, calling Quincy's name
every five yards.

There were more trees here, bigger ones. Dusk was starting
to fall and she was afraid they wouldn't find him tonight. He
might be stuck in a huge maple or nestled in the branches of
a gnarled oak. Not a soul strolled the sidewalk besides Chase.

At the second set of duplex condos, she saw a door

standing ajar to the unit on the left. Had Quincy gotten this far? Would he go inside a stranger's home? He didn't seem to be anywhere else.

Chase climbed the six steps, not making a sound, and searched for a doorbell, but didn't find one, so she pushed the door. It opened into a bare, unfurnished living room. The room was dark, but she saw light coming from the kitchen around the corner. All she could see from the front of the apartment was the refrigerator. She stopped, unsure of herself. This sure felt like trespassing.

Still, Quincy might be in there. The smell of meatloaf was strong.

"Quincy?" She said his name softly, hoping not to attract the attention of whoever lived here and whose property she was invading. The air felt dead, like the dwelling was empty.

The wooden floor planks creaked as she tiptoed across the living room. Chase flinched with each footfall, her nape hairs prickling. No one appeared at the top of the stairs to her right, yelling at her to get out, so she kept going.

She hoped Quincy was in the kitchen, where the food was. If not, she would have to think about exploring further. Quincy could be crouched inside an empty room, scared. For all his fierce bravado, he was a small animal, and vulnerable in so many ways. What if this household owned a pit bull? Or a mastiff? She almost whimpered aloud thinking about it.

Chase braced herself with a deep breath, inhaling another whiff of the delicious aroma, and peeked around the corner, into the kitchen. Sure enough, Quincy sat on the counter, devouring the meatloaf. But what caught her attention was the man, lying on his side on the floor beside some scraps of paper, his back to her. She knew him.

She breathed his name. "Gabe? Gabe?"

Quincy turned his head toward her and blinked his gorgeous amber eyes, then returned to his task.

Gabe must be injured, she thought. She knelt and shook his stiff shoulder. No response. She rolled him onto his back. Gasped. A steak knife was stuck in his chest. That couldn't be good! She reached toward the handle to pull out the knife, touched it, then hesitated and started to draw her hand back.

A soft voice from the doorway said, "What have you done?"

THREE

Chase dropped her outstretched hand to her side and spun toward the unknown man. He was middle-aged and had a preppy look, khakis, blazer over a polo shirt, sockless dock shoes.

"Should we pull the knife out?" she said. "He's not bleeding much. Maybe we should."

"You probably should have wiped your prints off and thrown it away before I caught you."

Chase rose and the guy took a step backward. "We need to call nine one one," she said.

"Why did you kill him?"

Now Chase took a step back. "Kill him? Is he dead? Why would I kill Gabe? "

Her mind raced. She had reason enough to kill him. This man thought she had. Her prints, as he said, were on the steak knife that obviously had killed him.

"Who are you?" she asked.

"Torvald Iversen. I'd shake your hand, but it's bloody."

Chase inspected her right hand. He was right again. "Then you call nine one one. What if he's alive?"

Torvald stepped around her and felt for a neck pulse. He gave her a dark scowl, then punched the three numbers into his phone. The man went out the front way to talk to the dispatcher, leaving Chase with the body . . . and her cat, still chowing down.

"Quincy, how could you?" She wiped her hand on a paper towel and stuck it in her pocket before she lifted her cat off the counter and nuzzled her face against his warm head. To her relief, he didn't try to return to his feast. He might be full, she thought. Half of it was gone. She chanced another glance at Gabe, but he hadn't moved. He had to be dead.

Being careful to avoid the body and the surrounding pool of blood, she followed Torvald Iversen onto the porch. He was slipping his phone into his pocket. "You're to stay here, not leave," he said.

This guy was annoying her. "Says who?"

"Says the dispatcher I just spoke to." His voice was quiet, but smoky, in a creepy sort of way.

"And I suppose you're free to go?"

He sneered, but halfheartedly.

"I thought not." Chase, being a better person, did not return the sneer. "I have to get my cat home." That sounded lame as soon as she said it. But what was she going to do with him while being questioned by the police? "Who are you?"

As the ambulance pulled up, lights and sirens at full speed, Quincy tensed in her arms. Chase tightened her grip and returned to the living room to shield him from the commotion a bit. The door, however, was standing wide-open and the noise made it into the living room just fine.

Her face buried in Quincy's soft, orange fur, she felt tears begin. Then her hands started shaking, which alarmed Quincy even more. This was the second encounter with

Gabe that had ended up with her shaking and distraught. But it would be the last. Deep inside, a small blossom of relief opened. He wouldn't release a rat in her store. He wouldn't report her to the health department (unless he already had). And he wouldn't shut her down.

"What were you doing here, anyway?" She jumped. That man, Torvald, had come up behind her.

She hoped she hadn't spoken any of her thoughts aloud. "Chasing my cat. He ran away and snuck in here."

"He knows how to open doors?"

Two uniformed men, and one woman, ran past them into the kitchen.

"What are *you* doing here?" she asked Torvald.

"I had a business meeting scheduled with Mr. Naughtly."

She wondered why he didn't buy his donuts during business hours like everyone else. "It looks like he was ready to eat dinner."

"It was a dinner meeting."

A warm, familiar voice came from the doorway. "Chase? What's the commotion?"

"Dr. Ramos! Am I ever glad to see you."

"I was on my way to the drugstore when I saw the vehicles on the street. Is Gabe okay?"

"You know Gabe?" Did everyone know him?

Dr. Ramos gestured to the south. "I live two condos away. What's happened? Are you feeling all right?" He must have noticed the tears on her face.

Torvald Iversen cleared his throat. "I arrived and found her pulling out the knife she stabbed Gabe Naughtly with."

Chase whirled toward him. "That's not true!" Quincy tightened his claws on her sweater.

A policeman with a deep five-o'clock shadow joined the group. "Who found the body? The call said someone named Iversen?"

"No, I found him," said Chase. Her cat squirmed.

"Why don't I take Quincy to my place until you're done here." Dr. Ramos took control of Quincy and, after assuring the policeman that he'd just arrived, walked down the stairs and into the night. Chase was sad to see the only friendly face disappear.

An hour later, after she told the policeman what happened, and after a detective arrived and she related everything three more times, she started walking toward home. She wondered how she would find Quincy and Dr. Ramos, but he hailed her from his screened-in front porch, two houses down.

Ten minutes later, ensconced in a recliner of fake—but very nice fake—leather, wrapped in an afghan, and sipping hot chocolate, Chase had almost finished going over the events of the afternoon to Dr. Ramos, who urged her to call him Mike.

"I told the exact same story to the policeman and to the detective, who showed up after you went home. That awful man, Torvald Iversen, kept interrupting and contradicting me the whole time we were questioned by the police officer, but the detective took us into upstairs rooms and talked to us separately. That man thinks I killed Gabe Naughtly!"

"You're shaking again." Mike hiked the afghan up her shoulder where it had slipped off.

She wasn't shivering from cold, but it felt nice to have Mike Ramos fuss over her like that. What she was shivering from was harder to get over than cold.

"Do you think they'll believe him?"

"I imagine they'll check everything out. Lots of people must have seen you outside, trying to find Quincy."

The cat caught the sound of his name and picked his head up off Chase's lap. She wasn't so sure lots of people had seen her. The five of them had separated—she, Anna, Julie, and Laci to search and Vi to guard the back door. She hadn't seen anyone on this street before she reached the condo.

The chirrup of Chase's phone sent Quincy shooting to the floor. He leaped into Mike's lap.

"See how he moves?" she said, digging her cell out of her pocket. "So graceful? He's not all that fat."

She ignored his frown and answered her phone. She had let the other dozen or so calls in the last couple of hours go unanswered.

"Where on earth are you?" Anna asked. "We've been worried sick." Anna sounded on the verge of tears.

"I'm okay and Quincy's okay." She heard Anna let out a long breath. "It's a long story. I'll be home in a few minutes. Is that where you are?"

"Yes, we're at your place. We've been going door-to-door trying to find you two. There's something happening at one of the condos up the street, too."

"Yah, that's where I've been. I'll tell you all about it."

Mike asked if she'd like a ride after she ended the call, but she thought the walk would be good to clear her head.

It was nice to be alone for a few minutes before answering still more questions. Quincy snuggled his head into her neck with his paws over her shoulder for the short trip. His long whiskers brushed her neck. Night had fallen. The tree-lined residential street was dark and quiet. The vehicles with flashing lights had departed. A crime scene van waited outside Gabe's place, but its engine was turned off. She took her time covering the two blocks to her place. The business district of Dinkytown at nearly ten o'clock was more brightly lit than the blocks to the north, bustling with returning college students and, this week, some families.

She headed up the stairs in the rear of the building and found Anna and Julie inside her apartment. Anna grabbed Quincy and Julie hugged Chase, then they traded. When everyone had been hugged, Chase scrubbed her hands with water as hot as she could stand it. She kept imagining she could detect traces of blood, but Anna pronounced them clean. Chase accepted a cup of cranberry herb tea and settled into her chair with her feet on the hassock.

"Where are Laci and Violet?" she asked.

"We sent them home after an hour of searching," Anna said. "They both looked dead tired. Young women have no stamina these days."

Chase knew she herself couldn't keep up with Anna and wasn't surprised that her two employees had the same failing.

"I'm not sure yet," Anna said, "but we might have an accounting problem."

Accounting problem? Chase was the one who did the books. "What sort of accounting problem?"

"I'll have to go over what I think I saw again. I don't want to worry you for nothing. Just thought I'd mention it. Now tell us what's going on."

When Chase had told them everything she knew—that Gabe was dead, that Torvald Iversen was a jerk, and that Dr. Ramos was now Mike and, on second thought, fairly good looking—she remembered she hadn't finished the cleanup in the shop. Quincy crawled into his cat bed and gave his collar a good scratching while she talked.

"I'll go, you sit," said Anna.

Julie sat on the floor beside the cat's bed and patted her lap. Quincy left off scratching and accepted the invitation.

"I have to go downstairs to get a scoop of diet food for Quincy anyway. It won't take but a few minutes."

Anna protested, but let Chase leave.

Chase flicked the light switch at the top of the stairway and made her way down to her shop. She didn't have to exit to the alley, since there was a door into the shop at the bottom of her steps. This door was rarely locked, but it was tonight. Vi had been guarding the alley entrance to the shop. Maybe she had locked everything when she'd left.

After Chase ran back up the stairs to get the key she

hadn't brought with her, she noticed that Quincy was crouched on the kitchen counter and Anna was holding something behind her.

She's slipping him treats again, Chase thought. She'd deal with that later.

She ran down the steps again and opened the door into the dark kitchen.

Two dots of light glowed red in the light that came into the rear window from the parking lot streetlamp. The dots were near the floor. Chase stopped, puzzled. She saw another pair of glowing embers, then another.

She switched on the light and three huge white rats scurried out of the kitchen, pushing through the doors into the showroom.

Swallowing a scream, she stomped the floor, trying to flatten an imaginary Gabe Naughtly to a pancake. She let out some choice words aimed at the man, then stood still, remembering he was dead. Murdered.

Julie and Anna both clattered down the stairs in response to her stomps.

"Now what?" Anna and Julie could see the rage on her face, she was sure.

"Rats." She pointed at the swinging doors.

FOUR

Julie and Anna stood frozen in the doorway from the apartment stairs into the shop.

"There are rats in there," Chase said, staring into the kitchen. Her body vibrated with anger. "Three of them, at least."

"How do you know, Charity? Did you hear them?"

She assured both women she'd seen them. They believed her when one poked a head into the kitchen, whiskers twitching. Chase saw some of Quincy's cat food scattered on the floor. The bag sat on its customary shelf. Someone must have strewn the food on the floor to keep the rats where she would be sure to come upon them immediately.

"Look," said Julie, pointing to the corner. "Whoever put the rats here left their cage."

"I guess we could lure them into it with Quincy's food. That's what they've been eating. I'm glad somebody likes it."

"I have a better way." Anna opened the cleaning closet. She pulled out the large bucket they used for mopping the floors. She swept up the food on the floor and dumped it into the bucket, adding another scoop for good measure. Then she removed a rack from the oven and propped it against the bucket with a ringing sound.

"Now we go away for a bit," Anna said.

When they returned, half an hour later, the tall bucket held three large white rats and one black and white one. The food was gone and the rats seemed lazy and content, not at all distressed by the steep, unclimbable sides that confined them.

"What's that little clatter noise?" asked Chase.

"It's called bruxing," Anna said. "That black-and-white one is chattering his teeth together."

"Is he mad?"

"He's probably content. It's usually a happy sound. They're obviously from a pet store. I'll see how tame they are." Anna bravely stuck a hand into the bucket. One rat sniffed her fingers. She picked it up and put it into the cage.

"Aw, he's so nice and soft," Anna murmured.

Chase was impressed. "This is a skill I didn't know you had, Anna. Where did you learn to handle rats?"

"One summer in college, I worked in the science lab. These are tamer than those were, by a long shot."

When all four were contained, Anna said she'd take them to the pet store on the next block over tomorrow morning.

Chase had dreams all night long of swirling, flashing lights, dead bodies rolling over, rats climbing her kitchen counters, and her own bloody hands. Morning took forever to arrive.

As she showered, she began to wonder when Gabe could have put the rats inside. How long had he been dead when she found him? His shoulder wasn't warm when she touched it. His body was starting to stiffen. Didn't that mean he'd been dead more than a few minutes?

So how could Gabe have done it? The rats were put there

while everyone was searching for Quincy. Gabe had to have been dead at that time. Who else hated Chase—or Anna—or the shop—enough to commit such horrible sabotage?

Early Wednesday, Chase got her bike out and took a turn around Dinkytown. Since they were so busy at work this week, she was missing Chase Time, some moments to unwind by herself and get some sorely needed exercise. Standing in a kitchen or hunched over a computer were the opposite of exercise.

She pedaled out of the large parking area behind her store, past the trash bin where Gabe had once planted the other rats. Since the rodents had been released this time inside her store, she expected a visit from the health department. The oven could probably use cleaning, especially the rack Anna had used to trap the rats, but everything else was neat as apple pie. Anna always saw to that. She and her husband, when he was still alive, had run the sandwich shop where the Bar None now did business. After his death at the early age of sixty-eight, she had closed the business down and the property had stood vacant for several years. The experience had given Anna the sharp business sense she now possessed, and the knowledge of what the health department came looking for.

Chase steered her bike south, down Fifteenth Avenue, past the campus substation, then along University Avenue with the campus on her left, pedaling to Tenth Avenue and onto the bridge, where she could catch a glimpse of the Mississippi River.

A light breeze came from the west and the air promised a warmish day. It was still August, after all. Chase loved autumn and fall colors, and couldn't wait to get her sweaters out of the under-bed box in her apartment. She spied a small sumac, beginning to flash its brilliant red leaves. Soon the others would follow, then the bigger trees, until Minneapolis was kissed by the jewel tones of turning leaves.

The sight of the Mighty Mississippi always calmed her. She stopped, straddling her bike for a few moments, watching the progress of the water that was near the beginning of its two-thousand-mile journey. When she was a child, she'd floated paper boats on its surface, then imagined their trip, picturing them making it all the way to New Orleans. Now that she was an adult, she knew a piece of paper would never make it that far. Still, she could imagine the voyage. She took a deep breath of the clear, crisp-tasting air over the cool water and pedaled to the shop, renewed and ready for another long day.

In her apartment, showered and dressed, Chase poured the diet cat food into Quincy's bowl and called him.

"Come get your din dins, little guy. Yummy, yummy."

Quincy, who had been lying on the floor five feet from his dish, turned his head toward her with all the speed of a snail and stared. He didn't even glance at the cat food.

"Quincy, baby, you have to eat something." Chase knelt and held a piece of kibble before him. If a cat could look disgusted, that was Quincy's expression.

Chase sighed, plunked the morsel into the bowl, and headed downstairs to work.

Chase had asked both Vi and Laci to work on Wednesday. Her inclination last night had been to shut the shop down for at least a day, but she didn't know why she felt that way. Respect for the dead? She hadn't respected Gabe when he was alive, so why should she start now? At any rate, she'd ignored that inclination. This week was too profitable to close down for a day.

The two young women weren't respecting anybody, but started in on each other almost as soon as the shop was open.

"No, Laci."

Chase listened in from the kitchen where she was helping Anna get out the ingredients she'd need for today's baking.

"Why can't you remember where the big bills go? Are you defective or something?"

Anna rushed to the front. When she returned to the kitchen she was tugging Vi by the arm. "That's enough. You can't speak to her that way."

Vi shook Anna's hand off and drew herself up to her full height. She looked down on Anna, which only made Anna stand taller and stick her chin out.

"You'll speak respectfully to Laci," Anna said, "as long as you're both working together in the shop. Do you understand me?"

Vi glanced away. "You're right, I was rude."

"I can always hire someone else."

That was true, Chase thought, but she would hate to lose Vi. She had such a way with the customers. Maybe Anna was being a little too hard on her. Sometimes Anna made Chase feel like a junior partner. Yes, she was a lot younger, but she wanted to be treated as an equal. Chase was going to stand up to Anna and tell her they needed both of them, as soon as she summoned the gumption. She was not fond of conflict by a long shot. She'd had enough lately.

Now Vi looked worried. Her hand flew to her neck. "I need the job, Mrs. Larson. I really do."

"Then don't make me fire you. Now go sell some goodies. The front is full of college students and their parents. And lay off your coworker."

"Laci doesn't remember anything I tell her. I think she does it on purpose sometimes."

Anna closed her eyes and took a breath. "It doesn't matter that much where the bills go in the cash drawer. We'll get it all straightened out at night. Don't worry about it so much."

Vi pursed her lips, glossy pink today and matching her silk blouse. Her blouses always bore either matching or contrasting cloth-covered buttons. Today the buttons were lilac. "I'll try to be patient."

The rest of the morning went smoothly. Chase had fun helping bake one of their best sellers, Lemon Bars. She hummed "Oh, What a Beautiful Mornin'" from *Oklahoma!* as she zested the lemon peels and juiced the lemons. Such a fresh smell.

At lunchtime, Laci came to the kitchen to eat the lunch she'd brought in. She perched on a swivel-top stool at the island and munched her sandwich while Anna cleaned up her bowls and baking utensils in the huge sink. Chase finished dusting the cooled lemon bars with powdered sugar, took her yogurt from the refrigerator, and sat beside Laci.

"How are sales today?" Chase asked.

Laci fiddled with a loose bobby pin. She'd come to work with her long hair in a complicated but stylish updo. It looked nice on her. "We're selling tons. We might run out of the Peanut Butter Chocolate Bars."

"I have some in the oven," said Anna.

They ate in silence for a bit while Anna clattered in the sink. Chase drew in the chocolaty smell of the baking goodies as she ate.

"Some people were asking if there were any rats in the kitchen," said Laci, wadding up her plastic sandwich bag and shooting a basket in the big wastebasket at the end of the island.

Anna froze with a soapy hand in the air and Chase stopped eating midbite.

Anna turned from the sink slowly. "Who was asking that?"

How would anyone know about the rats? thought Chase. Anna had whisked them away to the pet store early in the morning.

"I don't remember." Laci bit into a crunchy apple.

"No," said Chase. "We don't have rats. You told them that, didn't you?"

"Sure. There was just that one time, and Gabe put them there."

"Put what where?" Vi pushed through the swinging doors.

"You remember when Gabe put those rats in the alley?" said Laci.

"So he's the one who put the last ones here?" Vi asked.

"Chase says there aren't any more."

"It's your turn in front," said Vi to her coworker. Chase was glad they were being civil to each other. For now. "I'm ready for my lunch."

When Laci had left, Chase turned to Vi, perched on a stool and unwrapping her sandwich with a self-assured air. "What's this about rat rumors? Do you know who started that?"

Vi raised a smooth, perfectly groomed eyebrow.

How could the girl look so sophisticated? wondered Chase. She was almost ten years younger than Chase, but Vi made her feel awkward and young sometimes. Laci, who actually was younger and more awkward, probably felt ten times less capable around her. "What have you heard?" Chase said.

"Do you think Laci released the rats?" Vi said. "As a favor to Ted's dad, to make Ted like her more?"

"That's crazy," said Chase, pushing her yogurt carton away, no longer hungry. "There aren't any rats, and if there were, Laci wouldn't be involved."

"You should see those two," said Vi. "I had to tell Ted not to come behind the counter. He's got his hands all over her."

"It doesn't sound like Laci needs to curry his favor, then."

Chase wondered if Vi was jealous. After all, Laci had a

steady beau and she had none. That was probably because, as Vi had told them, she dumped every guy she dated after a few weeks. Anna thought Vi was waiting for one with a lot of money, trying them out to see how deep their pockets were.

The phone sounded in the office and Chase gladly quit the conversation to answer it. It was a paper-product supplier trying to get her business, and she made short work of the call.

While she was there, she opened the business spreadsheets to double-check something she thought she'd seen last time she balanced the books. Chase frowned. That was odd. Something wasn't adding up.

As she quickly reached for the door to have Anna look at the computer, she heard Vi speaking in the kitchen, near the closed office door.

"I'm talking about the money. It's not there. No, I don't have it, Felix."

She seemed to be speaking on her cell phone, probably unaware of how little soundproofing the office door provided.

"No, I can't. She's the owner. . . . Okay, co-owner. Same thing. I need to talk to you."

Did Vi know something about missing money? Which co-owner was she referring to? Anna? Herself?

"Yes, I know it happened, but I can't prove it."

The door was thin enough that Chase heard Vi let out an exasperated breath, then stomp away. Chase cracked the door open after another minute and Vi was gone. She picked up her iced-tea glass from the counter. Anna had finished the dishes and was slipping another batch of bars into the oven.

Chase didn't dare speak about the rats—or the accounts—with Anna when either of the sales workers could come in at any time and catch them. She'd ask her later if she was sure no one saw her returning the vermin this morning.

Anna had come back from the pet shop this morning saying that the owner hadn't sold any rats lately, but he'd taken them from her. Anna and Chase wondered if they should bother to find out where they'd come from. Had the owner told someone else that the rats had been in their kitchen?

"No," Anna had said. "He promised to keep quiet. He was upset about the dirty trick someone played on us." The man had gone to high school with Anna and she trusted him.

Now Chase wondered if Anna's trust had been misplaced and he'd let it slip somehow.

Anna went into the office to give Quincy some petting and keep him company for a few minutes between batches.

Vi pushed the doors open and returned to the kitchen. "There's a guy out there," she said.

"And?"

"He says he's an environmental something."

Chase gasped. "Environmental health inspector."

"Oh." Vi's eyes grew wide. "What should we do?"

"Business as usual. Let him wander around wherever he wants."

Vi turned to go.

"And Vi, don't talk to him at all. Act like he's not there."

Anna emerged from the office. Chase ran over to her and inspected her for cat hairs. She plucked three off Anna's shoulder and stuck them into the wastebasket. "Health inspector's here," she whispered.

"Oh, that's just great. I hope everyone out front isn't discussing you-know-what."

"Me, too!"

In a few minutes, the man entered the kitchen, clutching a leather folder and a pad of paper with a pen clipped to it.

"Harold Johnson," he said, heading for the sink. He was tall and thin with a full mustache, dressed in jeans and a long-sleeved green shirt. His round glasses emphasized his large, wide eyes.

All the better to see your rats with went through Chase's mind, and she gave a slight shudder.

After scrubbing his hands, he peeked into the tiny employees-only restroom in the corner. He emerged with a slight frown, then rescrubbed his hands. He went straight to the oven and whipped a fancy thermometer from his fanny pack.

Chase tried not to hold her breath or appear nervous. She had the idea that a health inspector could smell fear. When she imagined telling Anna or Julie about that, she smiled. They would probably point out that, despite the large bristly growth under his nose, the man was not a bear.

In fact, he was extremely polite and didn't write a thing on his pad of paper. After he'd taken the temperature of the oven (which Anna had cleaned first thing in the morning, scrubbing the rack thoroughly) and the refrigeration unit (which had been emptied and cleaned last week) and poked around among all the shelves, he nodded, gave them a smile, and left.

Chase and Anna toasted each other with Sprite to celebrate. Not that they knew for sure they'd passed the inspection, but if Harold hadn't made any notes, that was a very good sign.

Yesterday, at the scene of the crime, Chase had been told to come into the police station at two o'clock the next day to give a statement. It was well after one, so she left the shop in the hands of Anna, Laci, and Vi and drove to the Second Precinct building. She found a shady parking space on the street, before the imposing stone-faced brick building. She walked past the Eastside Guardian statue, three figures representing police officers and a lost child. The authority figures in the sculpture, although they were a bit bigger than life-size, didn't seem forbidding. That reassured Chase, who was irrationally nervous about being in a police station. Or maybe not that irrationally. After all, there may have been outstanding warrants for her in Chicago.

After a brief wait in an outer room, she was ushered into a small, green-painted room with one table and four straight-backed chairs. The detective from last night sat in one chair and pointed her into one across the table from him.

She hadn't noticed much about him last night at Gabe's condo. Now she could see that he wasn't as old as she'd thought, and was better looking than she remembered. The cut of his light brown hair was shorter than Chase thought looked good, but his very dark blue eyes, giving her an earnest but not unfriendly expression, were compelling.

Almost mechanically, Chase recited again what she'd told over and over the evening before. She'd gone out searching for her cat. The condo door was ajar. She'd entered and found her cat, and the dead body of Gabe Naughtly. Yes, the knife was already in his chest. Yes, she touched it. Yes, it was bloody. But she hadn't killed him.

She fidgeted a bit while she talked, trying to find a comfortable place for her hands. She put them in her lap, on the table, and then ended up sitting on them.

The detective, who told her his name was Niles Olson, was almost gentle with his questions, apologizing for making her go over everything she'd said one more time.

"This will be the last time," he said. "You're doing well. I appreciate the effort."

"I'll never have to tell this story again?" Chase immediately regretted using the word *story*. It made her recitation sound like it might be made up.

Detective Olson gave her his clear, direct gaze again. "I won't say never. You might have to testify in court. The defense might want to see if what you say when you're in court matches your statement today."

Chase wasn't worried about that. "I could never forget a bit of what happened. It's etched into my mind, like it's carved into a piece of stone." She shuddered.

Detective Olson leaned forward and raised his hand. She thought he might be thinking about patting her shoulder. She realized she wouldn't mind if he did. His hand dropped before touching her.

"What did Torvald Iversen tell you?" she asked. "Do our stories match?" There she was again, saying *stories*.

He didn't answer, merely turned off the recorder and told her to come in and sign her statement when it was typed up. They'd call her.

He looked disappointed in her question. Well, maybe that had been a dumb thing to ask. But why did she care what Detective Olson thought about her?

"I'd like you to stop at the counter before you leave, too," he said. "We need to get your prints."

She was relieved that the procedure was electronic and didn't get black goo all over her fingers, like she'd seen on TV.

That evening, after the shop closed and the bickering employees had left, Chase sipped a cup of decaf in the kitchen with Anna. Anna had baked most of the day, until the traffic had slowed in the afternoon, giving the women a chance to get ahead on chores. Now the cooking equipment was all cleaned and put away, ready for Thursday morning. The sweet bakery aromas of the day lingered, giving the kitchen a close, homey feel.

"About the rats . . ." began Chase.

"Bill wouldn't have said anything." Anna seemed to be reading Chase's mind again.

"How did Laci hear about the rats, then?"

"Vi heard, too," said Anna. "Did they both seem evasive about telling us who's been talking?"

"Maybe it's Ted," said Chase. "Do you suppose he released them, for his father? I can't see Laci doing it, just because they're seeing each other, but Ted's a strange guy."

"I don't know about strange, but he is troubled. He's had a problem with light fingers all his life."

"I didn't know that. Is that why he got sent home from college? Doris said it was his grades."

"No doubt it was. I don't think you get expelled for shoplifting."

"That's an ugly word," said Chase. "But I have noticed some of the boxed treats near the front of the store have been disappearing. Our count has been short three times. Do you think Ted's pilfering them?"

Anna shrugged. "Wouldn't surprise me. After all, who does he have for parents?"

"What is it with you and Doris?" Chase knew they didn't like each other, but with the recent events, she wanted to know more.

"Ancient history." Anna waved a hand in the air. "Have you found out anything about the missing cash register money?"

"No, of course not. I'd tell you if I did." Chase hadn't exactly said money was missing, just that she couldn't get the accounts to balance.

Anna rose to wash out her cup in the sink. Quincy was doing his nightly counter prowl. He patrolled for stray tidbits, acting like he was just out for a walk, his tail held high as he sauntered.

Tonight didn't seem to be the right time to find out about Doris and Anna and what the animosity was about. Ted was also an enigma to Chase. Laci proclaimed how sensitive he was, and how upset by his parents' impending divorce. Chase couldn't tell that he was bothered by anything, though. Was his apparent indifference a self-protective façade? If he had a history of shoplifting, he'd probably been troubled for quite some time. Maybe his parents' relationship had been stormy for a long time—maybe always.

Chase yawned. "I'd better go close out the cash drawer."

"No need. I'm sure that session at the police station tired you."

"It must have. I'm beat."

"You go upstairs and rest," Anna said. "I'll close."

"We agreed I'd do that," said Chase.

"I know, but I'm perfectly capable of it and you're worn out. I'll make you do extra baking tomorrow."

Chase knew Anna wouldn't enforce that, but accepted her offer. It felt just a tad odd that Anna was insisting on doing the books, but the gesture was appreciated. Chase knew Anna didn't like doing them.

"Thanks loads, Anna. I *am* tired. Maybe you'll have better luck. I'm not looking forward to battling Quincy into eating his healthy food. This morning he gave me the evil eye when I tried to feed him. I'll bet he hasn't eaten a thing all day."

"We'll have to come up with something that's good for him that he likes. Have you smelled that cat food?"

"Cats like dead birds and mice. They surely can't tell what smells good."

"Go on. I'll lock up and wipe the counters."

Chase picked up her cat and dragged herself up the steps, suddenly weary from all the events of the last two days and looking forward to a snuggle with her guy, Quincy.

The pudgy cat purred to be back upstairs, in the apartment with the soft furniture and the warm human lap. The surfaces in the office were so hard. It was time for what the humans called din dins. However, something vile was poured into the bowl where goodness used to be. He lapped up some water and walked away from the food bowl. No longer purring, his tail twitching and his ears low, he jumped onto the bed

*and shunned the warm lap for the rest of the evening. There
were good smells in the apartment, but nothing good was
being put into his food bowl.*

A light knock sounded on Chase's apartment door. She
opened it to find Anna on the landing, a worried frown on
her face.

"What is it? Come on in," said Chase.

"I want you to come downstairs and see something."
Anna turned and headed down.

What on earth? Chase wondered. Anna sounded so serious. She followed the older woman.

"There aren't more rats, are there?" she said to Anna's
back.

Anna didn't answer, but led the way into the office. She
pointed Chase into the chair behind the old wooden desk,
which had come from Anna's house when they opened shop.
Leaning toward the computer screen, Anna pointed to a
column of figures on a spreadsheet.

"There," Anna said.

Chase saw it immediately. There was an obvious discrepancy in the two numbers that should balance. "You've
checked this?"

"And rechecked and rechecked. We're short one hundred
dollars in cash. It's probably not an error making change."

Chase remembered Vi complaining that Ted had been
behind the counter with Laci. "You think Ted took it?"

"I have no idea. Someone took it."

The silence hung between them with a somberness that
made Chase squirm inside. "Could you talk to Ted?"

"If you think I should," said Anna.

"Someone should."

"If you insist, I'll do it."

"I'll let you." Chase couldn't imagine how she would

start that discussion. She stood so Anna could sit down and close the computer program.

"Quincy didn't eat a thing tonight," Chase said as they entered the kitchen. "I'm getting worried about him."

"Poor thing. He's starving."

"I don't think he is. Otherwise he'd eat his dinner."

Was Anna still slipping him treats during the day? She'd have to watch for that tomorrow.

FIVE

Chase had gone over the numbers at least five times Thursday morning. Anna was right. Money was missing. She'd been hunched over the keyboard in the tiny office for a couple of hours, enduring Quincy's plaints while he sniffed and pawed at the bottom of the door, trying to hook the corner with his claws. At one point, he even jumped onto the two-drawer filing cabinet that sat next to the door and tried to turn the slick brass doorknob.

"If you had opposable thumbs, you'd be dangerous," she told him. He had the right idea and apparently knew exactly how to open the door, just couldn't physically do it.

Her eyes were blurring from concentrating on the screen for so long. With a huff of exasperation, she pushed her chair away. Careful to keep Quincy confined—who knew when another health inspector might come by?—she left the office and went to the front to see how the day was going. It was almost lunchtime and she'd heard the front door chimes as the door opened and closed almost nonstop. This week was good for business, but she'd be glad when it was over.

When she entered the salesroom, Anna was at the cash register and Doris Naughtly hovered nearby.

"Where are Laci and Vi?" asked Chase. She and Anna had hired those two so they wouldn't have to work in the front themselves.

"Vi got what she said was an urgent call and said she had to leave," said Anna. "Laci is by the front window with Ted, who is probably stealing our merchandise."

Doris whirled on Anna. "What did you just say?"

"I said," answered Anna with measured tones, "that it's highly likely that your son, the thief, is stealing from our store."

"You shut your mouth! Don't you talk about my son that way!"

Chase cringed at Doris's shrieking. "Please—"

"Shall I talk about his thieving mother instead?" Anna still held her voice low.

Doris got even louder. "I never stole him! He wasn't yours!"

Anna closed her eyes for half a minute. "Doris, it all turned out okay. But please pay attention to what your son is doing."

Doris huffed at Anna and clamped her mouth shut. "I'll raise my son my own way, thank you very much."

Chase was beginning to hyperventilate. Every customer in the store, and there were at least a dozen, had paused to listen to the altercation. At least Anna didn't answer her back.

Doris's face flushed to match the raspberry stripes on the walls and her fists were clenched tight.

"Doris. Please." Chase held up her hands, palms out, and stepped in front of Doris to put herself between the two women.

"I'm sorry, Doris," Anna said. "I know you've just lost your husband. Chase, will you take over?"

Anna shoved the cash drawer shut a little more forcefully than necessary and returned to the kitchen. Chase had no choice but to slip behind the counter as Doris pointed to the dessert bars she wanted. "One dozen."

"The thing is," Doris said, leaning over the counter to confide in Chase, "I wasted all that money on a divorce lawyer." Even though she was bent close to Chase, she didn't lower her voice one bit. At best, you could call her normal tone strident. Now, complaining, it was bitter, too. One of her buttons caught on the edge of the display case. Chase heard it hit the floor with a tiny ping.

Chase could hear Anna muttering through the double doors, but she couldn't understand what she was saying. That was good, she figured, because then Doris couldn't either.

Chase couldn't help but cringe at the woman's cold heart. Doris had thrown Gabe out and he'd ended up dead.

Chase was flustered, but tried to sound calm and reasonable as she told Doris the amount. "Are you going to pay for Ted's purchases?" she added, trying for a wide-eyed innocent look. Chase peered around Doris to see that he held a hand behind his back. He hung his head, came forward, and deposited on the counter the two boxes he held.

He *had* been going to shoplift them, Chase realized. Anna was right. But then, she was usually right.

After the Naughtlys had paid for everything and left, Chase called an embarrassed-looking Laci to work the counter so she could try to talk to Anna in the kitchen. A bit of the history between Anna and Doris had come out, but she wanted to know the whole story. She wanted some leverage to prevent another scene like this one.

Chase perched on a stool at the kitchen island with a glass of iced tea while Anna pulled a bowl of dough, partially mixed, from the refrigerator. "Anna, did you date Gabe?"

Anna's back, which was turned to Chase, stiffened slightly. "Why would you think that?" She gave the dough she was kneading a vicious whack.

"You just now said to Doris—"

Vi rushed through the back door. Both Anna and Chase turned to stare. "Sorry. I had to take care of something." She ran through the kitchen, into the front room.

Anna said it first. "What on earth is the matter with Violet?"

"I don't know. She's usually so well groomed."

"Her hair's a mess."

"And it's not easy to mess up that short bob," Chase said.

"I've never seen her with her shirttails out. Sometime this afternoon, I'll try to take her aside and see what's bothering her."

"Let me," said Chase, not trusting Anna's instincts today. She was afraid Anna would terminate Violet. She couldn't read the look Anna gave her as the older woman stuck a metal bowl on the mixer and lowered the beaters with a clang.

"If you insist," muttered Anna.

Chase heard the office phone and went to answer it, shooing Quincy from the door. A glance at the caller ID told her it was the Minnesota Department of Health. She steeled herself to hear the results of the inspection and answered the call. Her spirits fell as the woman told her there was a problem. But when she said it was minor, Chase relaxed a bit. The sign cautioning employees to wash their hands was missing from the restroom, the woman said.

Chase hung up and went to check. Sure enough, it had fallen off the wall and slipped behind the wastebasket. She put it back up, using more tape this time, then went to see what needed doing in the shop.

The atmosphere was chilly in the kitchen, though the air was actually warm, full of the smell of baking cookie dough.

Anna was making Almond Cherry Bars. They almost always made Chase's mouth water, but today her tongue felt dry. Something was bugging Anna, something beyond the issue with Doris.

"Who was on the phone?" asked Anna, not looking up from her task.

"Health department. One teensy violation and I just fixed it." She told her about the sign and Anna suggested they use tacks or nails.

"Good idea," said Chase. "They didn't say when they'd reinspect."

"Speaking of health and cleaning up," said Anna, "our delivery seems to have shorted us on paper towels. Could you please do me a favor and run out and get some?"

Why was Anna being so formal? Getting paper towels wouldn't be doing *her* a favor. They both needed the shop to have supplies. Chase shrugged and went out the front door. She crossed the street and walked down the block toward House of Hanson. Right before she entered through the recessed red door, she caught a reflection in the door's glass that made her stop cold.

Dare she turn around? The man across the street had come from the direction of the video shop and was walking toward the apartments in the next block. The man was tall and blond. He looked too much like Shaun Everly. The man entered the door to an apartment building. She refused to think that Shaun was here, in Minneapolis. She gave a shudder and entered the tiny grocery to pick up some paper towels.

Shaun Everly was the reason she'd left Chicago. She never wanted to see him again. Ever.

SIX

As Chase trudged up the steps to her apartment at the end of the day, her cell phone trilled. The caller ID said "MN Police," so she figured she'd better answer it. She clicked the button, juggling Quincy while she unlocked and opened her door.

"Miss Oliver?" It was the cute detective, Niles Olson. Her heart quickened. If he wanted a date, she'd go, she decided right then. His voice was lovely over the phone.

"Yes?" There was, she was sure, a big smile in her voice. "This is Chase." She drew her name out. She realized she was flirting. With a policeman! What had gotten into her?

"We have a match on the prints."

"The prints?" She kicked the door shut and set Quincy on the floor. "Fingerprints?"

"Yes, yours match the ones on the murder weapon."

"Well, yes, I told you I touched it." She opened the fridge and pulled out a package of cheese. Quincy displayed mild, dignified interest.

"They're the only ones."

She froze with the refrigerator door open. The cat moved closer and put his front paws on the bottom shelf.

"Miss Oliver? Are you there?"

"Yes. What are you saying?" She returned the cheese to the refrigerator drawer, shooed Quincy out, and closed the door with a whomp of the gasket. Some of the air seemed to go out of the apartment, making it hard to breathe. Quincy stalked off as if he had never displayed any interest in the refrigerator.

"I'm saying you'd better not leave town any time soon. If you must, please clear it with me first."

"Oh." She clicked the phone off. Not leave town? The only fingerprints on the weapon? She was a *suspect*?

Chase sat in her stuffed chair and hyperventilated. Quincy seemed to sense her real distress and climbed into her lap, purring loudly. She stroked his silky back absently.

After what may have been minutes and may have been an hour, it registered that Quincy felt heavier than ever.

Chase needed to talk to someone. Not Anna. She called her best friend, Julie. She and Julie had taken skating lessons together, had camped out at Lake Minnetonka every summer, cross-country skied on the golf courses every winter, had shared the stories of their first kisses in eighth grade, had cried together when Julie got stood up at a junior high school dance, and knew all of each other's secrets. Chase needed to hear a friendly voice, so she did what she usually did. She called Julie.

There was no answer. She texted, "Call ASAP SOS."

Within five minutes her cell rang.

Chase opened the connection without checking caller ID. "Julie?"

"No, this is Dr. Ramos."

Chase pictured his dark, curly hair and those liquid brown eyes. Her heart lurched slightly. "Yes?"

"I'm calling to see how Quincy is doing."

"Oh." He was just interested in the cat. "To tell you the truth, something isn't working. I don't have a scale, but it seems like he's gaining weight."

"You're feeding him the prescription meals and treats?"

"Oh yes. I am, Dr. Ramos." Other people may not be, though. Other people, like Anna.

"Please call me Mike. Do you think he's getting into anything else to eat?" Was he a mind reader?

"He . . . may be getting . . . something." She scratched between her cat's ears, right on his stripes, where he liked it.

"Would you like to come in tomorrow and weigh him here?"

"Sure, I'd— No, I can't tomorrow. It's Friday. The shop will be tremendously busy until school opens next Tuesday."

"What time do you close?"

"At six."

"I can stay late for you, if you'd like to come by then."

She'd prefer to meet him somewhere that wasn't furnished with stainless steel tables, but that would do for now. Maybe she'd bring him some Almond Cherry Bars.

"I also called to see how you're doing, Chase."

"Not all that well."

"I'm concerned about you being mixed up in a murder mess."

That was sweet. The man *was* good looking. And hadn't accused her of embezzlement. So he was a huge step up from the last guy she'd dated, Shaun Everly.

"I'm holding up pretty well, Dr. Ramos."

"Mike."

"Okay, Mike."

"If there's anything I can do, don't hesitate to let me know."

She couldn't imagine what that would be, but she thanked him for his kind offer.

"I'll see you about six thirty?"

After she hung up, Chase had a warm, fuzzy tingle that Mike was thinking of her. She picked Quincy up and danced around the small room with him, being careful not to stomp her feet too heavily so Anna wouldn't come up and ask what she was doing. Quincy seemed puzzled by the activity, but went along with it, although he flattened his ears a bit.

Anna had offered to do the books again. Chase hoped there wouldn't be more money missing tonight.

After a light supper and another attempt to convince Quincy that his diet food was delicious, she tried Julie again. Still no answer.

As she crawled into bed with a book she was sure she wouldn't be able to concentrate on, her cell rang. She saw Julie's ID. At last!

"I have so much to tell you," Chase began.

"I have some news, too, but you go first."

"You want the good news or the bad news first?"

"Bad," said Julie. "Get it out of the way."

"This isn't *too* bad. We had a violation on the health inspection, but it's an easy fix—just the sign missing that tells us to wash our hands. Stupid regulation anyway. Here's the good news. Sort of. I think Quincy's vet might like me."

Quincy raised his head and blinked at the mention of his name. Chase scratched the short, soft fur between his ears and he closed his eyes, purred, and leaned into her fingers.

"You're not sure that it's good news?"

"Not really. He aggravates the heck out of me. He's so critical of Quincy."

"Chase, I think he's trying to keep your baby healthy. That's not a bad thing."

"I suppose. Now, what's your news?"

"I have a new case, a big one."

"Ooo, great! Can you tell me about it?"

"Not yet. It'll be a high-profile trial, so you'll read about it. I'm excited!"

"Are you going to be superbusy?"

"Probably. Why? Do you need something?"

"How can you tell?" Chase smiled. Her anxiety must have been transmitting through the phone waves. "I was wondering if you could find out what the police file says about me. Detective Olson told me not to leave town. He said mine were the only fingerprints on the murder weapon."

"There you go! You didn't murder Naughtly. This is the proof."

SEVEN

As Chase walked slowly down the stairs to the shop on Friday morning, she pondered what Julie had said. Why hadn't she thought of the fact that Gabe's prints should be on the knife? That is, they should be on it if he'd used it to, say, slice onions or bell peppers for his meatloaf. If the killer had pulled it from a drawer or a knife block, and had used gloves, then sure, hers would be the only prints. Could she get the lab to test the knife for traces of onion? Didn't everyone put onion in meatloaf?

At least Julie said she would try to access the files and see if there was anything in the parts available to her that she could pass on to Chase. Julie was such a good friend. Not only didn't she have time to do this right now, she shouldn't be poking around in cases she wasn't working on. If only Julie were in criminal defense, instead of prosecution. Except she wouldn't be able to spy for Chase if she were.

Quincy purred in her arms as she reached the bottom of

the steps and reached for the door into the kitchen. She hesitated a moment. Anna hadn't come up to say good-bye last night and they hadn't parted on good terms earlier. Chase determined to patch things up today.

She threw the door open and sang a cheery "Hi" to Anna, who was on a stool at the island.

Anna's chin was in her hands, elbows propped on the granite surface, a glum expression on her face. The expression was so unusual, Chase wondered at first if the woman dressed in Anna's bright yellow T-shirt and wearing Anna's shiny gray hair, staring at the bars on the baking pan that sat on the counter in front of her, was really Anna.

"How's it going?" Chase asked, regretting her wording the moment she said it. It was obviously not going well. "What's the matter?"

"Taste this." Anna took a square off the pan and held it out, then drew her hand back. "No, don't. I'm not that mean."

It looked like an Almond Cherry Bar from the batch Anna had made late yesterday. "Something's wrong with it?"

"Something's wrong with the cook. I must have doubled the amount of almond flavoring."

Chase took the confection from her and sniffed it. It smelled wonderful. She nibbled a corner, then ran to the sink to spit it out. "Um, maybe you tripled it."

"Next, I'll be confusing sugar and salt." Anna shook her head to clear her mood and got up to start baking. Chase, not wanting to go over the ledger figures, started a batch of Strawberry Cheesecake Bars herself, humming "Ya Got Trouble" from *The Music Man*. The sweet baking smells soon dispelled the gloom that Anna's early morning mood had thrown over the room.

Near lunchtime, Laci poked her head into the kitchen with a plea for help.

"We're slammed. Every freshman on campus, I swear,

is here. Some of them brought their whole families." Her pinned-up hairdo was drooping and she shed two bobby pins on the floor.

"I'll be right there," said Chase. She zipped into the office to pour a bowl of diet treats for Quincy. He'd been right inside the door, but ignored the bowl. He turned his back and walked away, rather stiff-legged, his nose and his tail in the air. "You just be that way, then. We'll see what the doc says tonight. You'll see. He might put you on the cat equivalent of bread and water." Something crunched under her shoe as she left the office.

She snatched up Laci's fallen bobby pins and stuck them on the small shelf under the counter, then ran to the front. The room was crowded with college students and relatives. "Keep baking," she called to Anna as she left. The shelves were half-empty and getting barer.

Chase made several trips back and forth from the freezer to replenish the stock, but the freezer was far from full. Just three more days until classes started. Then it would slow down and they could take time during the day to breathe.

It hadn't helped, of course, that Anna had to throw out the huge batch she'd made last night. Oh well, there was nothing they could do about that now.

The cat strolled to the door of his prison, the restaurant office. It may have looked like a strange place for a feline to call home during working hours, but the pudgy tabby cat never failed to purr when he was deposited there. Maybe that was because of the basket, lined with a soft blanket, in the corner. Or it could have been because one of the humans invariably brought bits of cookie bars to him at regular inter-vals during the day. This day, however, she was late. The cat knew it was past time for a num num. He sat erect, with his

*ears pricked forward, his tail wrapped around his front paws,
but twitching at the very tip. At last, someone was coming.*

The older woman cracked the door open and slipped in.

*"Here's a good boy," she crooned, sprinkling cookie bits
on the floor in front of him. "We don't want you to starve to
death, do we?"*

*He settled down to licking them up, hardly noticing her
leave, closing the door behind her.*

Chase froze with her hand outstretched to receive a twenty
from a student's mother. That man coming in the door, the
pale, thin guy wearing a blazer—was that the awful man
who had found her with the bloody knife? The sound of a
crash unfroze her arm and she took the money, then looked
down to see what had fallen to the floor. Vi had knocked a
stack of cartons off the shelf behind the sales counter.

As Vi knelt to pick them up, Chase followed the progress
of the man. Yes, it was Torvald Iversen, the one who had
called 911 and accused her of killing Gabe. She inhaled a
deep, cleansing breath and made change for her customer.
The woman thanked her sweetly and left with her daughter,
obviously a freshman, a skinny girl who could probably eat
the whole bag of Lemon Bars and not gain an ounce.

Iversen strolled around one of the front tables, lifting
boxes and setting them down. Chase waited for him to
acknowledge her, but he didn't glance toward the back of
the shop. Next, he perused the shelves of wares on the side
wall, fingering the knot of his tie with his creepy, long, pale
fingers. Finally, he left the shop without a glance in Chase's
direction and strolled toward the coffee shop.

Vi peeked over the counter after the door closed and
watched Iversen depart, her eyes wide.

"Do you know that man?" asked Chase.

"What man?" Vi stood up and nudged at the stack of boxes she'd finished reshelving. "Oh, the one who just left? No, why?"

Chase felt sorry for the girl. She was lying, Chase was sure. She'd probably had a bad experience with the horrid man, but Chase couldn't imagine what that would have been, what the connection between them could be.

Chase was still gazing out the front window, half expecting Iversen to pop in again, when she spotted a familiar figure walking down the sidewalk across the street. He turned into the coffee shop. Now she was sure Shaun Everly was in Minneapolis. What was he doing here? Was he here about the note she'd left him? Did he know she was here? She hoped not.

"**You'll have to** do something different, you know." Dr. Ramos, Mike as Chase was beginning to think of him, lifted Quincy off the scale. "Whatever you're doing isn't working. He's gained nearly a half a pound. That's a tremendous amount in such a short time. He's in danger of becoming diabetic. If that happens, you'll have a real problem on your hands."

"Just what do you suggest?" Chase sounded, she thought, shrill. Really, what more could she do? "I'm feeding him the exact amount of the food you prescribed."

"You can't be. He can't gain weight on that."

Chase fisted her hands on her hips. "Are you calling me a liar?"

"No, no. Calm down. I'm not calling you—"

"I am *not* giving him extra food . . . but . . ."

He put Quincy into his crate and gave the cat a scratch behind his ears with a thoughtful frown. "But someone else is?" he said.

Chase's mouth dropped open. How did he know? Anna was sneaking treats to him. That had to be it. When Chase had released Quincy from the office after the shop closed, she'd seen the cookie crumbs on the floor. She hadn't thought anything of them at the time, since cookie crumbs got everywhere. But now she put it together. When she'd gone to the front this afternoon, Anna had probably indulged him.

Mollified somewhat, Chase admitted that maybe someone else was feeding him. "I'll talk to Anna again. I'll make it clear that she shouldn't give him cookie leftovers." She dug a plastic container out of her purse. "By the way, I brought you these." She held out the bin.

"What's that?"

"It's a dozen Lemon Bars."

He accepted the gift and set it on the desk in the corner of the examining room. "Are you trying to make me diabetic, too?"

Chase didn't think that was very funny. He was attractive, but his jokes were lame. "I'd better get back and see if Anna needs any help," she said, lifting Quincy's crate.

"How many hours do you put in at Bar None?" He opened the door for her to exit and they walked down the hallway to the waiting room in the front. "It seems like you work day and night."

"Sometimes we do. But there are slow periods when we relax a bit and even get caught up with the baking. Are you going to eat the Lemon Bars I brought you?"

"Of course. Why wouldn't I?"

"You're afraid of becoming diabetic?"

He gave her a warm glance. "I was only kidding. Sorry if you took it wrong."

He told her that his grandmother had been a baker, had baked bread every day, and cookies often. He'd grown up near the Iron Range, in the northeastern part of Minnesota. His father had been one of the few Hispanics to venture that far north for work. His mother came from a Swedish family that had lived in the area for a few generations.

Chase took that friendly conversation as Mike trying to make up for his lame joke.

As she walked through the outer waiting room, a tall, svelte redhead with a short, spiky hairdo rose to greet Dr. Ramos. He met her with a huge smile and put a hand on her arm. Chase noticed that she didn't have a pet with her.

So Dr. Ramos had a girlfriend. She was disappointed, she had to admit. The man was devilishly attractive.

Anna had left by the time Chase got home, but there was a sticky note from her on the apartment door: "See me in the morning about the accounts."

The note was like a splash of cold water in her face. Were they short of money again?

Quincy started meowing the moment she came in. She poured diet food into his bowl. He turned away and meowed again.

"What is the matter with you?" Chase caught herself. It wouldn't do any good to yell at a cat. Especially at Quincy. He replied to her with a disdainful nose lift and disappeared into the bedroom.

Chase kicked off her shoes and sat in her favorite armchair to make a mental list of what she needed to worry about: Quincy, Anna, the missing money, her prints on the murder weapon, Laci and Vi squabbling. Anything else? Oh yes, the unexpected arrival of Shaun Everly. That was probably her most immediate problem right now.

As she reached for the TV remote to take her mind off her worries, her cell phone rang. She saw Laci Carlson's ID.

"Ms. Oliver?" She sounded worried, upset. "Could you do me a huge favor? I need to talk to you."

Now what? "I'll try. What do you need?"

"I need to tell you . . . to talk to you. Can you meet me somewhere?"

"Tonight?" She was so comfortable.

"Maybe early tomorrow? Al's Breakfast opens at six."

Chase groaned inwardly. Laci's voice was growing higher, tighter. Distress was obvious in her tone. Had Anna fired her? She was so itching to get rid of one of them—or both. Chase thought she had better meet the young woman. "How about six thirty?"

"Sure. I'll get there earlier to get a table."

"See you." Al's Breakfast had only fourteen stools at the counter, so even arriving at 6:30 didn't assure you a seat. But it gave you a fighting chance.

Chase checked her clock. Six thirty would arrive in a few short hours. She drew a bath after she ended the call, promising to show up, and wondering what had gotten Laci so upset. A nice, long, soaky bath with bath oil and a scented candle would help put her to sleep better than television. Anna would probably get to the shop at around 7:30, her usual time. Chase had to be there to answer Anna's summons, but surely, talking to Laci wouldn't take more than an hour.

In spite of her steamy bath, accompanied by a cup of chamomile tea, Chase slept fitfully.

EIGHT

Chase had finally fallen into a deep sleep at five, so the alarm startled her at 6:15. It startled Quincy, too, who stiffened beside Chase, then jumped off the bed and scooted out of the room.

Chase groaned and slapped the alarm off, then got up, dressed, threw food into Quincy's bowl, and stumbled down the stairs. She was looking forward to the university classes starting on Tuesday and the parents going home so she could relax and maybe get more sleep.

Al's Breakfast, a tiny place but a Dinkytown institution, was across the street and down a couple of doors from the Bar None. Chase went through her shop and out the front door, locking it behind her, and made it to the restaurant a few minutes after 6:30.

Laci sat on one of the red-vinyl-covered stools, halfway down the narrow dining room. She had done her hair up again, in spite of the early hour. How long must it take to fix it that way? She was staring down at the counter. Chase suspected she wasn't seeing the napkins standing at attention in their basket, or the plastic dinosaur that, inexplicably, lived on the counter. She had on a high-necked dark red blouse with lace on the collar and cuffs. She looked like a child playing dress-up, trying to be Queen Victoria.

Chase lifted Laci's huge cloth purse off the seat next to her and gave her the best greeting smile she could this early in the morning. Laci merely tented her eyebrows. Her eyes glittered, full of tears ready to spill.

"What is it, Laci? What's wrong?"

Before she could answer, they were interrupted by the server, a middle-aged woman in a white shirt as plain as Laci's blouse was fancy. Laci sighed and ordered coffee and toast. Chase gazed longingly at the eggs Benedict on the plate of the man beside her, but ordered the buttermilk pancakes. If they were going to do a lot of talking, she wouldn't have time to do justice to her favorite.

"It's Violet," Laci began, then halted with a loud sniff.

"Just a couple more days. It's Saturday and classes start Tuesday. We need you both there until then. After Monday, why don't you take—"

"No, it's not that. I'll work when you need me. It's Ted."

"All right." Chase was puzzled. She sipped her coffee. Laci had just said "it" was Vi. Now "it" was Ted?

"She's spreading rumors. It's not true!"

"What rumors? What's not true?"

"About him stealing things."

Chase braced herself. "Laci, dear, he was taking the boxed merchandise. I saw him."

"Not that. The money. Oh, I'm not explaining anything, am I? Vi says Ted is taking money from the cash register."

Anna had said she would talk to the young man about that. Chase wondered if she'd had time to do that yet.

"He's not," said Laci, still on the verge of tears. "He wouldn't do that."

What world did Laci live in where Ted would shoplift at college and steal boxes of cookie bars, but wouldn't steal money?

"Ted's always felt so out of place and awkward, he says. He was a late baby and his parents are more the age of grandparents. I think that affects him psychologically."

Sure, thought Chase. That makes perfect sense. Most late babies steal things and flunk out of college. Not.

Their food arrived and Chase busied herself applying butter and syrup to her pancakes.

"Can you please tell Violet to stop? She's upsetting Ted." Laci bit into her toast as if she were biting off Vi's ear. Chase knew that Ted was a sensitive soul in Laci's world.

"I'll speak to Vi." She lifted her fork. The first bite was always the best. She closed her eyes so she could taste the buttery, syrupy concoction to the fullest.

"Hm." Laci looked suspicious, as though she understood that Chase wasn't going to tell Vi to stop spreading rumors just because Laci asked her to. "The stuff with his parents is so devastating. Ted has so much anger toward his father. Sometimes he scares me when he talks about him."

"Laci, I said I'll talk to her. That's all I can do. When the rush is over, you won't have to work together."

Laci's half smile and nod made Chase sad. She probably thought they were going to fire Vi, when Laci seemed to be the one Anna most wanted to fire. Chase finished as quickly as she could and hurried to the store for her next confrontation, this one with Anna.

Even at this early hour, the sidewalks were filling with college students and their families, moving their children into the dorms. At the end of the street, a number 6 bus rumbled along University Avenue, flashing its blue and yellow stripe in a stray band of light from the newly risen sun. In an hour or so, the sun would climb above the buildings where it now hid behind the Bar None. This would be a beautiful day if Chase didn't have so much on her mind. She squared her shoulders as she unlocked the door and entered her shop from the front.

She found Anna in the office, sitting at the computer with the financial spreadsheet open on the screen. She was frowning.

Chase took a seat in the chair next to the desk, wordlessly, waiting for Anna to tell her why she'd summoned her.

"There's more," Anna said. Her blue eyes, usually warm and cheerful, were troubled.

"More money? We have too much?"

"More pilfering. Less money." Anna gritted her teeth, still staring at the screen.

"Have you talked to Ted?" Chase slipped her purse off her shoulder and set it on the corner of the desk. "I just had breakfast with Laci."

Anna looked up at her now, questioning. Her eyes were still clouded.

"She called last night and asked to talk to me. She's convinced Vi is spreading vicious rumors about him taking the cash and that Ted is innocent. And after we caught him red-handed stealing merchandise."

"Yes, we did." Anna spoke slowly. "He was, wasn't he?" She studied the corner where the wall met the ceiling for a moment. "But he hasn't been near the register since this last bunch went missing. Last bunch of money, not merchandise."

"How much?"

"You don't know?"

"Anna, I haven't been doing the books. You have. How would I know?" What was Anna getting at? Could Anna be . . . No, that wasn't possible.

Anna glanced away.

Then Chase got it. A coldness crept up her spine. "How long have you known me? Have I ever stolen anything?"

"Have you?"

"What?" Chase stood, trembling. "How can you ask me that?"

Anna's head sank into her hands and her head nearly touched the computer screen. "Charity, darling, I'm not sure what to think. No, of course not. How could I have thought that? I don't know what's wrong with me lately. But who could be stealing from us?"

Anna *had* thought Chase was the thief. The fact that she had thought that, even for a moment, turned something over inside Chase.

Chase stalked out and stomped up the stairs to her apartment. Her hands shook so she could barely get her key to work.

She stormed inside, slammed the door, and dialed Julie.

Julie answered right away and Chase let out a breath of relief. She needed to talk to her best friend so badly right now.

"You got a minute?" Chase asked.

"Maybe two. I'm due in a conference soon. Shoot."

"You're working on Saturday?"

"My huge case is coming up. We're working all weekend to prep."

"I don't know how to say this. Anna . . . have you talked to her recently?"

"Sure. She came over for coffee last night. Oh. Is this about the missing money?"

"Julie, she thinks I took it."

"What makes you think that?"

Should Chase interpret that last statement as a nondenial? "It's obvious. Did you get that idea?"

"I'm not sure what to say."

"Why is she doing this?"

Julie's deep breath came over the airwaves clearly. "Can I ask you something?"

"Of course. Anything." Why would Julie hesitate to con-fide in her?

"Are you doing all right with money?"

"What do you mean?"

"Are the vet bills expensive?"

Chase frowned. "Not especially. Should they be? Do you think Dr. Ramos is giving me a special rate?"

"No, no. But, well, Violet has been talking to Grandma and now she thinks that you're desperate for money to pay Quincy's bills and that, maybe . . ."

"Maybe I've been dipping into the till?"

"I told her that was ridiculous."

"It *is* ridiculous. Anna doesn't really believe Vi, does she?"

"I'm not sure. I haven't talked to her about it for more than a few words. Chase, let's talk about this later. I think that Grandma's having some other problems, but she won't talk about it. I gotta run, really. I'll call after work."

The cold that had entered Chase's spine downstairs now spread inside her. Her very heart felt chilled. It seemed Anna didn't find it hard to believe she would steal money from her business partner. From her own shop, for that matter.

Now she had to spend the entire day in Anna's company, knowing she'd harbored those thoughts about her, and ref-ereeing her incompatible employees. A few tears of self-pity escaped her nondescript blue-gray eyes. All she could see before her were Anna's periwinkle blues, giving her a steely stare of suspicion.

She splashed cold water on her face and returned to the fray.

After a couple of hours of pure torture—working in her kitchen had never been this hard before—her cell phone rang. She didn't recognize the ID, but it seemed official.

"Detective Olson here." Niles Olson, the good-looking policeman working on the murder case of Gabe Naughtly.

"Can I help you?"

Anna started paying attention when Chase used that polite, formal tone. She stopped mixing dough and cocked her head toward the counter where Chase had been sprinkling coconut onto some cooled Lemon Coconut Bars.

"We need to ask you a few more questions, Miss Oliver. Could you make it down to the station today?"

"Not . . . not right now. We're terribly busy."

"After hours, then. Give me a time and I'll be here."

"We . . . we're staying open late tonight. It's one of our busiest days of the year."

"What time?"

He was going to make her come to the station no matter what she said. "I'll be there at eight."

Could anything else go wrong today?

The cat was bored and hungry. He heard welcome sounds outside the office door. It sounded like a delivery person had entered the rear of the shop. That usually meant the back door would be propped open. The last time the older woman had darted in to leave him some cookie crumbs, the office door hadn't shut properly. He'd bided his time to use this knowledge, but now was the right time.

Hooking a claw around the protruding bit of the door, he nudged it open, just far enough for him to slip out. Slinking along the wall, no one saw him until he was at the rear door. The commotion and din made him move faster and he dashed through it. The alley and parking lot beckoned.

"**There goes Quincy**," said Anna. She pointed toward the back door with a spoon that dripped creamed butter and sugar.

"Not again." Chase shook her head and dashed out the

door the delivery man had come through. She almost knocked the boxes of cleaning supplies out of his arms. Twisting to help catch his wares, she felt her back wrench.

"Sorry, 'scuse me," she called, scrambling after her cat. Right outside the door, she halted. He hadn't gone far and she didn't want to frighten him into running away. Quincy crouched next to the trash bin, peering at something beneath it. Chase tiptoed to him and scooped him up, wincing at the pain that shot through her spine, hoping rats weren't under the bin staring out at her and Quincy, ready to invade her shop.

"Such a bad, bad boy," she cooed, cradling him and stroking his back.

The sounds of an argument reached her from the other end of the parking lot. A man and a woman stood on the other side of a car, only their heads visible above the roof of a small Toyota. The woman raised her arms and chopped the air repeatedly, her voice rising. She had a cute, short haircut.

It was Vi! Chase strained to hear what was going on. Was this guy the source of her recent distress? Chase wondered if she should go confront the young man—he looked to be the age of a college student or younger—and tell him to quit upsetting Vi. But Chase was holding Quincy. She needed to put him in a safe place first.

Back inside the kitchen, she deposited Quincy in the office and made sure the door was latched securely.

"I think that might be my fault." Anna cringed. "I might not have closed the door hard enough when I came out."

"When you came out from sneaking treats to him?"

Anna's softened demeanor vanished and her hostility returned. She turned her back to Chase and hit the button on the mixer with a vicious stab.

Way to go, Chase. Anna had started to apologize and Chase had immediately put her on the defensive. "Anna?"

She raised her head, but didn't look around and didn't reply.

"I'm sorry I snapped at you. We need to have a talk. I'm worried about you."

"Don't be. I'm all right." Anna's shoulders tightened and rose a notch, contradicting her words. "I just have some things to work out for myself. I seem to be taking it out on you."

"I didn't steal the money."

"We do need to have a talk. I need to tell you—"

Vi burst through the back door. "Sorry, I had to duck out for a minute." She hurried through the kitchen to the salesroom. Within seconds Laci rushed into the kitchen, sobbing.

"She's so mean! I can't work with her."

Now what?

NINE

Chase didn't get another chance to speak to Vi about the parking lot confrontation or to Anna about being suspicious of Chase before closing time at 7:30 PM. She'd soothed Laci by telling her she would give her a week off, starting Tuesday, when their rush would be over. Laci had considered that a whole week without seeing Violet Peters would be a much-needed balm for her. Chase hadn't pointed out that, after the rush, there would be no need for them to work together until the holidays. By that time, Chase hoped to have stood up to Anna about the situation. She would have to make time to speak to Vi about her treatment of poor little Laci, though. Vi had told Chase that she'd seen Ted making out with someone else. Even if she had, there was no need to tell Laci that, knowing she'd go off the deep end.

At precisely 7:30, Chase shooed the two women out the front door and turned the sign on the door to say they were closed. She flicked the overhead lights off and leaned her poor aching back against the door, but only for a moment.

The wood partitions for the little glass panes dug into her sore spine. She pushed away and strolled through the darkened shop humming "Tomorrow" from *Annie*. Stepping behind the counter, she pulled the trays from the display case, wincing each time she bent over. Most of them were empty, but three held a few bars that she would package and freeze to take to the homeless shelter when she had time.

Anna had left at 7:00, pleading an appointment, so Chase quickly did the cleanup that remained and headed for the police station. Walking through their parking lot at night was scarier than doing it during the day. The building was more forbidding, too. It loomed dark and gave her the chills.

She was buzzed through from the lobby to a sea of desks. Most were empty, but a lamp shed a pool of yellow on a desk at the far side of the room. Detective Olson's chestnut hair caught an edge of the light as he bent over some paperwork. The sound of her echoing footsteps alerted him to her presence in the otherwise empty room and he waved her to a seat beside his desk. This was much better than the stuffy interrogation room she'd been in before, although the stale air held odors of sweat and, possibly, fear.

She sat and noticed that his dark blue eyes looked weary.

"I just have a few more questions. I know I said we were done, but I want to try something."

She nodded. That didn't sound too ominous.

"Close your eyes and think back to the day you discovered Gabe's body."

"Okay." She bowed her head and squeezed her eyes shut.

"You're searching for your cat, you said."

"Right. Quincy is missing."

"Where are you?" His soft, smooth voice soothed her. She felt tension seeping out of her body.

"I'm searching for him. Walking down the street. Coming to the condos."

"Look around you. Is anyone else there?"

She shook her head. "I'm not looking for anyone, any people, I'm only looking for Quincy."

"Go ahead."

This felt almost like a hypnotism session she'd watched onstage in Chicago once. "There's a door standing open."

"Wide open?"

"No, just a crack. I walk up the steps and push it open."

"Why do you do that?"

She let out a puff of impatience. "To see if Quincy is in there." Why else would she enter a condo where she didn't know the resident?

"Why do you think he might be?"

"The way the door is barely open. He likes to squeeze through narrow places. It's a cat thing." She opened her eyes and stared at him defiantly. "Why do *you* think I went in there? To kill Gabe Naughtly?"

"You're sure you didn't see anyone else? No one on the sidewalk or across the street?"

"I didn't kill him." Her voice caught. If she started crying right now, she'd never forgive herself. "Just because I didn't see his killer doesn't mean I killed him. The killer had time to wipe his fingerprints off the knife. He probably left long before I got there."

Detective Olson leveled those serious eyes at her.

"What? What did I say? You're the one who told me about the fingerprints."

He drew a deep breath. "There was a lot of blood on that knife. I'm sure you remember that." Yes, she did. "That knife wasn't wiped after the blood got there."

"Oh." Her mind worked on high speed. "So . . . the killer wore gloves."

"Possibly."

"But Gabe's prints weren't on it either?"

Detective Olson shook his head.

"Was it even his knife? Did you test it for onions?"

"Onions?" He looked at Chase like she was crazy. "He wasn't killed by onions."

"Did his meatloaf have onions in it? Or bell peppers? That's what I put in mine. If the knife was his and was out of the knife block, he'd probably chopped onions with it. If not, maybe it's not his."

"Miss Oliver, I want you to concentrate on what you saw that night. Over the next few days, if anything occurs to you, let me know right away."

"Why do you think I saw someone?"

He didn't answer.

An idea popped into her head. "Because someone saw *me*, right? If they did, then they saw I didn't have time to kill him, right? Right?"

He handed her his card. "Call me if you remember anything."

On her way home, her hands started hurting from gripping the steering wheel so tight. She was livid, so angry at the detective she felt like squeezing his neck instead of the steering wheel. Why couldn't he at least tell her exactly why he was suspicious of her? He seemed to think she was lying. She had to convince him she wasn't. But how?

She called Julie as soon as she was in her bathrobe, settled in her favorite cinnamon-hued chair with a glass of red wine. She tucked a pillow behind her to ease her sprained back muscles. Chase held her breath as she listened to Julie's cell phone ringing away, afraid she wouldn't pick up. In the moment before it would have gone to voice mail, Julie answered, breathlessly. "I only have a minute. We're down to the wire on some paperwork."

"Two? Could I have two minutes? Please?"

Chase thought she must have sounded pitiful because Julie gave a light chuckle and said, "Aw, poor baby, what's the problem?"

"I just got home from being cross-examined by that Detective Olson."

"He has to question people, doesn't he?"

"But he doesn't have to suspect me of murder."

"He thinks you killed Gabe Naughtly? For real?"

"I'm not a hundred percent sure. But he intimated that someone saw me leave, or maybe enter, the condo. He acts like he doesn't think I'm telling him the truth about when I was there and what I did. I need to know what that person is saying. If they're lying about the times, it could look like I did it." An additional thought occurred to her. "Maybe that person is even the killer, trying to throw suspicion on me." Chase gulped some of her tart wine. It felt good.

"How awful! That would be hard to defend against."

"Could you find out who it is?"

"Well . . ."

"It has to be in a police report somewhere. Have you been able to get to those?"

"I can, but—okay, I'll try. I'll tell you, though, I may not be able to. I have no business being in those files, so I'll have to sneak."

"Love you, Jules. I understand. Don't jeopardize your job."

"I'll try my darnedest, Chase. I can't have you accused of murder!"

"Maybe, if I can find out who this is, there might be more information that hasn't been given to the police. This person might have seen someone else besides me."

"Then why wouldn't he mention it?"

Chase heard Julie's name being called.

"He might have seen someone familiar who belongs there," Chase said, in a rush. "Someone more likely to kill Gabe. One more quick question. What's with Anna lately?"

"She won't tell me. It's so aggravating! Gotta go. Talk to you later. Maybe tonight, late."

It was already too late to be considered early. Poor Julie, slaving away all weekend. Chase wished she'd had time to complain about her back. Julie's sympathy would make her feel better, she knew. Quincy jumped with one fluid motion into Chase's lap as she cut the connection. He bumped his head against her arm and her wine sloshed onto the sleeve of her robe.

"Quince! Now look what you did."

He turned his round, staring, all-knowing cat's eyes on her, the picture of innocence.

"I know, you didn't mean it."

Her robe was dark blue, so maybe the wine wouldn't show too badly. She scratched the top of his head. "I guess you want your treats, although I know you won't eat them."

She set her glass and her cell phone on the side table and went to the kitchen to sprinkle some diet cat treats into his dish. Quincy sat on his haunches and wrapped his tail around his front paws. He made no move toward the bowl on the floor. Chase shook her head. "What am I going to do with you?"

After rinsing the wine spot from her robe sleeve, she went back to her chair and picked up her phone.

"Dr. Ramos," Mike answered on the first ring. "Is that you, Chase?"

"You know it is. My number is right there."

"It's dark where I am. Couldn't quite see it before I answered."

"Where are you?" Immediately, she wished she could retract those words. It was no business of hers where he was. Or who he was with.

"I'm looking over some X-rays before I leave. It's been a long day. What do you need?"

X-rays. Right. Not a date in a dark restaurant. Come to think of it, maybe she needed X-rays herself. "The treats aren't working for Quincy. Neither is the diet cat food. I'm going to have to feed him something."

"Has he lost any weight at all yet?"

Chase squinted and thought, recalling the cat jumping into her lap. Was he lighter? "It doesn't seem like it."

He didn't answer.

"I know. Anna is slipping him things that he shouldn't have. I don't know how I can stop her. But can't I feed him something that tastes good to him? Then he wouldn't play on her heartstrings like he does."

"I'll dig around and see if there's anything new on the market that might work better. But you're a baker, aren't you? Maybe you could make something for him. Meanwhile, I want you to bring him in every couple of days so I can weigh him."

Unbidden, unwanted tears sprang from Chase's eyes. It was too much. Nothing was going right. She sniffed loudly.

"Are you all right?"

"No, I'm not all right," she wailed. She took a breath and calmed her voice. She was sounding like Laci. One more sip of wine. "Everything's going all wrong. Two of my employees hate each other. It's all I can do to keep them in the same room. Someone is stealing money from the cash register. My cat is miserable. And Detective Olson thinks I killed Gabe Naughtly."

"Why does he think that?" Mike sounded incredulous, which made Chase feel a smidgen better.

"Someone says they saw me that night, either entering or leaving the condo."

"So that makes him think you killed the man? Sounds far-fetched."

"If I could find out who the witness is, maybe I could see if he or she saw anyone else."

"There was someone else hanging out on the sidewalk earlier, before you got there."

Her heart leaped. "There was? You saw someone?"

"That guy Torvald Iversen. He was standing on the

sidewalk outside the condo when I got home. I noticed him because he wasn't doing anything, wasn't going anywhere, just standing outside Gabe's unit."

"That was before I got there, then?"

"Oh yes, quite a while before. Let me see if I can remember what time that would have been."

Torvald was there earlier? Had he already had his business meeting by the time Chase got there? Had he killed Gabe during their meeting? It would make sense that he was trying so hard to frame Chase if he were, in fact, the killer.

She heard Mike shuffle some pages. "What are you doing?"

"I keep an old-fashioned appointment book in my pocket. It's the only way I can organize my life. That day I had a three thirty appointment, so I would have been coming home about four. That's when I saw him. Then, when I went out later, sometime after eight thirty, I saw the commotion at Gabe's and came over and took Quincy."

Chase felt better after her call to Mike. She started humming "Everything's Coming Up Roses" from *Gypsy*. She hoped Julie could find the name of the nosy eyewitness. Surely the person would have seen Torvald, too. She wondered if he was being questioned as strenuously as she was.

TEN

It was Sunday, but not a day of rest for Chase and her crew. It was September 2 and classes would start Tuesday, the fourth. The Bar None would close at six on Tuesday. They would stay closed on Wednesday to recover from the onslaught of the last week. It would be relaxing with just Vi working on Tuesday, and Laci gone for a week. After that, Anna had told Chase she was going to tell the girl she was no longer needed. Anna had said they needed to replace her with someone less histrionic. Chase hadn't spoken up, but she was determined to do so, if they could get some uninterrupted moments. She wished they could hire a third worker, but they couldn't afford that.

These were Chase's thoughts as she pedaled her bike south along Fourteenth Avenue on her way home from an early ride. She'd taken a couple of pain pills at bedtime and two more this morning. The pain seemed to be easing up in the small of her back. The song "Any Dream Will Do" from *Joseph and the Amazing Technicolor Dreamcoat* was on her lips.

The day was fine. The warm, clear autumn weather was holding. She had felt the humidity today on her ride. Crisp days weren't too far away, though, and cooler temperatures. Brilliant fall days with bright leaves swirling from lofty tree branches were her favorite times in Minneapolis.

Her cell phone rang as she stopped for a red light at Fourth Street. It was Julie. She hadn't called back last night. Chase would suggest a getaway for the two of them when their crunch times were over. Maybe Julie had found the identity of the witness. Chase hoisted her front tire onto the curb and answered the call.

"I came in early, before anyone else got here." Julie was almost whispering.

"Won't that look suspicious?"

"No, I still have lots to do today. I need to get an early start on that anyway."

"So?"

"Yes, I found her."

"Her? For some reason, I've been picturing a 'him.' "

"The name is Hilda Bjorn. She lives almost directly across the street from Gabe Naughtly's condo. If I'm not mistaken, she has a small house with a nice front porch. I think I've seen a rocker there. I'll bet she's as old as the hills and sits and watches everyone and everything."

"I hope you're right, that she sees everything. Then she'll have seen Torvald Iversen, too. Mike says he was there quite a bit before I was. But if she's too old, her memory might be bad."

"Yah, there's that. Let's hope not. Are you going to talk to her?"

"I sure will. This should be a superbusy day in the shop. Maybe I'd better go over there right now." She hadn't worked up too much of a sweat. Her shower could be skipped and she could throw on her working clothes in a minute.

"Anything else interesting? Did you read Iversen's statement?"

"I did. Nothing much to it. He states that he's an investment broker, but it doesn't say who any of his clients are. He made a point of saying he hadn't been to the condo that day until he arrived and saw you with the dead body. The way this is written, it sounds like they don't believe him. Let me know what you find out from the woman. I hear voices. Some of the others are showing up. Gotta go."

"Thanks a million. Love you, Jules."

Chase's heart lifted as she stuck her phone into her jacket pocket. She turned around and rode her bike to the block where Gabe's condo was. Iversen lied in his statement! Would an innocent person do that? Dr. Ramos had said he'd seen him there earlier. She'd have to think of a way to use this.

Meanwhile, she'd talk to Hilda Bjorn. Sure enough, right across the street was a cute little house, painted red, with a white wicker rocker on the porch. Chase leaned her bike against the railing and mounted the steps to knock on the front door. After an interval, she knocked again, but not a sound issued from inside the little red house. The front door of the neighboring house flew open. A harried young man with a disorderly mop of hair clattered down his steps, then noticed Chase on the porch.

"Are you looking for Hilda?" he asked, peering through thick glasses.

"Yes, Hilda Bjorn. Do you know when she'll be here?"

His brow puckered in thought. "Don't know. She's in the hospital again. Sometimes she doesn't stay long."

Her hopes were dashed. She couldn't invade an elderly woman's hospital room to interrogate her. "Okay," said Chase, descending the wooden steps.

"Do you want me to tell her you were here?" He seemed anxious to be helpful.

"No, no, I'll catch her later."

"She might appreciate a visit. She's at the U Medical Center."

Chase waved her thanks and hurried back to open up her shop. She pedaled across the parking lot behind her store and picked up her bike so she could carry it up the stairs. The pain meds seemed to be wearing off.

A movement caught her eye at the edge of the parking lot. The sun glinted off a head of blond hair. A tall man faced her, staring intently across the top of a sedan. The man turned and walked away quickly. Shaun Everly! He'd been standing behind a car, watching her. He knew where she lived. She unlocked her door with an unsteady hand and carried her bike in.

She was still breathing more quickly than usual when she came down to the shop with Quincy. Anna had gotten in before her and made coffee. After Chase deposited Quincy in the office and shut the door tightly, she saw Anna notice her tremor as she poured herself a cup. Well, if Anna could have secrets, so could she. Anna hadn't told her why she'd left before closing the day before, what the appointment was for, or what was bothering her so much that she couldn't look Chase in the eye this morning.

Soon, the Bar None was thrumming along and almost felt normal. Anna was mixing up batter for Amaretto Lemon Bars, Laci and Vi were swamped with customers, too busy to bicker, and Chase was humming "Circle of Life" from *The Lion King* and cutting up a batch of Cherry Oat Bars and placing them on a tray to slide into the display case in front.

The sight of Shaun, staring at her across the pavement, stayed with her, though. Every once in a while, she shivered and broke off her song. She had no idea what to do about his presence.

In the middle of the morning, the strident tones of Doris Naughtly drifted to the kitchen. Chase saw Anna's back stiffen, but neither of them commented . . . until Chase heard Torvald Iversen's disturbing, spooky voice no more than two minutes later. Doris raised hers, becoming even louder than usual. Was she upset? Chase wondered. She wouldn't put anything past that horrible man.

Chase wiped her hands on her apron and poked her head through the double doors. Doris was backed up to the pink shelves on the side wall, hemmed in by Torvald. He stood over her, leaning in, his long, thin arms surrounding her, with his hands on the shelves. She wasn't making an effort to escape. In fact, she was tilting her head and giving him coy looks. Evidently, thought Chase, she wasn't wasting any time getting over the death of her husband.

Stealing up behind the man, Chase asked, "Can I help you?"

She stifled a smile when he jumped at her being so near without his detecting her arrival. He threw Chase a glare and straightened up. Doris smiled at Chase and smoothed her hair, although it was sprayed so vigorously that it couldn't possibly be disarranged.

"Yes, please," breathed Doris. She grabbed a carton of Lemon Bars from the shelf behind her. "I'd like these, please."

"Violet will help you at the register, Mrs. Naughtly." Chase gestured toward the sales counter in the rear of the shop.

Torvald had no choice but to step aside, glowering, and let Doris proceed to the cash register.

Chase kept her voice low. "I need to ask you a question."

He gave her a haughty look, easy to do from his height.

"What were your dealings with Gabe? I know you and he were doing business together. I also know you weren't there for a dinner meeting, like you told me." It was a bluff. Would it work?

She seemed to have penetrated his armor. A line of worry

appeared between his pale eyebrows. "What are you talking about?"

"I know he wanted to buy my shop. Were you helping him do that?"

"Ha." It was a mere syllable, devoid of humor. "It's none of your business."

"Is that what you killed him over?"

"The man led me to believe he could pull his weight, financially. I was a fool to believe him. It was nothing worth killing over."

He spun on his heel and left the shop.

Would Torvald be in hot water for not securing the deal for his client? Would it be worthwhile for him to kill Gabe? It didn't seem too likely. But the man *had* lied to the police. Something was very off-kilter about that man.

Chase returned to the sales counter, where Vi was ringing up Mrs. Naughtly's purchase.

"What was that about?" Chase asked her.

"That horrid man was coming on to me," Doris Naughtly said. "He wanted to have dinner! And my husband still warm in his grave, poor soul."

Chase shuddered. For one thing, she was sure the man in his grave was not still warm. Graves were cold places. For another, the thought of being hit on by Torvald Iversen made her skin itch. For yet another, Doris hadn't acted upset about him until Chase had interrupted them.

After Doris calmed down and left, Chase went back to the kitchen.

"Doris was being a drama queen again?" Anna asked. She drew out the word *drama* with an unattractive sneer.

"Anna, I wish you'd tell me what's going on."

The older woman walked to the storage shelves and ran her fingers along the bins, examining them, probably not for anything except an excuse to ignore Chase.

"Doris was . . . well, Torvald Iversen was . . . He had her cornered."

"Good." She kept her face away from Chase. "She's probably sleeping with him."

"She didn't seem to mind it until after he'd left. Anna, I love you. You're like my grandmother and my mother. I couldn't make it without you. It hurts when you shut me out."

Chase's grandparents had passed away before her parents' deaths. She had one dim memory of watching her grandfather fill his pipe, but didn't even remember her grandmother at all.

Anna turned from the shelves slowly, dropping her hands to her sides.

"I suppose I'm overreacting. But Doris is . . ."

"Yes?"

Anna slumped onto a stool and propped her elbows on the counter. "She's always been like this. I should be used to it."

Chase sat beside her business partner–cum–beloved substitute grandmother and waited for her to continue. Chase lifted a hand to pat Anna's back, then hesitated. Maybe she'd wait for Anna to get whatever it was off her chest first.

"We went to high school together. I did date Gabe a couple of times. Nothing serious. But Doris, for some reason, has always been jealous of me. She lured Gabe away, then dropped him. Years later, I found out they were getting married. I actually went to Gabe and told him I didn't think it was a good idea. He laughed, so that was the end of that."

Now Chase patted Anna's shoulder. Anna put her own warm hand over Chase's. "I can't ever complain about the man I ended up with. My goodness, that man could dance. We went out almost every weekend when we started dating, not very long after high school."

Anna's face softened and the haggard look of the past

few days fell away. She tilted her head upward, remembering her young romance. Chase didn't have a hard time picturing Anna dancing the night away with Allan. She was in her seventies now and still looked capable of it. In fact, Chase was sure Anna would be able to outdance her.

Anna smiled, then a couple of tears ran down her weathered cheeks. "I still miss that man."

Vi pushed the double doors open. "Almost out of Cherry Almond."

"There's a batch ready in"—Anna checked the oven timer—"two minutes." Anna jumped up the get the oven mitts.

Chase didn't get another chance to find out more about the history between Doris and Anna that morning.

The long Sunday morning bustled on until it was time for the sales clerks to take lunch breaks.

Chase rubbed her back. If she got a chance, she'd run upstairs for another pain pill. She stuck her head into the store. "Who's first today for lunch?"

Vi waved her hand. "I need to run out. Can I have the first break?"

Laci assumed a put-upon pout that said she disapproved, but she didn't say anything. Vi grabbed her big tote bag from under the counter and dashed out the front door, almost knocking over a pair of gangly freshman women.

Seeing her flee, apparently in no better shape than she'd been in the past few days, Chase was reminded that she still needed to talk to Vi about her troubles. She hadn't gotten far talking about Anna's with her yet. Laci was another matter. The poor girl's heart was on her frilly, lace-trimmed sleeve. Anna probably hadn't talked to Ted either.

Ted Naughtly chose that moment to enter the shop. With only Laci to tend to sales and customers, Chase decided to stay out front. She whipped off her apron and stowed it beneath the counter when Laci minced her way to the front of the store to greet Ted.

As the two of them spoke, heads together and nearly touching, a gang of college students swarmed in. It seemed like a whole fraternity, at least a dozen good-size potential football tackles.

They scattered, browsing the tables, the shelves, and some perusing the glass case.

"Hey, lady, could you tell me what these are?" One curly-headed giant beckoned from the front of the store, on the opposite side from where Laci and Ted communed. Laci wore a frown instead of her usual besotted look in Ted's presence.

Chase sighed and left her post of guarding the cash drawer from Ted and went up front to tell the young man what the contents of a box labeled Cherry Almond Oatmeal Bars contained. She assured him there was no coconut and he gathered up three boxes. For the next ten or fifteen minutes she was kept busy reciting contents for the others. She would never get upstairs for a pain pill at this rate.

When she returned to the cash register to ring up their purchases, Ted and Laci were there. At least the cash drawer wasn't open.

Chase drew a deep breath. She didn't want to lose her temper in front of these very good customers. She yanked Laci's arm and drew her close. "Miss Laci Carlson," she hissed under her breath, directly into Laci's ear. "Have I or have I not told you that Ted does not belong here behind the counter?"

Laci's eyes opened wide. "Well . . ."

"Have I or have I not?" Chase repeated through gritted teeth. "Tell him to leave the store right now."

She shooed both of them from behind the counter. Ted gave Chase a glum stare as he slid past her. Laci looked near to tears. The burly guy customers didn't seem to notice the scene, talking loudly among themselves and occasionally punching each other's arm.

After they left with a considerable number of purchases, Chase and Laci were alone in the salesroom. What would Anna say? Chase wondered. She tried to summon up the older woman's wisdom and experience. She also needed to make sure Anna didn't fire Laci.

Laci shrank as Chase faced her. "That will not happen again. Do you understand me?"

"What do you have against poor Ted?"

"Poor Ted is stealing from us! I've told you that. I'm about to ban him from the store. You will tell me if he comes in here again." Was she going overboard? If only her back didn't ache so. It was making her extra grouchy.

Laci started sobbing.

"Go into the kitchen until you can straighten up and do your job."

Chase felt like Cinderella's evil stepmother as Laci slunk through the double doors with her hands to her teary face. It occurred to Chase that this was perfect passive-aggressive behavior on Laci's part. Chase disliked being manipulated. She heaved a sigh. What next?

One more rush day, Chase told herself that night as she brushed her teeth for bed. She just needed to get through Monday.

ELEVEN

Monday was humming along and Chase was feeling that she would make it through the day. She watched the clock in the afternoon. The hour hand crept toward six. At seven thirty they would close up and the rush time would be over.

She had brought plenty of aspirin and Tylenol downstairs to the shop today and alternating them was helping her back pain. Her mood was better because of that, she was sure.

Anna and Chase had stocked the shelves for the last time at five and were both working the front of the store. Many last-minute freshmen were moving in and finding they needed something sweet to tide them over until dinnertime. Vi had asked to take an extra break at five, an inconvenient time given the number of customers in the shop right then. Chase wondered if Anna would try to replace both of their sales clerks.

At five forty-five, Vi was returning when Ted Naughtly showed up. Chase's good mood was fast evaporating. It was time to be direct.

She stood in front of the young man and blocked his way. "You are not welcome here, Ted. Please leave."

"I don't want to stay. I just need to tell Laci something." He glanced over his shoulder, out the front window, to the sidewalk.

Chase followed his gaze. A young woman closer to Ted's age than Laci's, maybe midtwenties, dressed in a very short skirt and very high-heeled shoes, stood on the sidewalk, her nose in the air, seeming interested in the top of the gingko tree that grew through a round hole in the pavement in front of the Bar None. Her bosom threatened to spill from the low-cut top.

"I promise I won't be back," he said.

Something in his manner made Chase stand aside and let him pass. Laci was near the rear of the store, holding a stack of boxes for a student's matronly relative who seemed to be stocking up for winter. The poor, slight girl struggled to contain the cartons in her thin arms as the woman, unconcerned, piled on a few more.

Chase watched as Ted walked to Laci's side. Laci turned her head and gave him a huge smile, bobbled, but didn't drop the boxes. Ted put his head near hers, as he always did. This time it had a different effect. He couldn't have said more than a dozen words before her smile vanished. Her expression continued to deteriorate as Ted left the store.

The young woman on the pavement took his arm and snuggled against him as they disappeared down the street without a backward glance from either of them.

Chase turned at the sound of a crash. Laci lay on the floor in a dead faint, surrounded by the scattered boxes she'd been juggling.

After a split second of shock, Chase rushed to her inert form. She knelt and shouted Laci's name a few times. Anna rushed in from the kitchen. Vi stood frozen for a few minutes, then grabbed the showcase for support.

"What was that noise?" asked Anna. "It sounded like something hit the—" She spied the two of them on the floor, one unconscious, and whipped out her cell phone. Chase breathed a sigh of relief that Anna was taking charge. Now everything would be all right. What else could go wrong that day?

Not more than two minutes passed before an ambulance pulled up, sirens blaring and lights flashing. Laci's eyelids fluttered and she turned her head. When she tried to struggle up, Chase put a hand on her shoulder. "Don't get up, Laci. Wait until the EMTs check you out."

The uniformed medics rushed into the shop and started working on Laci with the tools of their trade. One pumped the blood pressure cuff while another inspected her eyes, skin, and heartbeat.

Within a few minutes they decided to transport her to the hospital for observation. "Her blood pressure isn't what it should be," said the crisp blonde woman with the cuff. "She may be dehydrated." Her partner, the guy with the stethoscope looped around his neck, brought in a gurney and they carefully lifted Laci onto it. Chase and Anna followed them to the rear of the ambulance. Anna thought to ask which hospital she was being taken to. It made sense that she was being transported to the nearby University of Minnesota Medical Center.

"I'll drive," said Anna. "Come through the shop."

Chase started to follow Anna inside so she could go to the parking lot where Anna's car was, but a hard hand clamped her forearm.

"Where did they say she was going?" It was Ted.

"Ted, what happened?" Chase shook off his hand. "After you talked to her she passed out. Right after you went out the door. Do you know if she's sick?"

"Oh no. I did it."

"What did you do?"

"Don't shout at me," he growled. The buxom miniskirted woman lingered in the crowd of gawkers that had gathered, her wary, puzzled eyes on him. "I told her I was breaking up with her. I've been trying to tell her, subtly, but she wouldn't get the message. So I brought Krystal with me so Laci could see her, and I told her flat-out."

"She's . . . delicate, you know."

"Boy, do I. Where are they taking her?"

"U of M."

Ted hurried away. Chase, after calling to Vi to mind the store, ran through the two rooms and out the back door to Anna's car. As they sped southward, toward the hospital, Chase's cell phone rang with a call from Vi.

"Chase? Miss Oliver?" What was wrong with everyone? Now Vi sounded distressed, like the world was ending.

"What is it, Vi?" She knew she had snarled at her. She softened her voice. "We'll be back before closing."

"The health inspector is here. He says he needs to reinspect."

"Now? He has to do it now?" She could hardly expect the inspector to know that her employee was being rushed to the hospital. "Can he do this later?"

"He says not. His schedule is tight."

Chase told Vi she'd be there in ten minutes. She told Anna to drop her back at the store. When would she learn to quit asking herself what else could go wrong?

TWELVE

Anna let Chase out in front of the Bar None and continued on to the hospital to see about Laci. Chase entered her own shop through the front door, something she didn't usually do during business hours. Today she paused to appreciate her place. Seeing the cheery striped walls, the pink shelving, and, in the rear of the room, the shiny glass display case lifted her spirits momentarily. Customers eager to satisfy their sweet tooth milled about, creating a low, pleasant murmur. With the alluring aromas in the air, the first impression was nice for visitors, she decided.

She hoped it worked on health inspectors. Her insides tightened a bit, thinking about him poking around in the kitchen with no one else there.

Vi waited patiently while a couple of giggling upperclasswomen made up their minds what to purchase. Chase was glad to see that Vi was her usual put-together self, poised and polished. It had been a few days since she'd seen the old Vi.

She hurried through to the kitchen to find the same inspector as last time, the lanky, bespectacled Harold Johnson, this time in a blue plaid shirt, standing in the middle of the space scribbling on his pad of paper. He glanced up at her entrance and gave her a smile. She hoped that was a good sign.

"I see the sign is in place," he said.

Chase held her breath. The job Anna had done tacking it up again had worked, probably because she'd used pushpins, not trusting Chase's tape job. Now the employees could read about how they had to wash their hands every time they visited the restroom, something Chase was sure they appreciated.

Could the reinspection be this easy? He was still peering at her through his round glasses lenses, smiling underneath his bristling mustache. She nodded.

"All done, then." He clicked his pen shut and extended his hand.

Chase grabbed it and pumped the handshake. "Okay, then, good, good." She probably sounded like a babbling fool, but it was a relief to have something go right.

After he left, Chase helped Vi in the front until the stream slowed to a trickle at around 7:00.

"We have officially made it through the rush," she said to Vi. "Let's call it quits. I'll flip the sign and you can leave as soon as these last few are waited on. I think I ought to get to the hospital to see Laci."

"I hope she'll be all right." Vi wasn't heartless after all.

"I do need to see her. Will you do okay here by yourself?"

Vi glanced at the three people left in the Bar None, all elderly women, for a change. "I'll make it."

"See you tomorrow, then. It should be relaxing." Classes started on Tuesday and their business at the shop would be a fraction of what it had been for the last couple of weeks. At least she had Vi to depend on, to close up the store.

Chase went out the back, trying to tamp down an irrational feeling of unease, and drove to the University Medical Center.

She sped down East River Parkway, turned left on Harvard Street and zipped into the parking garage, sliding into a space fairly near the pedestrian tunnel. She ran down the long tunnelway to the main hospital and rushed to the emergency desk to find out where Laci was.

A very short older woman with gleaming snow-white hair was talking with the desk clerk. Chase got in line behind her since only one clerk was in evidence. A noise from her purse startled her—it was her cell phone. The desk clerk glared at Chase and pointed to a sign on the wall that said "Silence Cell Phone's." Chase sighed at the misplaced apostrophe, but followed the instructions. A glance showed an unfamiliar number, so she stuck the cell into her purse.

"Yes, dearie, thanks for asking," the woman said, her voice strong in spite of her elderly looks and her diminutive size. She wore a pink velour pantsuit under a puffy down-filled jacket. "I'm feeling so much better."

Chase couldn't hear the soft-spoken woman behind the counter, who was typing and swiveling back and forth between the older woman and her computer screen. Chase hummed "Get Me to the Church on Time" from *My Fair Lady* and bounced with impatience, anxious to see how Laci was doing. That sent a twinge to her spine, so she stopped and stood still, changing her tune to the more sedate "Ol' Man River" from *Show Boat*.

The white-haired woman glanced up at Chase. Her light blue eyes sparkled behind wire-rimmed glasses. "I won't be much longer, dear. Just checking out."

The woman turned to the clerk and spoke again. "Yes, that's right. . . . That's right. . . . No, I live on Fourteenth Avenue Southeast. I believe you entered Southwest." She leaned to one side to see the computer screen better. "And my name is spelled with a *J*. Yes, Hilda Bjorn."

Then it clicked for Chase. This was the woman who had reported seeing her! Anna was with Laci; she'd be fine. Chase needed to talk to this woman.

As the woman finished her business and turned away from the window, Chase waylaid her.

"Ms. Bjorn? Could I speak with you for a few moments?"

She peered past Chase, out the glass doors. "I don't think my ride is here yet. What do you need?"

"Would you like to sit down?"

"I'm old, dear, not dead yet. I can stand up. I was just in for a tiny infection in my insulin pump hole. That's what I call it, my pump hole."

Afraid she'd insulted the woman, Chase hurried to apologize. "I didn't mean . . . No, I don't think—"

"That's all right. It was rude of me to get snippy. Now, what's on your mind?"

"I'm Chase Oliver. I'm the person you saw coming out of Gabe Naughtly's condo the day he was murdered."

"Oh my. Yes, you are, aren't you?" She peered at Chase closely. "Yes, I can see that you resemble her." The woman drew back a bit. "Should I be afraid?" She peered around. "We are in a public place."

"I didn't kill Gabe Naughtly!" The clerk at the counter glanced up and Chase lowered her voice. "I thought that maybe you might have seen someone else that same day."

"I see lots of people every day. But that day? Let me think. Andy, of course. That's my next-door neighbor. His name is Anderson Fear, Professor Fear." Chase wondered if that was the somewhat fearful-looking man who had told her that Ms. Bjorn was in the hospital. "He comes and goes between his classes and his office hours. That day there were a lot of people at that condo. A young man looked like he was coming to see Gabe, after Gabe got home, but he didn't go in, just hung around on my side of the street. Oh yes, and that young woman had gone in already, the one that dresses kind of like, well, like a floozy. You know, those tight clothes, all those tattoos, and those horrid shoes. It's a wonder she's never broken an ankle in those things. She didn't stay as long as she usually does and she came out while the young man was still hanging around. She's been there a lot lately."

"Anyone else?"

The woman frowned in thought.

"Did you see the tall, thin man, very pale, wearing a blazer? He came in right after me that day." Chase would love to nail Torvald Iversen for the crime.

"Maybe. I'm not quite sure. I'll have to think about . . ." She looked outside. "Oh, there's my ride. Come see me sometime, dearie."

Chase saw the man she had already pegged as Professor Fear get out of a small Japanese car and come inside. He smiled when he saw Ms. Bjorn. "Ready to go?"

She nodded, turning to Chase before she left. "I'm sorry I couldn't help you, dear. I'm sure you didn't kill anyone."

It would be nice if more people were sure of that, thought Chase. So, a young man and a floozy. Who the heck would they be?

At the counter, the woman wouldn't give her Laci's room number, so she texted Anna and got it. The woman did tell her where the elevators were, so she took one up to Laci's floor. When she found Laci's location, Anna stood in the doorway, looking ready to leave. Chase raised her eyebrows and Anna nodded to the interior of the room.

Ted Naughtly sat on the edge of the bed, leaning in close and stroking Laci's hand. They were gazing into each other's eyes and neither had noticed Chase's arrival. The breakup hadn't lasted long, she thought.

Chase cleared her throat. They both kept gazing. "Hi, Laci," she finally said.

Ted jerked upright.

"Hi, Miss Oliver," said Laci wanly. Chase had asked both Laci and Vi to call her Chase, but it had never taken.

"How are you feeling?" Chase asked.

Laci batted her eyelashes at Ted. "Better with Teddy here." She managed a weak smile.

"I'd better go," he said, standing up. "Mom probably has dinner ready."

"Buh-bye." Laci sighed and gave him a limp wave.

"See you." He pushed past Chase and disappeared down the hallway.

Chase entered the room and sat in the visitor's chair while Anna still hovered at the door. The hard plastic seat didn't do anything for her back pain, and it flared up again. "Are you going home tonight?"

"No, they're keeping me until tomorrow morning for observation." She didn't seem to approve of that. Her weakness suddenly vanished as she propped herself up and poured a glass of ice chips, maneuvering around her IV. She'd been putting on an act for "Teddy," Chase realized. The little vixen.

"What's the reason for keeping you?"

"Oh, they said I was dehydrated."

"And her heart rhythm is a little off," said a nurse, bustling into the room with a blood pressure cuff. She wrapped the sleeve around Laci's arm and pumped. "She'll go home tomorrow if the scan for a concussion comes up normal and if nothing else happens."

"But she's okay?" asked Chase.

"Basically." The cuff deflated with a whoosh. The nurse unwound the Velcro, then noted Laci's numbers on an electronic pad and left.

"I've been dieting," Laci said. "I guess I overdid it."

"Dieting?" Anna spoke up at last. "Girl, you don't have an ounce to lose. What were you thinking?"

"Teddy's mom is so thin. I think he probably likes really thin women."

Chase pictured the miniskirted woman he'd gone off with just before Laci fainted. She wouldn't win any skinny contests, not with her top half, anyway.

"Laci," Chase said, "your job is to rest up and feel better. Let us know if you need anything."

"Laci!" A woman rushed in and ran to the bed, followed by a slower man who looked at Laci with deep concern. "Baby doll! We came as fast as we could when we heard."

"We were at the cabin," the man said. "Traffic was terrible."

"Oh, you always say that, Dad. Mom, Dad." Laci gestured around the room. "These are my bosses, Ms. Oliver and Mrs. Larson."

After all four shook hands, Anna and Chase left Laci with her parents.

"Vi should have closed up by now," said Chase. Weariness descended on her, pushing her down farther than the elevator was taking her. "Laci seems to have fairly normal parents. I wonder why she has to take up with a guy like Ted."

"Who knows anything about anybody?" This wasn't the cheerful, upbeat Anna that Chase knew.

"What do you mean?"

"It seems like you never really know someone, anyone. A person you think you know, a person close to you, could be, for instance, an embezzler."

It was an effort for Chase to keep her jaw from dropping.

"Who wants to go over the books?" Anna asked, leaning against the rear wall of the elevator as the floors dinged past. "You or me?"

"I can. You've been doing it every night for a while." *Only because you suspect I'm pilfering our money.*

"Go ahead. I'm whipped."

Chase looked at Anna directly. She seemed tired, maybe even more tired than Chase felt. The elevator doors opened, and before Chase could say anything else, Anna hurried out to the emergency parking lot, where she'd left her car.

How was she ever going to find out what was bothering her dear Anna? How were they ever going to get back to their easy, relaxed relationship? How was Chase going to find out if Anna truly thought Chase was stealing money?

THIRTEEN

The cat rested in one of his favorite spots, his owner's lap. The computer desk did make it a little cramped, but it would do until she came to and realized she hadn't fed him yet. The sudden ringing of the bell was too much, though. He jumped down and began ignoring everything in favor of cleaning his whiskers.

Chase could tell, from Quincy's swishing tail and his swiveled ears, that the doorbell on the back door startled him as much as it did her. It was an odd time of night for someone to be coming by from the parking lot.

When Chase opened the door, a frigid gust blasted her in the face. Julie burst in, slapping her arms with ungloved hands.

"A front came through," Julie said. "I didn't dress for this today."

"You look like you're dressed up for something," said

Chase, slamming and locking the door against the wind. "Come into the office. It's toasty warm there. Or do you want a hot drink?"

"I'm still dressed for court. Do you have some of that orange spice herb tea?"

"You'd better come upstairs for that. I'm tired of doing these numbers anyway."

Quincy followed them up the stairs to Chase's apartment.

"I have so much to tell you." Julie tossed her light jacket onto the back of Chase's leather couch and rubbed her hands together.

"Me, too," said Chase. "But you go first." Chase scooped food into Quincy's bowl. He gave her a sniff of disdain and stalked away.

Julie gave Chase a second look. "Are you in pain?"

"A little. It comes and goes. So, your case."

"We went to court today. In fact, we've all been celebrating for the last couple of hours."

"Hence, the odor of gin."

"Just a couple of G and Ts. Or three. I took a cab here."

"I would have picked you up. Why didn't you call?"

"I've been trying to for ages."

"Oh." Chase remembered she'd turned her ringer off in the hospital. After she set her kettle on the burner, she turned her sound back on. "I'll tell you about this. But go ahead. What's your case?"

"You know who Bill Shandy is?"

Chase shook her head, rummaging in her pantry for the tea that Julie liked.

"You know. Bill. The guy with the pet store." Quincy jumped into Julie's lap.

"Oh, *that* Bill. The one Anna took the rats to."

"Bill and Grandma knew each other in high school, and I think they were quite the item back then. But they married other people. Bill's wife died about a year ago. I know that the stepchildren wanted half of Bill's money at that time. They weren't entitled to it, but he did give them some."

"Some of this is beginning to sound familiar. I remember Anna talking about him. Didn't the dead wife have some children before she married him?"

"Yah, she had two children by her first husband, a marriage that only lasted three years."

"How old are the children?" The kettle whistled and Chase poured the water over the tea.

"One is forty-eight, the other fifty."

"And you know this, how?"

"It's our case. The oldest of Bill's stepchildren, Marvin, has been in and out of politics most of his life. After his mother's death, her son Marvin founded a charity organization called PCP, Pennies Can Provide."

"An unfortunate acronym. It's gotten a lot of press, though."

"The whole thing is unfortunate. The group collected donations to buy books to give to hospitalized children. Only problem, no children ever got any books after the first month."

"How did he think he could get away with that?" Chase handed Julie a steaming mug, redolent of citrus and cloves.

Julie cupped her hands around its warmth and sipped. "Marvin's been skating on the edge for years. He was elected to the school board in Minnetonka, but they booted him because they suspected he was stealing money. They could never prove it, so no action was taken."

"So I guess the legal people have been watching him."

"Bill Shandy is just about continuously arguing with that stepson about money. It's enough to give a person an ulcer." Quincy butted his head against Julie's wrist. She avoided spilling the tea, so he tried it again. "Bill feels he has to save something for his own son."

"You know Bill well?"

"Grandma's been dating him. She's pretty smitten. And

she's awfully upset about this whole thing, since Bill is taking it so hard. She says he feels responsible for what Marvin does. After all, he did raise the guy for most of his life."

Chase was surprised Anna had been able to keep this from her. Why hadn't she told Chase she was dating Bill? "Is that what's been bothering her?" It bothered Chase that Anna hadn't said a word to her about this.

Julie nodded and gulped down the tea, now cool enough to drink. "It's been bothering me, too, I have to tell you! I didn't know they were dating when I was assigned to this case, otherwise I wouldn't have worked on it. Grandma's keeping it quiet, though, and this is a big chance for me. This is going to be in the headlines tomorrow. Well, probably on the TV tonight. It's already all over the Internet. Then it'll be worse than ever for Bill."

"Is that all?"

"What do you mean?"

"I mean, is that all that's bothering Anna? We're having money problems in the shop. Has she said anything about that?"

"A little, but I'm not clear on the details." Julie glanced at her wristwatch. "I'd better get going. Back in court tomorrow." She rose and grabbed her jacket. "I don't think she's said anything about the shop being in trouble financially."

"Can I drive you home?"

"We've both had long days. I'll take another cab. No problem."

After Julie left, Chase reflected on the fact that she hadn't exactly answered the question about Anna and money problems. But maybe, just maybe, the embezzler Anna had mentioned was Marvin Shandy, and not Chase Oliver.

She returned downstairs to finish up and shut down the computer. As the screen closed, she wrinkled her nose in disgust.

"Now what?" she muttered to no one, or perhaps to

Quincy. He ignored her and began licking a paw to swipe his ears. "I'm sure Ted didn't have a chance to filch any money from the cash drawer. It's not him. But there sure is money missing. Nearly a hundred and fifty this time."

The clock on the desk read 10:30. On a normal night, Anna would still be awake. Chase picked up her cell phone and called.

"Anna? We're short again."

When she gave Anna the figure, there was silence for a half a minute.

"I think I should tell you," Anna said, "what I overheard from Vi a few days ago. You were in the office and Vi was on her phone."

Chase wondered if this was the conversation she, herself, had eavesdropped on through the office door.

"I couldn't hear everything she said, but my hearing is sharper than she must think it is."

It didn't do to underestimate Anna, Chase knew.

"It was something about missing money—I heard those two words—so I tuned in. She referred to something that she knew about, but couldn't prove. And it had to do with you."

Chase remembered very well what she'd heard.

"I'm talking about the money. It's not there. No, I don't have it, Felix."

"No, I can't. She's the owner. . . . Okay, co-owner. Same thing. I need to talk to you."

"Yes, I know it happened, but I can't prove it."

Vi had referred to the co-owner, not necessarily to Chase.

"Charity, I've gone back and forth on this, then back and forth again. I almost got myself believing Vi thought you had taken the money."

Even though Chase had overheard the same conversation, she hadn't jumped to the conclusion that Anna was a thief. Or had she? Just for a moment?

"I've been thinking all along," Chase said, "that it was Ted."

"Some of it might have been. This is a lot more tonight than has been missing before. It may have been taken by someone else."

Chase reached down to rub Quincy's head, consolation for dumping him onto the floor. Her back spasmed and she must have let out a whimper.

"Charity, are you in pain?"

"I pulled my back the other day. I'll be all right. When I went to the hospital, I left Vi alone in the shop. I wonder if someone took it while she wasn't noticing. There were only three older women there and I turned the open-close sign over before I left."

"I suppose she could have let someone else in," Anna said. "Or Vi could have taken the money."

"I doubt that. She drives an awfully nice car and her clothes look expensive, too. That girl has money. I was supposed to talk to her about whatever was bothering her and I never did. I don't think I'll be able to tomorrow, but Thursday or Friday, I'll be sure and do that. And I'll ask who, exactly, was in the shop tonight after I left."

"That's about all we can do for now," Anna agreed. "But this can't go on. Our profit margin isn't large enough."

"I know."

Quincy narrowed his amber eyes in agreement.

Tuesday didn't start out well. At opening time, Vi hadn't made an appearance yet. Chase called her, but got no answer. She left a message, then texted that she was needed ASAP.

Immediately after Chase flipped over the sign and unlocked the front door, a half-dozen people rushed in. The students started class that day, but the local residents must have pent up their desire for dessert bars, and they now flocked in.

Chase was stuck behind the counter, ringing up an endless stream of sales. She noticed people on the floor who could probably have used some help, but there was no one to give it. Anna was baking two more batches of bars they were running low on, an essential function today. They didn't want to run out while all these excellent customers were willing to buy.

The Bar None's reputation must have shot through the ceiling this year. This was supposed to be a slow day, but the customers didn't stop.

A few people walked out without purchases. If Vi were here, she could have sold them, Chase thought.

Finally, an hour and a half after opening time, Vi came through the double doors from the kitchen.

"I'm here," she announced with a wide smile, looking her usual impeccable self.

Chase glared and motioned her toward a trio of boys inspecting boxes from one of the tables. The display would need redoing after they finished manhandling everything.

Vi waltzed up to the guys and wowed them. She deftly straightened up the display while talking, listening, and handing them the varieties she selected for them. They came to the register grinning.

A sharp pain stabbed Chase behind her right ear. It was a wonder she hadn't had a headache every day for the last week and a half. She rubbed her head, willing the ache to go away. At least it made her forget about her throbbing back for the moment.

There was no time for anyone to take lunch. Well after when lunchtime should have been, Anna came to the front, finished with all the baking for supplying the shelves that day. The three women worked well together during the afternoon, creating a nicely choreographed ballet of salesmanship, helpfulness, and actual selling, graced with smiles and small talk, just enough to make each customer feel special, not enough to hold up the works.

A glance at the clock over the front door told Chase there was an hour left. They would close at the regular time of 6:00 today. During a slight lull, with the store only one-third full, Anna stepped over to the pink shelves and rearranged boxes to disguise the empty spaces created by the flurry of success. She turned and shot Chase a smile of triumph. Today would be a good day when they counted up tonight. Maybe it would make up for the missing cash.

Chase had worked the till all day. There hadn't been a chance to switch jobs. Vi approached the counter.

"Want me to take over back there for a while?" She gave Chase a huge smile, even bigger than usual.

Chase opened her mouth to accept the offer, then thought better of it. Vi was so good on the floor, she wanted her to keep working there. "No, that's okay. I'll finish up here. We just have an hour left. You're doing great. We'll have a glass of wine in the kitchen when we're done."

"I'm not sure I can stay. I'll see." Vi turned away and approached some hesitant customers. Soon they were laden with dessert bars. Vi, Chase thought for the umpteenth time, had the touch of gold for sales.

FOURTEEN

The Bar None would close in five minutes. It was finally the end of the long day. And this was supposed to have been an easy one. Chase closed her eyes for a moment and pictured herself with Quincy purring in her lap, sitting in her favorite cushy chair enjoying a long, slow glass of wine and a Chocolate Peanut Butter Dream Bar. When she opened her eyes, the shop was still there, and still open. And her back hurt more than it had all day.

Also, Gabe's visitation started in an hour. His funeral was going to be tomorrow, Wednesday. The shop would be closed, so, theoretically, Chase would be able to attend the actual service. But she'd rather just sign her name on the book at the visitation. That way, she wouldn't have to face his family and their grief, and to pretend she was sad that Gabe was dead. She gave herself a mental slap for that last thought, even though it was true.

Anna had returned to the kitchen to start the cleanup and Chase was tending the register, waiting to check out the customers who remained in the store. There were quite a few. Today's receipts should add up to a lot, she told herself. Could the extra day of big sales make up for the pilfering?

Chase finished a transaction and checked the drawer. She raised her head as a large person blocked the light from the front windows. It was the last person she ever wanted to see again. She grabbed the edge of the counter to steady herself and felt the sweat springing up on her palms.

"Hi, Chase," the man said, giving her the devastatingly handsome smile she'd fallen for.

"Shaun." Tall, blond, ruggedly good looking, and all too real. She froze for a moment in the headlights of his dazzle.

"Oh, so you remember my name." The smile on his handsome face wasn't friendly. "I wondered where you were hiding out."

She wiped her hands on her smock. "I am not hiding out."

"I can't believe you're not locked up. Maybe you escaped from jail?"

The nearest customers, apparently the grandparents of the student fidgeting between them, stared openly. Chase couldn't stand a scene in her shop tonight. But what could she say to him to get him to leave? Or at least be quiet?

"Very funny." She tried for an amused smile. "I'm surprised you're not *in* jail yet. Come back and see the place. Vi, could you work the counter for a moment?" She beckoned him toward the kitchen. Anything to get him out of here, away from her customers. The older couple walked toward the door, trailed by their young student.

"Wait a minute," the young man said. "I wanna buy something."

"Let's come back later," said the woman.

Chase knew they'd never return.

She grabbed Shaun's elbow and tugged him until he followed her, a doubtful expression on his face.

Anna was drying the mixer attachments and stowing

them in the drawer. She looked up as they entered. "Who's this?" She raised her eyebrows and gave him a brilliant smile.

Shaun turned his charm on full force. "I'm Shaun Everly. Pleased to meet you, Miss . . . ?"

Anna wiped her hands on her apron and extended a palm. "I'm Anna Larson, co-owner of the Bar None." She gestured at the kitchen with a proud sweep of her hand. "You're a friend of Charity's?" She tilted her head at him. Was she flirting?

Chase said, "No," a fraction of a second before Shaun said, "Yes."

He chuckled. She didn't. Anna's smile faltered.

"We knew each other in Chicago," he continued. "We worked together. For a while." He turned toward the office door. "What's that awful noise?"

"Quincy, hissing at you, as usual," said Chase.

His ice-blue eyes narrowed. "You still have that mangy cat?"

The smile dropped from Anna's face. An enemy of Quincy's would be an enemy of hers.

"There's the back door," said Chase. "You're welcome to use it."

"I'm not surprised you don't want me around." There was a hint of menace in his silky voice. "Afraid people might find out what you did?" He walked over to stand next to Anna and talked to her in an undertone, then handed her something she stuffed into her apron pocket. Chase caught the sound of a sibilant and thought she heard the word *stole*.

"The only thing I'm afraid of," Chase said, "is that you'll spread more of your lies. Now get out."

He gave Chase an ugly sneer. "I'm not going far. Thinking of moving here." Then he left, giving the rear door a hearty slam.

"Who on earth was that?" Anna looked horrified for Chase. "What an awful man!"

"Yes." Chase's knees weakened in the aftermath of the confrontation. She grabbed for a stool and sat.

Anna glanced at the clock. "I'll go flip the sign and finish up out front."

Chase waited, unable to stir, listening to the voices in the front of the store. Finally, the last customer left and Vi and Anna came in.

"I really do have to leave," said Vi. "Have fun without me."

"Are you going to the visitation for Gabe Naughtly tonight?" Chase asked.

Vi paused on her way to the back door. "I'm . . . not sure."

"The funeral is tomorrow," Anna said. "Maybe you'd rather go to that?"

"We're closed Wednesday this week, right?"

"Yes, so we could all go if we wanted to."

"I'm doing the visitation," Chase said.

"Me, too." Vi continued toward the door.

"See you Thursday?" Anna said. "Since we don't know when Laci is returning to work."

They normally closed on Mondays and Tuesdays, except during freshman move-in time, when they only took Wednesday off. Next week they would close both of the normal days.

Vi left out the parking lot door, saying she'd be back on Thursday. Anna released Quincy from the office. He twined around her legs, then sashayed over to Chase.

"Can I get you something? Shall we open that bottle of wine?" She leaned down and rubbed Quincy's nape.

"That would be lovely. I've been looking forward to it all day. I haven't taken any pain pills since this morning."

Anna wielded the corkscrew, reached for two of the tumblers they kept in the kitchen, and poured them half-full. She and Chase clinked their glasses and Chase gulped down a hefty amount.

"Now spill," Anna said. "What was that talk of jail?"

"What did Shaun say to you?"

"That's not important." Anna glanced away.

"He's the reason I left Chicago. I've told you that."

"You never told me his name. Or how good looking he is. Or exactly what the details were."

"I know. It was . . . upsetting. We both worked at the same place."

"That German place in the Loop?"

"Yes, I was waiting tables there. The waitstaff took care of the dinner checks, no cashier, and we handled a lot of money. His uncle owned the place. Shaun didn't work there much, but showed up once or twice a week to help out in the kitchen."

"What else did he do?"

"He was going to school, I guess. At least that's what he said. Right now, I don't believe anything he's ever said. He asked me out a few times and I thought we hit if off pretty well, but I knew he wasn't someone I wanted anything permanent with."

Chase took another glug of her wine. Anna moved around the kitchen efficiently, putting away the day's equipment, stopping to sip her wine when she passed it.

"When money was missing," Chase said, "he convinced his uncle I had taken it. I tried to reason with both of them."

"Who did take the money?"

"I didn't know, at first. I just knew it wasn't me." It sounded like Anna was accusing her. "No matter what I said, Shaun's uncle was sure I'd taken it, and I got fired."

"That's when you came home to Minneapolis?" Anna put the last of the baking sheets in the cabinet and came back to sit beside Chase.

"No, not exactly. Before I left their place, I happened to see a deposit slip in the kitchen wastebasket. I thought that was an odd thing to be there, so I fished it out. Shaun was not only a jerk and dishonest, he was stupid. The receipt was for a large deposit to his personal account. It was for exactly the amount that had been missing the week before. I knew I didn't want to work with anyone in that family again, so I didn't use it to get my job back. But I did leave Shaun a sealed note about finding the deposit slip before I left the place.

"Then I tried to get another job. I applied at five different places nearby. One of them finally told me that Shaun had talked to them. I was blacklisted!"

"Blacklisted? That's terrible. Why would he do that?"

"Because he's a class-one jerk."

"You could have brought the deposit slip to the police."

"Yes, I know, but I just wanted to get far away from everything."

"So you came home." Anna's warm smile eased Chase's heart. "I'm glad you did."

Chase heard a car start up in the parking lot. She realized she hadn't heard Vi's car leave. Or Shaun's.

"Is that Vi, just leaving?" Anna said. "I wonder what she's been doing all this time."

Chase jumped off the stool and ran to the rear door. Her back didn't twinge at all. The wine was a good painkiller. She flung the door open and scanned the parking lot. Vi's red Z4 was pulling away. Another vehicle, a silver Porsche Boxster, drove out of the lot, turned north on Fourteenth, and sped off. Shaun's car, Chase would bet the store on it. Well, maybe not the whole store, but she was sure it was him. It was the same car he'd had in Chicago. She shivered in the cold night air and came back to the warm kitchen.

"Shaun and Vi both just left. They were probably out there talking. He's no doubt told her all his lies about me."

"We both know how fickle Vi is about men. She won't stick with him long."

"One day is too long with Shaun Everly." Chase plopped onto the stool and finished the glass of wine.

"Need another?" Anna didn't wait for her answer, but poured her a glass.

Chase didn't want to get to Gabe Naughtly's visitation too early. If no one else were there, she'd have to make small talk with Doris. That would be awful. She waited until 7:30, then walked the few blocks to the funeral home on Southeast Seventh Street. A brisk wind made her glad she'd worn a heavy jacket. She looked at the trees along the way, imagining them as they would look in a month, full of ochres, scarlets, golden yellows, and shiny browns for some of the oaks. For now, they were all still green, stirring in the breeze, giving off slight, breathy rattles as she walked slowly beneath them. She was in no great hurry to get to the visitation.

The parking lot beside the small, white, one-story building was half-full of cars. That must have meant a lot of other mourners were already there, so Chase deemed it safe. She wanted to duck in, sign the book, tell Doris and Ted that she was "so sorry for their loss," and get out quickly. She had never been fond of Doris, but the more she heard about her from Anna, the less she liked the woman. Chase hated duplicity. She would be forced to be two-faced to the woman at her husband's coffin, though—to be nice and act sympathetic. Chase would also be very conscious, while she was there, that some of the people present suspected she was the murderer of the deceased.

The guest book was on a wooden stand next to the front door. The pages were white with gold lettering, and a gold pen lay atop the book. Chase was sure Doris had picked out these things. Ornate was the woman's style.

Chase picked up the heavy pen, glancing at the names already entered between the gold lines. Violet Peters's name was near the top of the page. Torvald Iversen had scrawled his name five lines up. Under it was another Iversen name, Elinda, written in a loopy style. Since it was on a separate line, it didn't seem like it was Torvald's wife. Maybe a sister, aunt, mother? Chase shuddered at the thought of being married—or related—to the man. After she signed her name, she quickly found Doris, muttered her obligatory line, and walked home.

In her apartment, she settled into her comfy chair without that glass of wine she'd been looking forward to for hours, since she'd already had a couple in the kitchen with Anna after they'd closed up. Her phone rang and she jerked awake, realizing she had dozed off.

"Julie? How's everything going?"

"We're still picking the jury, but I think we'll finish with that tomorrow. The day after, at the latest." Chase heard Julie take a sip of something with clinking ice cubes.

"It sure is a slow process."

"Sometimes I think due process should be called glue process," said Julie. "There's something I need to tell you. Grandma talked to me just a few minutes ago and I'm not sure what she's trying to say."

"What were her words?"

"She didn't make a lot of sense. She was distraught. First, she told me she thought the receipts looked like they were short again today. Then she rambled on about Ted Naughtly's history, but when I asked her directly, she said she didn't think he took the money."

"Really? More was missing today?"

"Then she told me your nemesis from Chicago showed up. I remember you telling me all about him, the cad."

"What does Anna think of him? She didn't say much to him."

"She wouldn't say it right out, but I don't think she dislikes him enough." More ice cubes clinked. "I got the impression they had talked for at least a few minutes."

"Wait a sec." Chase went to the kitchen to pour herself a glass of Dr Pepper. The sound of Julie's ice cubes was making her thirsty. On her way back to her leather couch, Quincy wound around her legs, nearly tripping her. He felt so solid. He had to be gaining, not losing ounces.

"They must have talked after the shop closed. Did she say exactly what he told her?"

Julie blew out a breath into the phone. "He told her you stole that money in Chicago. The money you think he stole and blamed you for."

"And?"

"I still think you shouldn't have run. I could have come over and helped you with, I don't know, some sort of legal solution."

"I know, and I still appreciate the offer, but I was sick of the place." Chase took a noisy gulp of the pop, rather more than she'd intended.

"What was that sound?"

"Me, swallowing, silly."

"Swallowing what?"

Chase sighed. "Dr Pepper." Chase set the glass on the side table and tucked her feet under the afghan she kept on the back. Her toes were icy from the floor. "So, does Anna believe Shaun?"

Quincy jumped onto the arm of the chair, purring loudly. He scratched his neck with his hind foot, then curled up in her lap.

"No, she says you told her you had proof Shaun was the thief. But she's worried about you. Hey, I have a call from my boss. Talk to you tomorrow."

Quincy jumped down with a solid plop. He stepped daintily into his cat bed in the corner of the room and pawed at it before settling down.

"That's curious," Chase said to the cat. The bed shouldn't have made any noise, but there was a faint rustle when Quincy scratched at it. She recalled that he'd been doing that for a few days. Usually he climbed in, curled up, and settled down with no pawing.

"Let me see, little guy." She knelt, with a groan of pain as her back acted up with her movement, and lifted him out of the plush-lined foam bed, adorned with orange paw prints on the outside. A scrap of paper lay curled in the corner. That must have been what had rustled, she reasoned. She extracted it and Quincy hopped back into his nest.

It was a corner, torn from a larger piece of paper. She couldn't tell what it was, but it might have been a legal document. At the bottom, Torvald Iversen's signature and handwritten date were clear below a printed line that had his name, "agent for" with the rest torn off. Above that, the letters GABRI remained under the line and there was no signature above it. She would show this to Julie and see what she could make of it.

But it looked like some sort of agreement between Gabriel Naughtly and Torvald Iversen. It was dated the day Gabe had died. And someone, it seemed, had torn it up. In a fit of anger? Just before a murder? How had it ended up in Quincy's bed?

FIFTEEN

Chase gave herself the luxury of sleeping in on Wednesday. A whole day stretched ahead, free of the shop, to do anything she wanted. She thought for a while about the people Hilda Bjorn had seen outside Gabe's condo the day he died. Mike Ramos had said that Iversen was there before he said he was. Maybe Hilda missed that. She probably wasn't on her front porch all the time. If only there was a way to prove that he was there, beyond one person's suspicions.

And who were the others, a young man and a floozy? It sounded like Gabe had a mistress. Did he also have a stalker? The mistress didn't stay long, Hilda had said. Was that because she ran in, killed him, and fled? She said the young man didn't go in. How confusing!

The young man could have been Ted, but why would he stay outside and not go into his own father's place? Could the young man have been the mysterious guy she'd seen with Vi out back?

The floozy? Too-tight clothes—Laci and Vi both wore tops that fit snugly. All the girls their age did. But tattoos and extremely high shoes—that wouldn't be either of them.

As soon as Chase swung her legs off the bed to the floor, Quincy made it plain that she had duties. After pouring the food into his bowl—which he took three bites of before stalking away—she took a couple of pain pills and went downstairs to do some research on the computer.

She looked up *diet cat food* and found lots of ads and recommendations for commercial cat food. Adding the word *recipe* to her search netted more valuable results. Some of the webpages suggested using ground bone and canning the food, some debated between raw and cooked, one stressed the need to balance all sorts of vitamins, minerals, and amino acids, and sounded very complicated. None of them were specifically for weight loss, though.

Maybe she should just concentrate on treats. After another half hour, she began to get some ideas. To rest her brain from cat treats, she looked up the page for local news and found the headlines Julie had been anticipating.

LOCAL MAN ON TRIAL FOR CHARITY THEFT

The article didn't mention Bill's name, but did Marvin Shandy's, of course. Bill had adopted him and his sister and changed their last names to his. Chase wondered if he regretted that now. Poor Bill. Poor Anna. The publicity was going to affect both of them badly. She shook her head and returned to a bit more cat treat research.

Back upstairs, she poked around in her refrigerator to see what she could use for a tempting cat treat. She put a couple of slices of leftover turkey through her meat grinder and mashed it together with hamburger and low-fat chicken broth, adding a bit of oatmeal and an egg. She made two patties and stuck them under the broiler. She took the patties out of the oven before they were thoroughly cooked. Quincy had never liked well-done meat. The cat, lured by the turkey, rubbed against her calves a few times, then sat staring up at the stove, his eyes wide and his ears pricked forward.

"You think you'll eat this? I wonder. Should I call them Kitty Patties?"

While the Kitty Patties were cooling, she texted Julie to call her when she could. Two minutes later, her cell rang.

"We're on break." Julie's voice was hushed. "I'm out here in the hall, but we have to go into the courtroom in a few minutes."

"Still doing voir dire?"

"Yep. We should be able to finish that up today, if all goes well. Whatcha need?"

"I found a piece of paper in Quincy's bed." She picked it up from the kitchen counter where she'd put it, then walked to the balcony doors to inspect it again in the daylight coming through the glass panes.

"Oh yes, what is that? I remember seeing it there."

"You saw this? When was that? Why didn't you tell me?"

"It was the night Gabe was killed. It was bothering Quincy. I took it from his collar, but you discovered the rats and we all ran downstairs before I could say anything. I dropped it into his bed right before Grandma and I left to see what was upsetting you. Forgot all about it until now."

"Do you know where it came from?"

"No, just that it was stuck in his collar."

"I never saw it, and neither did Mike."

"It was folded up, tiny. I wouldn't have seen it except Quincy was scratching like crazy and I poked around to see why."

"Did you look at it?"

"Not really."

"Can you meet me somewhere for lunch and take a look?"

"Sure. Oops, gotta go. I'll text when we're breaking for lunch. I think I can get away today. I'm supposed to run to the office for some papers and some online research anyway."

Chase closed the call and looked out at the street below. She didn't often have time to stand and watch the city going about its business in the morning. The café directly across the street was open for breakfast. People who looked like professors—and several students—went in and out, carrying coffee containers as they left and headed toward campus. They all wore substantial jackets and a few had hats and gloves on as well. The weather was turning.

When she went back to the counter, where she'd left the Kitty Patties cooling, Quincy was crouched over the broiler pan, steadily chowing down.

"Finally, something healthy that you'll eat." She broiled up a few more to have on hand. She would give Anna strict instructions to feed him these instead of dessert bars.

At 11:30, she was in a seafood restaurant a block from the court building. Julie made it there only fifteen minutes after the time she'd given Chase in her text message.

"Sorry," she said, unbuttoning her coat and unwinding her scarf. "I got waylaid by my boss. I have to run to the office this afternoon and research a couple of points. I should have a few minutes now, though. Enough time to eat and chat."

"I ordered you a cup of clam chowder and the iceberg wedge salad." That was what both of them always got for lunch there unless they were splurging on the lobster bisque.

"Perfect." Julie threw her coat and scarf onto the seat and slid into the booth. "How are you feeling?"

"I'll live."

The waiter delivered the iced tea Chase had ordered and Julie held out her hand. Chase put the torn piece of paper in her palm. "Definitely some sort of contract to be signed by two people," Julie said, squinting at the tiny scrap. "Looks like Naughtly and Iversen, doesn't it?"

"I just wanted to make sure."

"Aha. It's also dated the day Naughtly was murdered."

"So, somehow, Quincy got this stuck in his collar at Gabe's."

"Most likely," Julie said.

"Which proves that Iversen *was* there before he said he was, just like Mike told me," Chase said. "The torn bits of paper on the floor next to his body must have been something that one of them tore up before I got there."

"Do you think they had a quarrel about some sort of agreement?"

Chase chuckled. "A disagreement about an agreement? Is there any way to find out what it was, exactly?"

"Do you know who Naughtly's lawyer was? Or who Iversen uses?"

"No, but the police would."

"I don't know if this has anything to do with the murder, but I happened to overhear someone say that Torvald Iversen filed a restraining order yesterday."

"Who is it against?"

"I didn't hear that. I'll try to find out if you think it's relevant."

"Probably nothing to do with this business."

Chase's next stop was the police station. After she asked for Detective Olson out front, she was shown back.

"Good to see you again." He motioned her into the chair beside his metal desk. It was just as uncomfortable on her back as it had been the last time. The room vibrated, full of bustling people this time of day.

His blue eyes were so dark, and so steady. She blinked and he broke his gaze.

She handed him the scrap of paper. "I found this caught in Quincy's collar."

He looked at it, turned it over, and set it on his blotter. "Yes?"

"See?" She leaned over and pointed to the print. "It's an agreement signed by Iversen, but not by Gabe, dated the day Gabe died. Iversen was there before he said he was, taking this to get Gabe's signature. They had a fight about this—whatever it is—and Iversen killed Gabe over it."

The unwavering gaze was back.

"There was probably a lot of money involved," Chase ventured. "Don't you think?"

"I think this is the rest of the document we found on the floor by the body. It *is* a document signed by Iversen, but that doesn't mean he was there that day, when he says he wasn't."

"Can you see if his fingerprints are on it?"

"They're on the other pieces, so they're probably on this one, too."

"He was there earlier! Michael—Dr. Ramos—saw him!"

"Yes, we have that information."

He leaned toward her and gave her a gentle smile. She felt something inside warming up.

"Ms. Oliver, we're still gathering evidence. This isn't proof of anything, but thanks for bringing it in."

She shot up out of the chair. "Am I still the main suspect?"

"Did I say you were?"

"You told me not to leave town." She winced and grimaced from the back spasm caused by her sudden movement.

"Yes, I did. And that still stands. Are you okay?"

"Fine. If I can find someone else who saw him there, will that nail him?"

"Please let *us* interview the suspects." There was no trace of that smile and the dark blue eyes glittered, looked hard.

"There were other people there, too."

He raised his eyebrows, encouraging her to go on.

She sat down gingerly and told him about Hilda and the young man and the floozy. She was almost certain the young man was Ted.

"We'll look into this," he said, but he hadn't taken any notes.

It was still up to her to clear herself.

SIXTEEN

Driving away from the police station, Chase wanted to talk to Anna. She called, but Anna didn't pick up. The lovely day that had stretched before her, free and empty, seemed dreary and weighty now. It was only midmorning. What would she do the rest of the day?

She headed for the hospital to visit with Laci. However, she had checked out early that morning and was, as far as Chase could tell, at home. Chase had never been to Laci's home and had to stop by the office to find the address.

Before she went into the office to look up the records, she flew up the stairs to check on Quincy. He lay in his bed, snoozing. The Kitty Patties she'd left atop his diet food were gone—and so was the food that had been beneath. His bowl was clean!

Quietly, not wanting to disturb whatever force was at work, she backed out and shut the door. Quincy slept on. He hadn't even raised his head. He must feel good, she thought, to have his tummy full of good food, finally.

She pulled the notebook out of the desk drawer below the computer. She hadn't balanced the books from yesterday, but she wanted to put that off as long as possible. Laci's information would be in Anna's handwriting, since she was the one who kept employee records. She preferred to keep them on paper, but Chase knew they were in the computer somewhere, too.

She paged too far and saw the posh address of Vi Peters's place. Flipping to the *C*s for *Carlson*, she found Laci's information. She froze when she saw the address. It was the same building she'd seen Shaun Everly walking toward, that first time she saw him in Minneapolis. If she went to see Laci, would she encounter *him*?

Why on earth did Laci drive her PT Cruiser to work when she lived that close?

Oh well, Chase was going to have to figure out if she was brave enough to chance running into her nemesis. She walked the two blocks at a brisk pace, then hesitated when she got near.

Chase loitered on the sidewalk opposite the apartment building, where she could see the parking lot that belonged to it, until she thought she might be attracting attention. Laci's PT Cruiser was there, but so was the silver Boxster that she thought was Shaun's.

A black Lexus idled next to the door. The driver had the hawk-nosed silhouette of Torvald Iversen, and his long, thin fingers drummed on the steering wheel.

Chase felt a brazen anger rising from her toes. She walked to the driver's window of the Lexus. It was open, and he turned when she approached, looking surprised to see her there.

"Some people have to work in the middle of the day," she said.

"I am working," he said, his eyes half-lidded and his manner cool. "Are you?"

"What kind of work is this, sitting in your car? Looking for someone else to attack?"

"No, as a matter of fact, I'm looking for someone else to partner with my client."

Shaun's car was nearby. Could these two creeps be cooking up a scheme together?

As if her thoughts of him had the power to conjure up the man himself, Shaun Everly walked out the door of the building. He didn't go to his car, though. Ignoring Chase, he got into the passenger seat of Iversen's Lexus. The car pulled away without either of the occupants giving her another glance.

Good riddance, Chase thought. Those two deserve each other. Maybe Torvald would knock off Shaun when he found out what a cad he was. Maybe Shaun would steal money from Torvald and that would set things off. Maybe they were . . . what?

Puzzling over the association of those two bums, she marched up the front steps into the building. She pushed the door open and ran a finger along the name tags under each buzzer. None of them said "Everly." Maybe the building manager hadn't made up a tag for him yet. One was labeled "L. Carlson," so she pushed that one.

Laci's voice came over the intercom and she buzzed Chase in, not sounding upset to see her. How could Anna think about firing Laci? That would be like kicking a sick puppy.

After she climbed two flights of stairs, Laci ushered her into an apartment filled with ruffles and floral-patterned furniture. Chase decided Laci did resemble an ailing baby animal, maybe even a sick puppy.

Chase asked her how she was feeling and got a sigh and a woebegone expression. Laci lifted a limp wrist to wave Chase to a seat on the cabbage-rose sofa. She sat herself on a chair covered with Victorian striped fabric in various shades of pink. Laci's other wrist was wrapped in an Ace bandage.

"What's the wrapping on your wrist for? Did you hurt it?" Chase sank into the soft couch. When it bent her back the wrong way, she scooted to perch on the edge of the cushion.

"I sprained it when I fell, the doctors said." She rubbed the bandage with her other hand. "I'm lucky I didn't break it."

"How long do you have to stay away from work?" Maybe, if she had to take a lot of time off, that would make it easier for Anna to eventually terminate her.

"Not long. I might be able to come in tomorrow. I could have a little bit of a concussion, they said. They'll tell me when I can work again."

"Well . . . why don't you take another few days off. We can manage for a while. Business should be slower now."

"Until the holidays. Then you'll need everyone."

That was true. If Anna got rid of Laci, she would need another worker. She still hadn't talked to Anna about this.

"You know," Laci said, "how I told you Vi was spreading rumors about Ted stealing things?"

"Yes," Chase replied cautiously. She remembered. Also, Ted *was* stealing things.

"I think that's what started making him so upset." So upset that he dumped Laci? "He was bad then, but he's ten times, a hundred times, a thousand times worse now. He's almost been a different person since his father was killed. He totally blamed him for everything, you know."

Chase wondered if that was because he had killed his father. Laci said he got very angry about his parents' separation. Angry enough to do something to his father?

They both jumped when her buzzer sounded. When Laci answered the intercom, Ted's voice came into the apartment.

"Should I go?" asked Chase.

"No, maybe you can help."

"Help with what? What's his problem now?" She might need some background before he made it up the stairs and arrived at Laci's door.

"He's going through some horrible things. He's frantic."

Chase had seen Ted before when Laci thought he was upset. But she'd never been able to detect distress in the guy so far.

When Laci opened her door, Ted grabbed her and held her in a boa-constrictor clinch until he noticed Chase on the couch.

"Oh," he said, stepping back. "Hello, Ms. Oliver."

He looked awful. His light brown hair, usually combed to minimize the premature retreat at the forehead, stood up in places and lay in messy wisps in others. His carefully cultivated three-day stubble had grown to be a week's worth. Maybe he really was upset this time.

"Can I get you something?" Laci sounded formal toward him. Maybe that's because Chase was there, or maybe it was because she had so recently almost lost him to someone else.

Chase cast Ted for the part of Hilda's young man. She briefly considered Krystal, Ted's former companion, for the role of the floozy, but didn't think the woman had had any tattoos.

"A beer?" He sank onto the chair Laci had vacated.

When Laci brought him a can, Chase had to make an effort to contain her shock. Laci kept beer in her apartment? That was hard to picture. Although she did include a linen napkin.

"Tell Ms. Oliver about the . . . you know." Laci perched on the footstool next to Ted's chair.

Ted belted down half the can of beer and wiped his mouth on his sleeve, ignoring the napkin. "It's about my dad."

"Yes, it's terrible," Chase said. "I don't know how I'd deal with—"

"No, not that he's dead. Well, that's bad, but . . . just before he died, I mean, I thought maybe I could, I don't know, talk to him, get him back together with Mom. I mean make him come to his senses."

Laci was nodding slowly, her eyes large and soulful and sympathetic. Maybe she'd been right that he was broken up about his parents' impending divorce. Chase wondered why he would be appealing to his father when it seemed his mother had kicked her husband out. Maybe to improve his dad's behavior so she'd take him back?

"Mom was seeing that creep Iversen, and I thought Dad should know about it. I followed him home after he was in your shop that day."

Doris *was* seeing Iversen. Interesting.

"The day he was killed," Laci said, in case no one knew that.

"I wanted to go into his condo and talk to him, but right after he goes in, this woman shows up. I mean, I've seen her before, but I think I didn't want to admit it." He paused.

"Admit what, Ted?" Chase asked.

"That he has a mistress. Pretty sure that's what she is. Or a hooker."

The floozy that Hilda Bjorn saw? So Ted *was* the young man.

"So, after she goes in, I figure I'll wait until she leaves. But it's making me sick to think about them in there. . . . Anyway, she leaves pretty quick. I figure I need to go in now, but I'm not fast enough. Before I can cross the street, *Mom* shows up. She leaves even sooner. She runs out. She's all shocked-like. I've never seen her look like that."

Ted paused to finish the can. He handed it to Laci, who hurried to bring him another.

"Did you go inside then?"

After popping the new brew open and taking a sip, he replied, "Well, see, I mean, Mom has this, this big red splotch on her jacket when she comes out. It's her tan jacket, so it really shows up. She stops at the bottom of the stairs and notices it. Then she takes the jacket off and throws it in the bushes."

Big red splotch? Hiding the jacket? That sounded awfully suspicious. In fact, it sounded like Doris killed Gabe. If Ted was telling the truth.

SEVENTEEN

Chase wanted to talk to Julie about what Ted had said. If it was true, it sounded like his mother had to have killed his father. No wonder the poor guy was so distraught. After Ted had mentioned the jacket, Chase remembered it—light tan, with epaulettes held by huge gold buttons. She'd seen it when Doris was in the shop that day.

As she walked home from Laci's apartment, she pondered what Ted might be saying after she left.

A sudden gust sent the fallen leaves dancing down the sidewalk before her. The weather was not only turning cooler. The day had turned darker as low clouds rolled in to hide the sun.

The lovebirds had cried out for privacy with their lingering glances and deep breathing, so she'd left Laci to comfort Ted. Chase would be beside herself if she were in his situation.

But had he told her the truth? Could he be rotten enough

to want to implicate his mother in his father's death? He could, she thought, if he was the one who had killed him. His version jibed, somewhat, with Hilda's. But he could still have committed the murder and be blaming his mother. Hilda had left out Doris being there. And Iversen. Maybe she wasn't there, although Chase would bet Iversen was. She was beginning to think she should forget about relying on the old woman's witness. She didn't sound senile when you talked to her, but Chase had to admit she didn't know any senile people and had no idea what they should sound like. Maybe they sounded perfectly normal, like Hilda.

Chase kicked at a clump of oak leaves. The wind caught them and tossed them into the street. A ray of sunshine broke through the restless, milling clouds, then disappeared just as quickly. She pulled her jacket collar up. If only Julie were more available to her today. This was an important step in Julie's career, assisting on a big, public case (even if it was one that sent her grandmother reeling), but Chase wished it weren't happening right now. She had to talk to someone.

Almost home, she dialed Anna, who didn't answer. The wind blew more fiercely across the open parking lot, moaning through the tree branches. She could taste the crispness of the coming season in the air.

Next, as she crossed the lot to her door, she tried to call her new acquaintance, Mike Ramos.

"Chase, good to hear from you. Are you ready to bring Quincy in so I can reweigh him?"

She'd forgotten all about that. Was it Saturday he had suggested she do that?

"Oh, oh yes. Could I bring him in today? The shop is closed." She'd see him face-to-face, which would be even better than phoning. She'd talk to him there.

He said she could come right away since his waiting room

was empty, so she opened the door to the stairs to go up and get Quincy.

The tabby cat had noticed that the apartment door hadn't latched all the way the last time she left. He'd spent the morning searching the apartment, but hadn't been able to find any more of the treats, the best-tasting thing he'd had to eat for a long time. He nudged the apartment door open and expanded his search to the stairs. Just as he reached the bottom, the treat maker opened the door that led to the parking lot. He slipped through before she could react and ran outside, on the chance that there might be something good to eat out there.

Chase gave a sigh. She knew she shouldn't call after him. That would only excite him and make him run farther away. But he wasn't running. He scampered to the large trash bin and crouched, tail twitching, peering underneath with that intent predator cat stare. Chase crept up behind him. Before she could stoop to pick him up, he scooted, quick as a cat's blink, around behind the trash bin. She cursed under her breath at the pain that seared her back.

She called his name softly, wishing she had one of those Kitty Patties. Again, she snuck up behind him. This time, he stayed put, intent on his prey. He reached an agile paw behind the large bin and clawed, bringing out a scrap of material.

Chase swooped down and picked him up. A piece of tan clothing dropped from his claws. Chase stared at the shining gold buttons, caught in a stray ray of sunshine poking through the clouds. She almost dropped Quincy. It was Doris's jacket.

After she ran upstairs to shut Quincy into the apartment, she dialed Detective Olson.

"I've found the killer," she began, but he cut her off.

"Where are you? What are you doing?" His voice was curt, abrupt.

"I'm not contaminating the scene. The evidence is on the ground, right where my cat found it."

She heard him blow out a breath. "On the ground, where?"

"Right behind my shop. Come around the back and I'll be here."

"What is it?"

"You'll have to come and see for yourself. I think I know, but I don't want to say." What if it was someone else's jacket? She'd feel like a fool.

She was prepared for a crime scene team to arrive, but Detective Olson was the only person in the one unmarked car that idled to a stop beside her fifteen minutes later.

"Here it is." She pointed to the jacket as soon as he climbed out of the car.

"At least I'm not finding you cornering someone you think is a murderer. Tell me exactly what happened here." He pulled a small notepad and pen from his pocket. Good, she thought, he's going to take notes.

She told him how Quincy stalked the jacket and extracted it from behind the bin. "See the bloodstain? Ted Naughtly says he saw his mother wearing this jacket, with the stain, when she left Gabe's the day he died." She didn't mention that Ted also said his mother left it in the bushes in front of the condo. How did it get here, at her business? Was someone trying to implicate her? She was about to mention the discrepancy in location when he spoke.

Detective Olson hadn't touched the jacket yet, but he bent over it and sniffed. "Doesn't smell like blood."

"It's all dried up."

"Doesn't look like it either. Wrong color."

"How could it not be blood? Ted saw her run out with this stain on her."

"I'll call Ted Naughtly in for questioning right away."

"He's at Laci's apartment, I think. He was there a few minutes ago. Are you going to have someone investigate this? Is it evidence? I guess it could belong to someone else."

In answer, a white CSI SUV with a blue BCA logo on the side pulled up behind the detective's car. Beneath the bold initials were the words "Bureau of Criminal Apprehension" with a stylized map of Minnesota under the name of the state.

Chase observed while they took photographs and measurements, then answered their questions about exactly where the garment had been before Quincy pulled it out, as near as she could tell.

After they left, she realized that she'd stood Dr. Ramos up. Oops. She ran upstairs and called him from the apartment.

"Can you still see us?"

"I expected you about an hour ago." He sounded annoyed, for which she didn't blame him.

"Something happened. I need to talk to you about it." Was that true? She *wanted* to talk to him about it.

"I'm about to see a patient. I should be done in half an hour, then I'm free for an hour."

"I'll be there this time. I promise."

It was after lunchtime, so she gulped down a peanut butter sandwich, but would have preferred a bowl of hot soup. She'd gotten chilled standing in the parking lot for so long, watching the officials process the scene. The longer she had looked at the jacket, the less that stain had looked like blood to her, too. What was going on?

When Chase got to Mike's office at Minnetonka Mills, he was still with his patient. After a short wait, she hauled Quincy into the examining room in his carrier. Did he feel lighter? Not likely, since he'd still been getting treats from Anna as of yesterday.

Chase winced when she lifted the carrier onto the exam table.

"Is something wrong?" Mike asked.

"I hurt my back the other day. His crate feels extra heavy, I think, since I did that."

When the vet weighed him, though, it was worse than she expected.

"He's gained a few ounces, almost a quarter of a pound." He shook his head and gave Chase a stern glare. "That's not good. The crate feels heavier because it *is*."

"I should have waited longer. He'll lose weight by next week."

"Why would that magically happen?"

There was no call for sarcasm, she wanted to say, but bit her tongue. "I've put together a recipe, like you suggested. It's for a healthy cat treat."

"Tell me." His look softened.

She told him the recipe and he admitted, nodding, that it was a good one. "I have to keep Anna from sneaking desserts to him."

"Would you like me to tell her not to?"

Chase could imagine how well that would go over. "No, I can do it." It would work better now that there was an alternative. She hoped.

"Take care of your back. If Quincy were lighter that would help."

She wanted to stick her tongue out at him, but that would have been juvenile. As she left, she turned her head toward his closed office door and did it anyway.

Later, when Chase was dressed for bed in her favorite flannel nightie, she finally got a chance to confer with Julie. She'd been wanting to talk to her all day.

"You wouldn't believe how slow this thing is going," Julie

started out. "We finally finished voir dire today. I thought we'd be done with it two days ago."

"Still, isn't that pretty good for a major case? I think it takes longer than that sometimes."

"I know, I know. It's just that this doesn't seem *that* major. The evidence will be pretty cut-and-dried. I mean, I don't see how we can lose."

"So what makes it take longer?"

"I think everyone is being extra careful about everything they do."

Chase stretched and yawned. She was getting sleepy and hadn't talked to Julie yet about Doris's jacket.

"Why are they being so careful, do you think?"

"Oh, that's obvious," Julie said. "The press is all over this. They're swarming the courthouse. It makes a good, scandalous story, robbing money from charity."

"I guess that makes sense." Chase tried to picture Doris's murder trial when that day came. Or Ted's. Or Torvald's. Would she be called to testify? Would there be a gauntlet of reports and microphones to endure? "Listen, I want to talk something out with you."

"Shoot."

"I talked to Ted today, at Laci's apartment."

"I thought they broke up."

"I'm not sure about their status. It seems to be on again at the moment. Anyway, he told me he saw his mother run out of Gabe's condo, the afternoon he was murdered, with a huge red splotch on her jacket."

"Wow! Do the police know about this?"

"They do now."

"So she murdered him?"

"Not sure about that. Ted says she threw her jacket in the bushes right outside the condo. However, Quincy got out late this morning, after I came back from Laci's, and he found her jacket behind my trash bin."

There was a moment of silence. Then Julie giggled. "Quincy is quite the detective, isn't he? How did that happen?"

"Getting out or finding the jacket?"

"Never mind. So you called the police?"

"Yes, and they came and went over everything out there. But what do you suppose this means?"

"You mean how did the jacket get there?"

"I guess. I don't even know if Ted was telling the truth. Detective Olson doesn't think the stain is blood at all. Could Ted be cold-blooded enough to try to frame his mother?"

"If he is, he's going about it in an odd way. He told you where she put the jacket, but that's not where it was."

"I wonder if Doris moved it. If she knew Ted saw her stash it there and decided to . . . I don't know . . . try to implicate me?"

"But her jacket can't implicate *you*, can it?"

Chase grunted in exasperation. "I don't know. I don't know who to believe and I don't know what anything means."

EIGHTEEN

The next morning, Chase arrived downstairs before everyone else, carrying a plastic bin that contained Quincy's new treats. After she put it on the bottom shelf of the refrigerator, she busied herself in the kitchen, starting the coffee and getting out supplies for the day's baking. She was eager for Anna to get there so she could tell her about the treats—and about Doris's jacket.

When Anna finally came in, Chase had to look twice. She wore her usual vibrant sweater, this one of bright teal with turquoise swirls, but the rest of her was drab and colorless. There wasn't a hint of bounce in her step. Even her usually brilliantly shining gray hair was limp and lackluster. Chase wasn't sure whether to sympathize or to leave her alone.

Anna surveyed the bowls, the mixer, and the pans Chase had spread on the granite counter, and dropped to one of the stools, where she started swiveling back and forth, a dull expression on her face.

"I have something to show you." Chase's own voice sounded unnaturally bright to her, trying, as she was, to combat Anna's gloom. She presented the plastic container of cat treats and opened the lid so Anna could see them.

Anna leaned over and sniffed. "They don't smell too appetizing."

"They're not for you, silly. They're for Quince. These are healthy cat treats. Dr. Ramos says he should have only these from now on, and his diet food."

"Poor Quincy."

"He loves them! And you're to stop giving him desserts." Chase knew she was becoming shrill. Anna was being unreasonable.

Anna shrugged, glanced away, and picked a couple of cat hairs off her pants. The swiveling stool had developed a squeak.

"You're driving me nuts," Chase said, then softened her voice as she put the cat treats into the refrigerator. "Is there anything I can do?"

"Do you know about Julie's trial?" She quit swiveling.

"Yeah, that's gotta be hard on the family."

"It is! Bill is beside himself." Finally, a spark from Anna. "He has such ambivalent feelings toward Marvin to begin with. And, on top of everything, his own son is giving him a hard time."

"Marvin is his stepson, right? But he had a child with his second wife, Marvin's mother?"

"Yes. His only natural child."

"What a mess." The coffeemaker quit making its gurgling noises and Chase poured Anna a cup.

"Julie says it could drag on for weeks." She took the steaming mug and inhaled the strong coffee aroma, giving Chase a weary smile. "Thanks."

"So, you and Bill? You're . . . ?"

"Yes. We are." Her smile deepened. "I was hoping he

would, maybe, propose soon. I so wanted to surprise you with a ring." She frowned and started swiveling the squeaky stool again.

"That would be a huge surprise, since I didn't even know you were seeing anyone."

"I'm sorry to have kept this a secret. Julie didn't want me to broadcast it, since she's working on his stepson's trial. There's also the fact that his wife hasn't been dead that long, barely a year. I didn't want to tell anyone. It just seemed a little . . . icky."

"Oh, Anna." Chase gave her a hug from behind, resting her chin on Anna's dear, gray head. That effort didn't hurt her back a bit. "I'm so sorry you've been going through this alone. We shouldn't keep secrets from each other. And there's something else I have to talk to you about."

Chase felt Anna stiffen. She went on. "About firing either of these girls. We can't do that."

"And why not? We hired them. We can fire them." Anna got up and stepped away.

Chase took a deep breath. "Am I not a full partner?"

"Of course."

"Then you need to consider what I think."

Anna nodded and was about to say something else.

Vi came in and interrupted any further discussion. The changeable woman was, once again, her disheveled self rather than the usual suave, smooth Violet Peters. She even had a small stain on her dark blue satin blouse. Chase couldn't remember ever having seen a blotch on Vi's clothing. Her buttons today were two shades of pink. Sometimes Chase thought her clothes were a notch or two down from designer stuff, but those buttons made up for that.

Vi said perfunctory good mornings and passed through to the salesroom to don her smock and open up.

Chase raised her eyebrows at Anna, but she had turned her attention to beginning the day's baking.

Chase retreated into the office to go over the books from two days ago. She turned on the computer and glanced at the news page that came up.

She did a double take. The headline hit her.

PROMINENT FINANCIER FOUND DEAD;
FOUL PLAY SUSPECTED

The victim's name, Torvald Iversen, jumped out at her from the verbiage below the bold print. Chase let out a sharp yelp. Two seconds later, Anna opened the door.

"Are you all right?"

Chase pointed at the screen. "He's dead!"

Anna peered at the screen.

"You want to sit and read it?" asked Chase.

Anna pulled a chair over and they both consumed the short, uninformative article. Iversen had been found dead in the morning at his home by his cleaning lady. She usually arrived when he was gone, but this time she had found his body close inside the front door, partially blocking her entry. A quote from her was included ("I tried and tried to push the door open, and when I did, I almost threw up"), but there was no comment "at this time" from the officials.

"I'm calling Detective Olson," Chase said, and pulled up the number he'd reached her from on her cell. But there was no answer.

"I imagine he's busy right now," Anna said. "He's probably working on this case since it has a tie-in with Gabe's, don't you think?"

Chase nodded. That made sense. Chase decided she would go over the receipts later. She was a little too rattled to do it just now.

She and Anna shut Quincy into the office and both worked in the kitchen for a few minutes before Vi came in.

"What was the matter? The customers have left and I came back to see what's going on."

"Oh, you heard me yell when I saw the news?" Chase said. "I was surprised to see a report that Torvald Iversen is dead."

"Oh." Vi paled. "On the Internet? Isn't he the one who . . . ?"

"The one who's been accusing me of murder. Yes. I can't say I'm sorry he's dead." Chase immediately regretted her last statement, recalling that Vi had denied knowing him once before, the day he'd made her so nervous she'd knocked over a stack of dessert containers. "Now he can never admit he killed Gabe."

"He . . . he killed *Gabe*?" Vi looked shocked.

"Why else would he keep insisting I did it?"

"That's a good question."

The chimes on the front door tinkled and Vi left to greet the customer.

"What do you suppose is wrong with her?"

"I'm as puzzled as you are, Anna. We were going to have a talk with her, and with Ted, but I don't think that's happened either, has it?"

"Do you think that's a good idea? Maybe we should stay out of their personal lives."

"But Vi works for us," Chase said. "We should try to help her. That reminds me, we still need to talk, we two, about our other employee."

"Laci?"

"Yes. I know she and Vi can't work together without tangling, and Vi is the much better salesperson. But . . ."

"We should get rid of both of them."

Chase blew out a breath of exasperation. Why was Anna so obtuse sometimes? "No, I don't think we should. We can work all this out. And if we're going to make an extra effort to help Violet, then we have to do the same for Laci. They're both our employees. They're part of the Bar None family."

"I suppose you're right. But can we help Laci, somehow, without her working here?"

Chase shot Anna an exasperated look.

"All right, I'll make more effort." Anna returned to the kitchen, allowing Chase to catch a whiff of the tangy scent of the Lemon Bars that were browning in the oven before the office door swung shut.

There, she'd done it. She'd spoken her mind about Vi and Laci. They would keep employing them and would get them settled down so they could work together by the holidays. That was over two months away. Relief washed over Chase. She was sure she was doing the right thing.

Later that afternoon, Detective Olson returned Chase's phone call.

"I read about Iversen," she said. "That's why I called you."

"You have information about his death?"

"Not really. It's just that, well, he's been so vehement in accusing me, I figured maybe he killed Gabe. Was it suicide?"

"Is that what you read? Was that on the Internet?"

"No, it didn't say *suicide*. It said *foul play*. But if he was remorseful about killing Gabe, suicide would make sense."

"It's pretty hard to bash your own head in."

"He could fall on something sharp."

"Didn't happen. His skull is crushed, and the murder weapon has been removed. You don't need to concern yourself with Iversen's death. But I have something to tell you about the jacket you found."

"Is it Doris's?"

"Yes, but—"

"So she *did* kill him."

There was a pause at the detective's end of the call before

he continued. "As I was trying to say, the stain is tomato sauce."

"Tomato sauce? There was all that blood."

"Not everything you saw on the floor of the condo was blood. A bunch of it was sauce. It either spilled or was thrown. I suspect Naughtly threw it at his wife, from the amount on her jacket."

"Is there a serial killer?"

"I wouldn't say that. But I will caution you to be careful what you say to people who knew Gabe. That's why I told you some of this. I want you to stay safe. Keep away from his acquaintances and relatives."

Chase deflated after the phone call. It would be hard to avoid all of Gabe's acquaintances and harder to avoid his relatives, since her employee was dating one relative and another was a regular customer.

It seemed like Doris hadn't killed Gabe. Whoever had would probably have blood on their clothes. Too bad Hilda Bjorn hadn't seen anyone run out of the condo covered in blood. It didn't look like Iversen had done it either. In fact, Chase would bet her missing money that the same person killed both of them. Evidence against this was that the murder weapons were so different. They were both probably weapons of convenience, though, the nearest weapon to hand. That seemed to make sense. A small point for it being the same killer.

Not only should she stay away from people connected to Gabe, she should keep away from potential murder weapons.

NINETEEN

Laci showed up at the shop late in the afternoon. As soon as she walked through the rear door, Anna started making a fuss over her.

"Are you sure you should be running around? Did you drive yourself? Here, you'd better sit down."

Chase thought that, for a person who had wanted to get rid of Laci so recently, Anna was overdoing it a bit.

Anna pulled out a stool, but Laci shook her head. "I'm fine. I just saw the doctor at three. There's no trace of a concussion. At first they thought I might have a teensy one, but he rechecked me today. I'm all fine. He gave me a prescription to help me relax if I start hyperventilating or feel like I'm getting too nervous."

"Have you taken any of those pills?" Chase asked, thinking that maybe she shouldn't drive under the influence of relaxing medication.

"No, I haven't been to the drugstore yet. I wanted to check in here and let you know I'm doing better." In spite of her refusal a few seconds ago, she perched on the stool Anna had offered her. "I'm not sure when I can return to work."

"Don't worry about it," Chase said quickly. "We'll do fine. We're not superbusy." The customers had to drop off soon. Their rush was supposed to be over by now.

"It sounds like there are a lot of people out front," Laci said, fiddling with the flounce at the wrist of her sleeve. "I could maybe help out just a bit." When she swiveled slightly, Chase realized she was on the squeaky stool. They needed to oil it.

"Vi will call us if she gets swamped," Chase said. "Really, we're okay."

"But that's so considerate of you to offer," Anna said.

Good grief, thought Chase. Back down, Anna. "Are your parents still in town?"

"No, they had to leave yesterday." Laci's tone was flat and casual, but a sad look flitted across her face, then disappeared.

What kind of parents would leave when their daughter had a possible concussion? wondered Chase, horrified. She could tell Anna was wondering the same thing.

"Oh dear," Anna said, almost under her breath.

"That's all right," the young woman answered. "I'm used to being on my own. They don't hang around much."

"Still . . ." Anna patted Laci's thin shoulder.

Laci jumped off the stool. "I think I should go get my prescription filled."

"Let me drive you," Anna said.

"I won't take any until I get home. I know not to drive after I take a pill like one of these."

"If you think so." Anna seemed less than half-convinced.

Chase was surprised Anna didn't button Laci's jacket for her before she left.

"Oh my goodness." Anna's worried face reminded Chase of the care Anna had given her when her parents had passed away. She really was a kind and generous soul. Anna was about to say something, probably about what they should be doing for Laci, when she was interrupted.

"Paper man," called the delivery guy coming through the back door, a box of paper bags imprinted with the Bar None logo hoisted on his shoulder.

Distracted by her conflicting thoughts on her relationship with Anna lately, Chase opened the office door so she could stow them there. She neglected to stick a foot inside to prevent escape. Quick as a flash Quincy darted out, making it through the parking lot door before it completely closed behind the delivery man.

Darn it, thought Chase. Not this again.

The butterscotch tabby knew the enticing tomato aroma that had been behind the trash bin was no longer there. That was the first thing he sensed after he made it through the door. The second thing he sensed was a loud voice calling his name. Rather than voluntarily return to the office, he set out in the direction where he'd first found the delicious tomato saucy meatloaf. Now that he knew his way, his progress was swift and sure. It took no time at all to zip over there. When he found the condo door closed, he looked around for another way in. Instead, he spied someone across the street eating something that smelled good. He padded across the street.

Anna made it to the door first. "I think he's headed for Gabe Naughtly's again."

"What's wrong with that cat?" asked the paper deliveryman.

Anna threw Chase an accusatory glance. "He doesn't get enough to eat."

"I'll go," Chase said. "I think you have a batch ready to come out of the oven in a few minutes."

Chase trotted out of the parking lot, around the corner, and up the street, spying a small, fast-moving bundle of orange fur two blocks ahead. She got stuck waiting for traffic to clear so she could cross the streets, though, and by the time she got to Gabe's condo, Quincy was nowhere to be seen. She mounted the steps, to be sure he wasn't hidden behind the post, even though he was too fat for the post to hide him. Just to be sure, she jiggled the doorknob. Yellow tape still sealed the door. So did the dead bolt lock when she tried to open the door, thinking she could duck under the tape.

"He's not there, dearie," called a voice from behind her. Hilda Bjorn was sitting on a rocker across the street, on her front porch, bundled for the weather and holding a mug of something steamy. She also held a short-haired orange fur-ball in her lap.

Chase crossed the street and approached them with caution. "That's my cat. I've been looking for him."

"Oh, I'm glad he has a good owner." The woman set her mug on the table beside her and handed the purring Quincy to Chase. "He's a very nice cat."

"He's a very naughty cat right now." Quincy nuzzled her shoulder.

"He sure does like these cheese crackers."

Chase held Quincy out and inspected him more closely. Sure enough, there were crumbs the color of neon traffic cones stuck to his long whiskers. "He's supposed to be on a diet. How many did he eat?"

"Oh, just a handful. I'm glad you're looking for the cat and not for the man across the street. He's dead, you know."

"Yes, I talked to you about that. At the hospital. Do you remember?"

"I think so."

"You told me who you saw going in and out of the condo the day Gabe . . . died."

"He was murdered, you know."

"Uh, yes, I know." How much of what this woman said was reliable?

"So many people that day," she said. "The young man, the floozy, the older man who's been there a lot lately, and that woman with the nice jacket."

"Woman with a jacket?" Doris? "You saw her, too." Maybe her memory was sharper than Chase was giving her credit for.

"I couldn't understand why she took off her jacket and threw it into the bushes. It had gotten all dirty, but I'm sure it could have been cleaned."

Was Doris back to being a suspect now? In spite of the stain on the jacket being sauce? Could there be any others? "Can you think of anyone else who was there that day?"

Hilda aimed her bright blue eyes at the porch ceiling. The late-day sunshine glinted off her wire rim bifocals. She gave a slight frown. "No, I can't recall. There might have been more. Maybe I'll think of them later. It was a busy day over there."

Chase scribbled her number on the pad she kept in her apron pocket for Bar None orders. "If you think of anyone else, could you please call me?"

"Of course, dear, although I should tell the police first. That nice Detective Olson did mention that. I think I'll give him a call right now."

She rose to go inside.

"Thanks for corralling Quincy," Chase said.

"Oh, is that his name? What a nice name. I think he's a little hungry. Maybe you should feed him more."

"Ms. Bjorn, I'd like to thank you. I'll tell my workers"— of which she had exactly one at the moment—"to give you a dozen free dessert bars next time you come to the Bar None."

"How very sweet of you, dearie. I'll take you up on your offer."

Hilda went inside and Chase headed back to the shop.

Chase approached her building from the rear, through the parking lot, as usual. Quincy snuggled next to her neck, purring. Those whiskers tickled a bit. She wished she knew what went on in that little brain.

Halfway to the door, Chase stopped. Something was missing. Vi's bright red Z4 wasn't there. After depositing the cat in the office with some of her own homemade treats, being sure to firmly close the latch, Chase stuck her head through the doors to the front. There was Vi, smiling and talking people into buying twice what they'd intended. Where was her car?

The Bar None was closed for Thursday night. Anna had helped tidy the kitchen and Vi had straightened up in front before they left. Chase went to close and lock the back door, wanting to retreat upstairs and cuddle with her guy, Quincy. A silver sports car pulled up, stopping almost upon her, so close she thought it might try to go through the door. It was the last person she wanted to see—Shaun Everly.

He jumped out, but stood leaning on his open car door, not approaching her and not seeming to be a threat, for a change. He wore a nylon jacket, which he might need later in the evening, though the air was warm then. The jacket was cobalt-colored and brought out the color of his gorgeous light blue eyes.

He turned to Chase. "Where is she?" He sounded belligerent. His eyes might be gorgeous, but they were angry right then.

Chase thought she knew who "she" was, but she played dumb just to annoy him.

"Are you looking for someone?" Chase held the doorknob in her hand, standing half in and half out. She could retreat inside quickly if Shaun decided to go after her.

"Vi. Where is she?"

"I have no idea. She's not here. She left work over half an hour ago."

He blew a puff of exasperation through his lips. "She asks for a ride, then doesn't stick around to take it. I'm getting a little fed up with her."

"Maybe she found out what you're really like and decided not to have anything to do with you. She's pretty smart, you know." She thumbed the doorknob lock on the inside of the door.

"You Minnesota people are the worst! Vi is a tease and a two-timer. That Iversen guy—man, what a temper on him. No wonder someone killed him. I was trying to set up a simple little business transaction, but he dithered around way too long. And you."

Shaun took a step toward her. Chase tightened her grip on the door latch.

"You're something, you know that?" His sneer ruined his handsome face.

Chase pressed her lips together and refrained from blurting out the first thing that occurred to her, which was, *I know I am, but what are you?* In fact, the thought of the childish retort made her smile slightly.

"What's so funny? Are you hiding her in there?"

"Does she have reason to hide from you, Shaun? What have you done to her?"

"Me? Nothing! It's her! She stood me up last night, too. Look, I'll go away and leave you alone if you give me that deposit slip."

"Gosh, I would if I could. I'm not really sure where it is."

"Then I'll just stick around until you find it. I'll make your life miserable."

Chase straightened her backbone and stood as tall as she could. "You don't have any power over me here. Go back to Chicago, where you can wreck other people's lives."

"So you admit your life is wrecked?"

"Of course not. You're an ant to me, a tiny, insignificant ant." If only that were true. How could this man have the power to make her dread being next to him?

Shaun got back into his car, muttering, "I don't understand women."

Chase agreed with that thought completely. She couldn't keep a grim smile off her face at the thought of Vi dumping Shaun. Maybe she should give her a raise.

Shaun slammed his car door, and roared away. She stepped inside, closed the door, and slipped the chain latch on. It was past time to curl up with Quincy and a book. She would also see if she could find that darned deposit slip. She hadn't come across it yet after her move.

On Friday morning, it was almost time for Vi's break. Chase asked Anna if she could spell Vi. Anna said she'd finished baking for the day, so she'd be glad to. Anna didn't get out front as often as Chase did, being the main baker, and she welcomed her chances to do so.

When Vi came to the kitchen, she drooped onto a stool. Chase pushed a glass of lemonade in front of her, noting the strain on Vi's face and the circles under her eyes, poorly disguised by her makeup.

"Vi, I'm worried about you. What's the matter?"

Vi sat straighter and flashed her saleswoman smile at her boss. "Everything's fine. Nothing's the matter. It's you I should be asking about. I know you hurt your back the other day."

"Never mind that now. Where's your car?" The truth was, her back didn't feel very good at the moment.

The starch went out of Vi and she slumped, bowing her head until it almost touched the lemonade glass. "I . . . lost it." She sounded forlorn.

"It's stolen?"

"No. Not stolen. I missed too many payments."

"Why didn't you say something? We could have helped you out. A loan, maybe."

Vi sat silent for a good long while. Then she raised her head and seemed to make up her mind about something.

"Ms. Oliver, you and Anna *have* given me a loan."

Chase wrinkled her brow. Had Anna given her money? Then her eyes widened with comprehension. "*You're* the one filching cash from the drawer."

Vi looked down at her lemonade and nodded.

Chase struggled to contain herself. "Why? Why did you do that?" Chase pictured how easy it would be for Vi to stash the money in her huge tote bag that she kept under the counter that held the cash register.

"I needed to pay for things. My car, my apartment, things. Clothes, shoes."

"You're buying things you can't afford. I thought you must have a lot of money from your family, the way you live."

"No. My family doesn't give me anything. They don't have anything to give. I'm making my own way."

"This isn't how to do it."

Chase slid off her stool and went to fetch Anna from the front. There were no customers. "Anna. Please come into the kitchen. I don't know if I can talk civilly to her."

"To Vi?"

"Just come back here. I'll keep an ear peeled for the front door."

Anna joined Vi at the counter. "What's going on, Violet?"

Chase didn't let Vi answer. "She's the one who has been taking money from the cash register. It's Vi!"

"I don't have enough money," Vi wailed. "I can't make my car payments. I can't buy any new clothes. I didn't know what to do. I was being evicted. I was going to be homeless."

Anna took Vi's thin, cold hand. "Would you like us to help you set a budget?"

Vi gave Chase a wary sideways look. "Maybe."

"You've lost your car," said Chase. "Do you still live in the expensive apartment?"

"For now. I'll probably be evicted at the end of the month."

Chase and Anna exchanged a look. Chase decided to let Anna handle this since she was about to explode with anger.

"We'll think of something," Anna said. "Let's find a place you can afford, and maybe a secondhand car."

"I have one. I got a used Hyundai in White Bear Lake. But I don't know how I'll make the payments on it either. My credit cards are maxed out and I can't get any more. I don't know why. I've sent in some more applications, but they won't give me any more cards."

The poor girl knew nothing about supporting herself, about budgeting, about living within her means. "We have to sit down and do a budget for you. The next time you have a payment coming up, let me or Charity know. Don't just take the money from the drawer."

"I was going to repay you."

"How?" Chase demanded. Anna was right. They should fire Vi. Maybe Laci, too.

Vi shrugged and squeezed her eyes shut. "I had some money coming." Her eyes flew open and there was white-hot anger in them. "I was *promised* that money."

"What happened?" Chase asked.

Vi's face turned ugly. "It, well, it fell through. And the job . . ."

"What are you talking about?" Chase put her face close to Vi's. She wanted an explanation for her actions.

Anna gave Chase a look that said *back off.* "Do you want me to help get that stain out of the pretty blue blouse you wore yesterday?"

"No. I can do that much myself."

Chase didn't think Vi was going to let either of them help her with budgeting either.

"My break time's up," Vi said, slipping off the stool and hurrying to the salesroom.

Oh brother, thought Chase. What *now*?

TWENTY

"**I** wonder how she thought she was going to pay us back." Anna said. The three women had gathered at Anna's place after closing on Friday for a confab. She lived on Nokomis Avenue, an easy drive from the Bar None. Her modest white clapboard house had pastel blue shutters on the first-floor windows and two dormers poking from the roof on the smaller second story. Anna loved the location, a very short walk away from Minnehaha Creek, Lake Hiawatha Park, and the walking trail around the lake.

"I tried to get her to tell us, but after you warned me off—"

"Did I really?" Anna asked.

"You know you did. That look you gave me. I didn't bring it up again before she said her break was over." Chase stood at the tall double windows, watching a neighbor's red pickup truck go past as dusk fell. "She rushed off to return to the sales floor."

"Poor girl. I guess this is what's been eating her up."

"I'm not sure we can help her, Anna."

"I'm not sure you shouldn't prosecute her," Julie said. She'd come from the kitchen and joined them for the discussion of what to do about Violet Peters. She sat beside her grandmother on the pale blue couch, sipping the light white wine she'd brought along after work. Anna's preference for vibrant colors in her clothing didn't carry over to her decorating tastes. She chose pale blues and mint greens for every room in her house.

The dessert bars from the shop that would expire the next day were stacked on a plate and the three women picked at them. Business was slowing down to the extent that there were enough leftovers for the homeless shelter and a few for them, too.

"You think so?" Chase paced the room, too agitated to sit, let alone drink the wine. "That wouldn't help get the money back."

"Now we know who took the money, Grandma." Julie nudged Anna gently with her elbow.

"I could never press charges against poor Vi." Anna bit her bottom lip and gazed at Chase with tears in her eyes. "I thought you had stolen the money, Charity. I don't know how I could have even entertained the idea for a minute."

Chase stopped pacing and saw the stark emotion on Anna's face. Her own eyes teared up. "You know what's crazy? I thought you might have taken it, too."

Anna bolted up from the couch and the two women hugged, long and hard.

"We have to trust each other, Anna. We're in this together," Chase mumbled into Anna's soft gray hair.

They separated after a final squeeze. "I know," Anna said. "You are absolutely right."

"I'm beginning," Chase said, "to agree that we should look for new employees."

Anna chuckled. "And just when you've convinced me we should keep them."

"So when are you going to tell me the rest about you and Doris Naughtly? It might be ancient history, but it's still affecting you, when you don't want to be in the same room with her."

Anna grabbed her wineglass and took a healthy swig before answering, "It's Bill."

"Bill? Your future fiancé?" Chase sat in Anna's large, comfy, green striped chair and set her wineglass on the round marble-topped table at her elbow.

"Did you know we went out for a bit in high school? I didn't tell you that part. Doris dated him after me. We were never very serious. Doris dated him for a time, and she treated him so badly, I felt sorry for him. After I left for college, he married his first wife."

"On the rebound?" Chase said.

"Maybe. After Doris stole Bill away from me, she dumped him. He took it hard. Bill asked me out again, but I had fallen, hard, for Allan. I don't think Bill was happy with his first wife at all. I'm not even sure he was happy with his second wife, Marvin's mother. Her children were always such a trial for him."

Anna shook her head, recollecting the old history. "Doris was just never a nice person. She was always attracting guys with her cleavage and her flirty ways, then dropping them flat. Now that Bill and I are dating seriously, I've heard more about Doris. She really did wrong by him. She's even making another play for him. She shops for canaries every week and has never bought one. He sees through her by now, so it won't do her any good. But it still upsets me, for his sake."

Chase covered Anna's worn hand with hers. "I'm sorry."

"Marrying Allan and opening our sandwich shop was the best thing that could have happened. I feel bad for anyone who has never known what we had together."

Anna took another sip of her wine after that long discourse. "That's the whole story. She's an evil woman and

I'd rather she didn't shop here. And I'd very much rather she didn't stop in at Bill's shop every day, not that he would give her the time of day."

"Did Doris start making a play for Bill before or after her husband was murdered?"

"Before, but not long before. I think they separated soon after she started sashaying around Bill's shop acting like she wanted to buy a pet, flirting just like in the old days."

Chase wondered if wanting to renew an old flame, whom she had dumped, would be a motive for getting rid of her husband. She'd sure like to know what they were quarreling about when he threw tomato sauce on her.

As she drove home later, she realized they hadn't made a decision about Vi. They couldn't fire her right away, for the simple reason that they didn't have anyone else to work the salesroom.

Chase was ready for bed very early after a strawberry-scented bubble bath that soothed her frazzled nerves somewhat and eased her aching back. She pulled her duvet up and climbed in with a Bookmobile Cat mystery by Laurie Cass. Even though Chase had never seen a bookmobile, she liked the concept, and loved Eddie the cat.

Before she'd read five pages, Mike Ramos called.

"I've been thinking about you." That voice, so deep and rumbly. If she'd never seen his handsome face, she could have fallen for that voice over the phone. "How are you holding up with everything that's going on?"

"My back is a little better, but I'm awfully nervous about not knowing who is killing people around here."

"Would it help to know I'm a little worried, too?"

That was sweet of him to say that. After all, he wasn't nearly as involved as she was.

"Let me know if there's anything I can do," he said.

A vision of Mike rubbing her back, soothing her sore muscles, relaxing her, flitted through her mind. Something inside her tingled. "I will, I promise."

They chatted a bit about the murders and the suspects, then hung up. But now that she'd thought about a massage, Chase wanted one right away. She would work on that.

After her chat about suspects with Mike, Chase decided to organize her thoughts more clearly, if she could. She wrote out two names in pencil at the top of a piece of paper: Gabe and Torvald. Unfortunately, for her and for Torvald, he would have been the first named suspect in Gabe's column, except he was dead, too. She chewed on the pencil. Did the fact that he was dead mean he didn't murder Gabe, though? Could he have killed him, then could someone have killed Torvald because of that? Maybe Doris? Or Ted? Or Gabe's tattooed mistress? That mistress was a shadowy figure. Chase assumed she existed, but had never seen the woman herself.

All right, then, time to get down to business. She refused to put her own name anywhere on the paper. Under *Gabe*, she wrote *Doris* and *Ted*. Not knowing the mistress's name, she wrote just that: *mistress*. She repeated the same three names in Torvald's column, in case Torvald killed Gabe and someone exacted revenge on him.

She stared at the names for a moment. The shadowy mistress brought to mind the shadowy young man Vi had talked to in the parking lot last Saturday. She wrote down *young man*. It had looked like they were arguing. Chase had never seen him again, but that didn't mean he wasn't a killer.

That's ridiculous, she told herself. You can't suspect people just because you don't know who they are. She erased the young man from both columns.

Quincy noisily protested the fact that she was ignoring

him and that his next meal was late. Chase rose to feed him, but she was so absorbed in her task that she didn't look to see whether or not he ate.

Lacy had connections with the Naughtly family, all of whose names were on the lists, but Chase couldn't see her way to putting Laci's name down. Violet had even less connection.

But there was Shaun Everly. She had seen him get into Torvald's car. Did he have business dealings with Torvald? Gabe had, and Gabe was dead. There must be a tangled connection there somewhere. She put Shaun's name in both columns.

Except that Torvald's name was only in one column, the suspects were identical. This was getting her nowhere. She crumpled up the paper and got up to toss it in the kitchen recycle basket.

In the kitchen, she noticed Quincy hadn't touched his food. No wonder—she had forgotten to add the homemade treats. She mixed in the Kitty Patties and watched Quincy empty his bowl in record time.

Then she made herself a cup of herbal tea and carried it onto her balcony. She wrapped herself in a soft blanket and, watching the Friday night parade pass on the sidewalk below, she sipped her tea and stroked the contented cat in her lap, humming "It's the Hard-Knock Life" from *Annie*.

Hilda Bjorn didn't take long to collect on the dozen dessert bars Chase had offered her. She came in Saturday morning, right after opening.

Chase heard her voice in the front and came out to greet her.

"Vi," she said, turning to her clerk, who was more like her suave, confident self today. Her buttons were rose gingham against a purple satin blouse. "I want you to let Hilda choose a dozen, on the house. She helped corral Quincy the other day."

"Sure thing, boss." Vi beamed her golden smile on the old woman. "Would you like to taste anything?"

Chase left them to it, glad that Hilda was following through.

The customers were steady throughout the morning, but dwindling from the huge crowds of the week before, much to Chase's relief—and Anna's, too, since she could ease up on the incessant baking.

Vi asked to go out for lunch, so Anna clerked while she was gone. There was no reason not to let her go, with the amount of business they were doing.

Soon after Vi returned, Laci Carlson came through the rear door. Chase was surprised to see her there.

Anna reacted much more, though. "What on earth are you doing here, child? Shouldn't you be resting?"

"I'm rested, Mrs. Larson." Laci's smile made her look as lighthearted as Chase had ever seen her. "It's been nearly a week. I'm bored."

"What does your doctor say?" asked Chase. "Should you get a clearance to come back to work?"

Laci pouted like a four-year-old. "Yes, I'm supposed to."

"Did you think we wouldn't ask about that?" Anna's tone was gentle, solicitous. "Tomorrow is Monday. We'll be closed Monday and Tuesday. Maybe you can get in to see your doctor and come back to work on Wednesday."

"I guess so. I mean, I do have an appointment on Tuesday."

"That's settled, then." Anna pulled out a stool. "Have a seat and I'll get you a Peanut Butter Fudge Bar." They were Laci's favorite. Chase flinched. They'd been Gabe's favorite, too.

TWENTY-ONE

After they closed, Chase put off doing the books and decided to go out and treat herself to a frozen yogurt. She would get to balancing the books later. After enjoying her solitary creamy treat, she returned to her parking lot to find an old red Saab pulled up next to the place where she always parked her own little Fusion. Laci Carlson got out of the passenger side and waved to Ted as he drove off.

Chase said hi, noting that Laci's eyes were red-rimmed. "Are you all right?" Laci must have been waiting here to intercept Chase.

"I guess so," Laci said, not convincing Chase. "It's Ted. I think he's two-timing me. It's not his fault, though. He's just so distraught."

Chase wanted to shake Laci by her thin shoulders. Instead, she stepped within inches, invading the young woman's physical space so she couldn't ignore Chase's words. "Listen to me. If a guy is two-timing you, it's his fault. There's no excuse for not working out the problems between you."

"Oh, we don't have any problems between us. Ted is just, well . . ."

"Ted is just what?" Ted is just a first-class jerk?

"He's so upset about his mother, and that jacket thing." She fingered the pearl button on the frilly cuff of her blouse.

"Why is he upset?" The jacket didn't seem to incriminate his mother, having tomato sauce on it as it did, and not blood.

"He moved it from the bushes so no one would find it, then the cops did find it. They questioned his mother, and him, for hours and hours." She kept twisting the button. It was coming loose.

"*He* moved it? *He's* the one who stashed it behind my store?"

"He didn't want his mother harassed." The button fell to the ground with a soft ping. Laci didn't seem to notice it, but started fiddling with the one on her other sleeve.

"Questioning her is not harassment. She was one of the last people to see her husband alive. The police are just doing their job."

Laci shrugged, looking at the pavement.

"Laci, listen to me. It might be a good idea for you to stay away from Ted until the authorities find out who killed his father."

Laci's eyes widened. "What do you mean?"

Should she say it? Yes, she should. "I mean, what if Ted killed his father?"

Laci's took a sharp intake of breath. "He couldn't, could he?"

Chase shrugged one shoulder. "Who knows? What are you doing here? Did you come to see me?"

Laci nodded, still not meeting Chase's eyes.

"What about?"

"About working. I need to get back to work. My rent won't pay itself."

Chase knew she and Anna couldn't fire both Vi and Laci, at least not until they hired one or two other clerks to replace them. She hoped they wouldn't fire either one. "I can't talk right now. I'm on my way to . . . an important . . . meeting. Come over later and Anna and I will look at the schedule."

Laci sank a bit toward the pavement she still stared at.

"We'll get you going right away, okay?"

She murmured an assent and turned away to walk to her nearby apartment.

Why did Chase feel so rotten watching her small, thin form slowly trudge across the parking lot? How could Anna think about firing her?

Sunday crawled by so slowly, Chase wished they'd decided to close that day. The people of Dinkytown and the U students must have had much better things to do that day than shop for dessert bars.

After she'd eaten lunch, she got a phone call from Detective Olson.

"I want you to come to the station, Ms. Oliver, as soon as possible."

He sounded stiff and official, and he called her Ms. Oliver. That wasn't good.

"What's the matter?" she asked.

"How soon can you get here?"

His voice was not only stiff, it was cold. A shiver clawed at her, slithered around her torso, and tore at her stomach.

"Am I in trouble?"

He didn't answer, so she said she'd be right down. She called out to Anna that she had to go out for a few moments, not wanting to tell her what she feared—that she might be arrested for Gabe's murder.

She went upstairs first, to get her purse with her car keys. The chill she'd gotten when Detective Olson called was still with her. She slid her favorite soft gray cashmere sweater over her blouse, then donned her jacket and went downstairs.

Chase didn't break down in the parking lot outside the police station. She waited until she was in Julie's pickup truck.

Julie's own periwinkle blues filled with tears. Chase swiped at her own tears, feeling guilty she was making Julie cry, her shoulders heaving with the attempt to stifle her blubbering.

"Was it horrible?" Julie asked.

"Worse than horrible," Chase wailed through her sobs. "I was in that ghastly room for hours and hours after they let me call you. There was a table and a couple of very uncomfortable chairs. They locked the door. I had no idea what was going on. I didn't know if I'd have to spend days and days there."

"I wasn't sure what to do when you said you were being detained."

"Who was that good-looking guy that got me out?"

Julie waved a hand toward the car leaving the police station parking lot. "Oh, that's Jay."

"Jay? Jay who?"

"Jay Wright. I went to law school with him. When you said they were questioning you and had told you to make a phone call, I thought for sure you'd been arrested."

"I didn't know what to think. They didn't tell me much."

"Jay is working as a criminal lawyer, so I figured he'd be able to do something."

"He's awfully good looking."

"We . . . dated for a while, before we both got so busy in our new jobs. Anyway, he was glad to do me a favor. I'm just thankful you're not still in there."

"Me, too," wailed Chase. She sobbed with Julie's arms

around her, awkwardly, in the bucket seats of the small pickup. Eventually, her sobs turned to snuffles. Julie handed Chase some tissues from the box on the floor and drove Chase to her apartment as quickly as she could without getting a speeding ticket.

After a cup of hot chocolate, topped liberally with miniature marshmallows, Chase slumped in her cinnamon and mocha overstuffed chair while Julie sat on the hassock, warming Chase's hands, still cold, between hers.

"It was awful," Chase said. "That was worse than I could ever imagine."

"You poor thing. What exactly happened?"

"Detective Olson hammered at me for a long time. He was trying to make me say I murdered Gabe Naughtly! I think he was trying to railroad me."

"Did he say why he thinks you did?"

"He kept asking me if I was sure about the time when I was at the condo. How did I know it was that time? Wasn't I there earlier? He made me say everything I've already said. Over and over and over. The longer I sat there, the more my back hurt."

"How *is* your back?"

"I'll take some pain pills as soon as I can move."

Julie jumped up and brought her two tablets. Chase swallowed them with the last of her cocoa.

"Thanks, Jules. You're the best."

"So, here's what Jay told me. He says a witness placed you at the scene much earlier than you'd said."

"Did he say who the witness was? Some delusional, blind person? Or someone who hates me enough to want me in the pokey?"

Julie smiled.

"Why suspect me now? Hasn't everyone given their statements already?"

"Jay says Hilda Bjorn came into the station in the

afternoon and said . . . Here, I'll read it. Jay printed out part of her interview. 'I remembered another person I saw at Mr. Naughtly's condo the day he died. I just saw her again. It was that nice girl at the Bar None.' "

"That's what I get for giving her free merchandise! She already told them she saw me, didn't she?"

"No, now she says she saw you at a different time, much earlier, soon after both Doris Naughtly and Iversen were there. Here's what she said. 'It was right after that tall thin man, Einnar, or Ivanhoe. Iversen? Yes, that's it. After he left. Probably about four thirty.' She also says you had blood on your clothes."

"Why would she say that? That's simply, absolutely not true! I was there at eight."

"She sounds a bit confused at times. I'm surprised you were called in on her statement. She was questioned over and over."

"Not like I was, I'll bet."

"She stuck to her story every time. 'It was that nice girl who gave me the free dessert bars at the Bar None shop. The one with the cat.' "

"Well, I can tell you that I feel like killing someone right now." Chase set her empty cup down to give her full attention to her purring pet. He arched his back to encourage more petting and upped his volume a notch. Her ire subsided somewhat. "Maybe I could talk to her, to Hilda. Do you think I could help her remember a bit more?"

Julie hesitated a moment. "I think you'd better be careful or someone might think you're interfering with a witness."

"Well, anyway, please thank your friend Jay for me."

"Sure will. You've been through a lot tonight. It would be good if you didn't go to the shop tomorrow. You could stand to sleep in."

"Don't I know it. We're closed Monday, so I will. I think I'll get a massage, too."

"Oh, that's right. That should help your pain. Just remember, I never told you any of this about Hilda Bjorn. Jay was doing me a favor. He shouldn't be giving me this information."

"I need to do something extra nice for him. Or maybe you should do that."

Julie looked like she might like that idea. "Just so you know, I'd probably get fired if anyone knew I told you any of this. I want to keep my job a little longer. If I weren't so doggone worried about you . . ."

"I appreciate you sticking your neck out for me like this. No one will ever know."

Julie took both cups and put them in Chase's sink before hugging her good-night and leaving.

Chase got ready for bed, pondering. She would have to pump Hilda Bjorn carefully to avoid interfering with her.

TWENTY-TWO

On Monday, the shop was closed. It felt so good to sleep in, Quincy curled against her back in a warm, silky soft ball, that Chase wondered if she could stay in bed all day. Then her back reminded her that she needed to see about getting a massage. After a long soak in the tub with lavender bath salts—which didn't help her back at all—she called Mike to see if talking to him would cheer her up. But he could only talk for a half a minute, telling her he would be in surgery for a few hours with an emergency for a dog with some sort of problem. Something about X-rays and stomach.

It was past time for her to get a massage. She knew just the place, too. There was a parlor called The Refinery in the next block. Anna went there regularly for mani-pedis. Chase was tempted to go all out and get ninety minutes, but, when she got there, she opted for only an hour. It was late morning already and she thought she'd want lunch before an hour and a half, having grabbed only a fruit bar before her bath.

The fruit bar hadn't stayed with her. She should have eaten a Hula Bar.

The Refinery was a peaceful, soothing place, with an Asian symbol in the front window that, their sign said, meant "purify, cleanse, refine." If only she could do all three of those in the next hour. There was an appointment available immediately. Maybe this day would continue on a lucky note.

After she'd been kneaded and pressed and rubbed thoroughly to the soothing strains of ambient music, and the masseuse had quietly left and closed the door so she could get dressed, Chase rose from the massage table cautiously, not daring to twist her back and undo what she was feeling. It was so much better, she wanted it to last. She was careful getting dressed, just in case. No pain stepping into her jeans. That was good. No pain bending over to pick up her shoes. Even better.

She felt so good, she decided to walk to Hilda Bjorn's and talk to her before she lost her nerve. Julie had raised a point that Chase thought might possibly be valid. After all, Julie had a law degree. Just to check, Chase had gotten on the computer and looked up the term *interfering with a witness*, which looked like it had a lot in common with *tampering with a witness*. Tampering seemed to involve threats and physical force. She would avoid those two things.

She had to pass Mike's place on her way. She wanted to stop in and see if he had a moment to talk, since she hadn't had a chance to since she was brought in for questioning. She knew he came home for lunch sometimes. However, his extended-cab pickup was gone, so he was probably still in surgery at his clinic, fixing up the poor dog who had the problem, whatever it was. Maybe she could talk to him on her way back if his truck was there. He owned that big truck for the times he had to go to farms and take care of livestock and horses. He hauled a lot of equipment on those trips, she knew.

A new seriously cold front had moved in during the night and she'd had to bundle up for her walk to The Refinery. Going to the spa, she'd faced south, so it was cold, but not too bad. Now that she was heading north it was even chillier, a brisk wind making her glad she'd worn a wool scarf and her down jacket.

Hilda wasn't on her front porch today. That wasn't surprising, given the temperatures in the thirties. If the wind blew the clouds away, it might warm up. Chase mounted the porch steps and knocked on Hilda's door. Her wicker rocker moved a bit in a forceful gust. There was no answer. She tried again.

The man who lived next door, the absentminded Professor Fear, was walking to his home from somewhere. She figured he was coming home for lunch. "Do you know where Ms. Bjorn is?" Chase called.

He shrugged and shook his head. He didn't seem too concerned. "Maybe over at the church."

Disappointed, Chase retraced her steps until she was half a block from Mike's place. Both his truck and his car sat by the curb, so he was home. Her disappointment evaporated and she found her heart giving a slight flutter as she stopped. A matching sensation in her tummy reminded her of the small fruit bar she'd eaten, and that she'd been hungry again soon after she'd eaten it. She was ravenous now.

She had taken a step forward, toward Mike's condo, when his door opened and a woman stepped out. Mike followed her, his hand on the small of her back.

Chase halted, taken aback by the intimate gesture. She stood next to a tree that cast a shadow over her, so the couple wouldn't notice her.

The redhead she had seen in Mike's office leaned into him, then turned and threw her arms around his neck. He returned the embrace, hugging her tightly. Chase shrank away. The embrace continued. She reversed her course and stumbled to the corner. Circling the block and continuing by way of her detour, she found her way home.

She mounted the steps to her apartment and fumbled with her key. Quincy greeted her with an insistent meow that sounded hungry. Chase, however, found that her appetite had vanished.

TWENTY-THREE

When Chase answered her phone two hours after her thwarted attempts to connect with Hilda Bjorn and Dr. Mike Ramos, she was surprised to hear the voice of none other than Dr. Mike himself.

"Is your back feeling any better?"

She resisted the thrill his deep voice gave her and plunked down on her leather couch. "Yes, thank you. I got a massage earlier today." Her back really was a lot better. She flexed it and moved side to side. Yes, it was definitely on the mend.

"In that case, I'll go ahead and ask if I can take you out to dinner."

Huh. His lover-girl must have left. "What did you have in mind?"

"Chase, are you all right? You don't sound like yourself."

"How do I sound?"

"I'm not sure. Upset? Bothered?"

How perceptive of him. She didn't answer.

"Do you want to go to Moscow on the Hill in St. Paul to cheer up?"

Did she ever! She'd never been to the local purveyor of fine Russian dining, but that wasn't for lack of desire. The place was a little too rich for her struggling shop-owner pocketbook. Her pique vanished. "That sounds wonderful."

"How soon can you be ready? I skipped lunch and didn't have much breakfast. That surgery took it out of me."

"Give me twenty minutes."

As soon as she hung up she wished she'd said ten.

The meal at Moscow on the Hill was everything she'd thought it would be, from the piroshki appetizers, to the Duck Breast Ekaterina with Ukrainian dumplings, to the White Russian tiramisu. To say nothing of the wonderful Moskovskaya vodka. She had downed two glasses, but Mike had been more cautious and sipped only one, followed by strong coffee minus the traditional vodka. Chase was glad to see his restraint with the alcohol, since he was going to drive them home.

While Chase enthusiastically tucked into her dumplings, complete with caramelized onions and sour cream with dill, the conversation turned to what was on both their minds, the most recent murder.

"What have you heard?" asked Mike.

"Just that Iversen's cleaning lady found him dead." She longed to unburden herself about being a suspect in Naughtly's murder, but didn't want to ruin the meal by talking about the awful Detective Olson. "That's what it said on the newspaper's Internet site."

"I noticed the same report. When I read her name, I realized we share the same cleaning lady."

"You do? I'll bet there's a lot that hasn't been reported."

"I imagine so."

"The cleaning lady might have seen things that are important."

She was going to have to talk about this. After a nice hunk of duck washed down with a generous swig of the sweet vodka, she began. "I think Iversen is the one who killed Gabe Naughtly. Since I seem to be a suspect—"

"Whoa! You're still a suspect?"

"As far as I know." She didn't bring up her most recent stay in the police station. "I truly think Iversen might be the one who killed Gabe, though. So how can I clear my name now?"

"Don't you think it's more logical that the same person killed both of them? They had business dealings together. They might have crossed the wrong person in their under-handed attempts to take over other people's property."

"Like mine."

"They were after your shop?"

"Most definitely! That, and the fact that I put my finger-prints on the knife that killed Gabe, puts me in the spotlight. Or whatever they call that bright light in the grilling room."

"You were put in a grilling room with a bright light?"

"Well, not actually. It was a grilling room, but there wasn't a bright light. Being questioned by Detective Olson makes me feel like I'm in a cement room with no air." If she told him about being left alone for all those hours, she'd probably break down and cry.

"I can imagine."

"Can you see if your cleaning lady knows any details that might help clear me? For all I know, I'll be suspected of killing Iversen now."

"I'm not usually there when she comes, but I can leave a note for her to call me. Or, I'll tell you what, since I worked a good part of Sunday, I'll cancel some appointments tomor-row and be there when she comes."

Chase let out a breath of relief. "That would be wonderful."

After doing everything she could to get every last drop of the tiramisu, everything short of picking up the plate and licking it, Chase had a sudden thought.

"Something connects Gabe and Torvald," she said.

"Their business dealings, I'm sure," said Mike. "That's what I've gathered from the news sources. Several people have posted online about Torvald's possible shady business practices."

"True. But I'm wondering if anyone else is in danger. Maybe those close to them."

"Does Torvald have any family locally?"

"I'm not sure, but Gabe does." There was the person named Elinda, who had signed the book at the funeral home, but who knew where she lived? "Do you think Doris and Ted might be in trouble?"

"Are those his wife and son?"

"They were getting a divorce, but I doubt it had gone through yet."

"Since no one knows why either one was killed, I suppose it's a possibility."

Chase wondered if she should mention that to Detective Olson. Maybe her best strategy would be to stay away from both Doris and Ted so that if they were killed she wouldn't be right there, gripping the murder weapon.

The streetlights, charming imitation gaslights, lit the sidewalk outside the restaurant. Mike had managed to find a parking spot a half a block away. It would be a nice place for a romantic stroll, thought Chase, if the wind weren't blowing so hard and cold. Mike bustled her into the truck and slammed the door against the elements. He was quite the gentleman.

Coming down the hill on the way home, Chase loved the

way the lights of the city spread out before them. "Are you recovered yet from your awful day at the clinic?" she asked.

She studied his profile, lit from below by the lights of the dashboard. The hollows around his eyes looked deeper than they had in the restaurant.

"When I got the call, I braced for the worst, but the dog came through surgery just fine. His owner said he'd swallowed a whole chicken, but none of the bones punctured anything and I got him all cleaned up. He'll be good as new soon."

"Good news." Chase was sure he was an excellent animal surgeon. This seemed like confirmation of that.

"I know the dog will be fine, but his owner isn't—feeling guilty for not putting the thawing chicken where he couldn't get it. After all, it could have been serious if one of the bones had lodged wrong."

Was the owner the redhead he'd hugged on his front porch? She'd test the waters to find out.

"I suppose *he* would feel that way. Is *he* an irresponsible owner?"

"Not he, she. And no, she's not irresponsible. This could happen to anyone. She's usually conscientious, but she's had a lot on her mind lately."

The subject wasn't mentioned again, but Chase was left wondering if Mike was merely consoling an upset dog owner, or if there was something more between them. She also couldn't help but wonder what those arms would feel like if they were wrapped around her, instead of the spiky redhead.

Her mood shattered when Mike pulled up behind the shop to let her off at the door to her apartment stairs. Shaun Everly's silver Boxster was idling next to the building, exhaust smoke pouring from the tailpipe in the chill air.

"What's *he* doing here?" she exclaimed.

Mike gave her an alarmed look. "Is something the matter? Who is he?"

"He's someone I knew in Chicago. Someone I never want to see again. He's just moved to Minneapolis and, well, I wish he'd move back."

"Is he bothering you?"

Was he? "Nothing illegal. I just don't like the sight of him."

"Sounds like you two have a history."

Chase grimaced. "You could say that." She had a fleeting memory of seeing Shaun drive off with Torvald and wondered if Shaun could possibly be involved in the man's death.

"Do you want me to take you someplace else?"

That was a thought. A good one. "Yes, could you take me to Anna's? He doesn't know where she lives."

"I don't either, but I can take you."

Chase was relieved. Then she thought of Quincy. "Wait, I can't do that. I have to go in and feed my cat."

"All right, you do that. I'll go with you. If he's still here when we come down, I'll take you to Anna's."

"Perfect." Chase broke into a huge smile that turned into a slight giggle. Mike was so smart!

TWENTY-FOUR

Mike walked around the car to open the door for Chase. She climbed out of the big truck, studiously avoiding a glance at Shaun's car. His silhouette showed in the driver's seat. The exhaust sent a plume of ghostly vapor into the frigid night air. For a fleeting moment, Chase hoped something could plug the tailpipe so Shaun would asphyxiate. She scolded herself mentally for such an awful thought. She disliked Shaun Everly immensely, but couldn't go so far as to wish him dead.

She sensed his eyes on her as she led Mike to the rear door that served both the restaurant kitchen and the stairs to her apartment. With any luck, Shaun would assume that Mike was staying for a while and would leave.

As they mounted the stairs, Chase remembered that she'd left dishes soaking in the sink. And where had she thrown her underwear last night, or rather, early this morning after she'd left the jail?

"The place might be a mess. I had a rough night."

They reached the landing outside her door. "What happened?" Mike asked.

Chase fumbled with her key.

"You're shaking. Here, let me." It was a relief to let him take the key. Somehow, it didn't fit into the lock while she held it.

After Mike slid the door open, Chase stood where she was, sudden tears streaming down her face.

"It was awful," she whimpered. Yes, she was breaking down, just like she knew she would. And she was only *thinking* of being in the pokey.

Mike herded her through the doorway, kicked it shut with his foot, and put those nice, strong arms around her. She sobbed on his shoulder for a moment, then, mortified and embarrassed, pulled away from him and ran into her bathroom.

Dabbing at her splotchy face, she frowned at herself in the mirror.

What's wrong with you? Take hold of yourself, dummy.

She had been in his arms, right where she wanted to be. However, she hadn't wanted to be blubbering at the same time. She heard Mike talking to Quincy in her kitchen and Quincy meowing loudly, complaining that his din din was late.

When she finally considered herself presentable, she poked her head out the doorway. Mike was going through her cupboards! She cleared her throat and he turned around with a big grin.

"He thinks it's long past dinnertime. Where's his food?"

The cat and the vet, both looking at her for the important answer, made her laugh. It felt so good to loosen up like that. She opened the cupboard where a bag of Quincy's food was stowed—not the cupboard Mike had been searching—and scooped out his diet cat food. Her hands were holding steady now. She got her homemade treat from the refrigerator and mixed it in before she set his dish on the floor.

"That's impressive," Mike said, watching Quincy wolf down his food. "Maybe you should print up the recipe for that stuff and I can give it out to my clients with overweight, picky cats."

"Do you have a lot of them?"

"Do I ever. It looks like you've hit on something great."

Quincy continued eating, though his ears pointed at them, telling them he understood they were talking about something to do with him.

"Would you care for a cup of coffee? I have decaf." Mike was being so sweet, not mentioning her breakdown.

He was looking through to the living room and the balcony. "Sounds good. You have a nice place to drink it, too."

"The living room?" Chase started the process, measuring out the beans and pressing the button to start the noisy grinder.

"No," he shouted over the din, "your balcony."

"Isn't it too cold?"

"Do you have blankets?"

Great, thought Chase. He's a hardy outdoorsman. It didn't sound like fun to her, since it was probably in the twenties by now, but after the beans were ground and she started the coffee brewing, she got two eiderdown quilts from her linen closet. They were the warmest ones she had.

What Chase had failed to consider, was the need to snuggle in the cold. When she had filled two mugs with fresh brew, Mike settled himself on the chaise and beckoned her hither. Tingling a little inside, she nestled beside him and they tucked the quilts around themselves.

"Now," he said after a big sip, "tell me what's the matter."

Holding her lips stiff so she wouldn't cry again, she hoped, she told him she'd been questioned again last night. "Detective Olson wanted me to say I killed him."

"Killed Torvald?"

"No, just Gabe, for the moment. Do you think the police will think I killed Iversen, too? Julie and her friend Jay got me out in the wee hours this morning. I had to spend ages in a suffocating, empty room. I didn't know if I was going to be arrested, or thrown in jail, or what. First, I was questioned for hours. Then they left me alone there for hours. Detective Olson was trying to make me say I killed Gabe. I almost wanted to say it, too. I got so worn down." Her chin was crumpling, but she didn't let the tears fall. Her face got so ugly and red when she cried. She was *not* going to cry in front of Mike again.

"You poor thing." Mike put his mug down, cupped his warm hand on her shoulder, and caressed her upper arm through her sweater.

Chase wished she could stay like this forever.

"Why would he suspect you for Iversen's murder? You weren't around there when he was found."

Chase had no idea how it might happen, but somehow, the way things were going, she thought she would be a suspect.

TWENTY-FIVE

C hase was surprised she wasn't cold. Mike put out a lot of body heat and snuggling next to him kept her toasty warm. The life of the city went on below them, lit by the tall, curved streetlamps. The tree near her balcony, planted in a hole in the sidewalk, filtered the light with its gently rustling leaves. The wind was dying down. Cars droned by and people, talking to each other or to their cell phones, strolled past. The horror of being a real murder suspect was retreating to the far recesses of her mind.

"Isn't that the car?" Mike said.

"What car?" She lifted her head from his shoulder a quarter of an inch.

"There. The one that was in the parking lot." He pointed to a silver Boxster creeping down Fourteenth Avenue.

Chase jerked upright, dumping her coffee in Mike's lap. Mike jumped to his feet. Chase thought Shaun sped up a little. She hoped he'd gotten an eyeful of the cozy duo.

Mike grimaced.

"Oh my gosh. I'm so sorry. Did I burn you?" She jumped up and waved her hands, uselessly.

"It's not hot enough to do that. I'm all wet, is all." He gave her a cute grin. "No harm done. It'll wash out. Do you want to tell me what's going on with you and the guy in the Porsche?"

"Nothing's going on. I told you, he just moved here. I knew him in Chicago." She turned and paced the length of the small balcony.

"If nothing is going on, why is he spying on you?"

She might as well tell him. She kept pacing while she talked. "He's the reason I left Chicago." She told Mike about how Shaun accused her of pilfering money from his uncle, then got her blacklisted so she couldn't get a job anywhere in the city.

"Sounds like a jerk. Why did he trail you here?"

"He wants something that I have." She stopped and faced Mike. "It's something incriminating. I wonder if it's time to take it to the police. I just want him to stop talking to people I know and spreading lies about me. The same lies he spread in Chicago."

"I would think so. Is this something that would get him into legal trouble?"

"Criminal trouble. But then I'd have to get involved and testify and face him in court. There's something else I did, too."

Mike frowned. "What else did you do to him?"

She hadn't told anyone this, not even Anna or Julie. "I took out a restraining order against him. When he found out, he got so angry, it scared me. That's when I finally gave up and left."

"He's in violation, isn't he? He shouldn't be around you if it's still in effect."

"I don't think it is. It was a *temporary* restraining order, and it was only good for a week. I was supposed to go to court and get an injunction."

"But you didn't?" His tone told her he thought she was an idiot. Maybe she was.

"I never wanted to face him again. I decided to leave instead."

Mike shook his head. "Maybe that was a bad decision."

Chase nodded in agreement. "I can't change it now. But I do think I'll spend the night at Anna's. I'd better call to make sure she's there."

"Did you notice the other person in the car?" Mike said.

Chase stopped mid-dial. "Other person? No. Could you see who it was?"

"Just a silhouette."

"Male or female?"

"I couldn't tell. Shortish hair. Either a guy who needs a haircut or a gal who gets hers cut short."

Who would Shaun be associating with? He had so recently gotten here. He had seemed to know Torvald, though. And he knew Vi. Chase continued punching in Anna's number. Her call was answered right away.

"Charity! Julie has told me all about your ordeal. I'm so sorry I couldn't be there to rescue you."

"Julie did a fine job of that, Anna," Chase said, laughing. "She was my knight in shining armor."

"I was with Bill. His son came into town. Their meeting upset Bill so, that I went over there."

Chase wondered if she'd been there all night, and all day. "Where are you now?"

"I'm at home, of course. You just called my landline."

That made her feel a little stupid. Yes, she had dialed Anna's home phone. She heard talking in the background. Probably Anna's television.

"Do you need something, dear?" Anna asked.

"I'm having a little problem. I wonder if I could stay with you tonight."

"Just a moment." Anna muffled the phone and spoke with someone. Was Bill there? "How soon do you want to come?"

"How soon can he leave?"

"What? How soon can who leave?" Anna was put out. Chase shouldn't have been such a smart aleck.

"Just kidding. It sounds like someone is there. How about a half an hour?" She raised her eyebrows at Mike. He nodded.

"I'll be here. Are you in some sort of trouble again?"

"No, not with the police. I'll tell you everything when I get there."

They sat on the balcony another twenty minutes, mostly in easy silence, watching the street below, then Mike drove her to Nokomis Avenue.

Chase talked to Anna for over an hour before they bedded down. Over brandy nightcaps, Chase told her all about her date, then gave her the gruesome details about the horrible questioning when she thought she was going to be thrown into the clink. The more she shared her woe, the less of an edge it had.

Anna had read in the newspaper that Torvald's funeral would be the next day. She said she wasn't going to attend, but Chase thought she, herself, ought to do something. She wasn't about to zip over to the visitation that night, as she'd done for Gabe Naughtly, so she decided she'd have to drag herself to the service on Tuesday.

When Chase woke up in the morning, she'd slept so soundly she couldn't figure out where she was for half a minute. Then the powder-blue wallpaper, faintly striped, and the gauzy lace curtains on the guest room windows told her she was at Anna's. They split a banana and each had a bit of yogurt before they left. It felt like old times.

After Anna dropped her off Tuesday morning, Chase was acutely aware that this was her second day off. It had been a few weeks since she had had two days off in a row and she was at loose ends, not knowing what to do with the hours that stretched ahead. The funeral service was at two, so there was a lot of time to kill meanwhile.

Maybe she'd work on a new recipe for some treats for Quincy. Maybe not, since he liked the ones she had already concocted. Maybe she would go for a bike ride. The cold front that had arrived the day before was still hunkering over the city, giving the chilly air a blustery feel, with its wind gusts. Maybe she wouldn't do that either. Maybe she'd just sit around and read a book. That was a good idea. She had finished the Bookmobile Cat book, but had the new Lydia Krause mystery from Marilyn Levinson. The last one had been such a fascinating read, she'd gotten this one last time she'd been to the bookstore.

A light drizzle started in the afternoon, which reinforced Chase's decision to stay indoors as long as she could. She fixed hot chocolate for herself and fresh Kitty Patties for Quincy. Sitting close to the glass doors to her balcony, watching soft rain fall, and hearing light drumming on her roof, she read and drowsed until it was time to get ready for the funeral.

Chase dragged herself to her bedroom to put on something suitable for mourning a man—another man—whose death wasn't something she was sorry about. It was still dripping outside. She put on dark brown slacks and a white blouse. Should she wear dressy shoes? Because of the continuing rain, she had decided to drive, even though it wasn't far to walk. But she knew the parking lot at the funeral home—the same one where Gabe had been—had enough dips and waves in the pavement that the dry spots would resemble an archipelago. She'd have to hop from island to island if she wore shoes she didn't want to get wet. So she slipped into a pair of sturdy brown oxfords. They had weathered many a puddle with no ill effects. No one would look at her feet anyway.

The parlor was nearly full, but Chase found a seat in the

next to last row, on the aisle. She'd completely forgotten how
early one must get to a funeral to get a "good" seat. The
creamy ivory walls and the heavy silk curtains in the front
and along the side wall gave her a peaceful feeling. That
was probably the purpose of all the décor, from the plush
beige carpeting to the softly glowing brass chandeliers
depending from the rather low ceiling.

An elderly woman noodled on a small electronic organ
at the front of the room for ten minutes after Chase arrived,
playing sad, slow songs, then launched into a piece even
more dirgelike.

That must have been the signal for the procession. Everyone on the wooden pews rose. The funeral workers, two men
in dark suits, wheeled Torvald's casket down the aisle on a
gurney. Barely audible under the organ music, one of the
wheels squeaked, complaining about carrying such a nasty
man, Chase was sure.

The casket was followed by six men, the pallbearers.
Chase didn't recognize any of them, but that didn't surprise
her. She hadn't known Torvald, himself, until he barged in
at Gabe's and accused her of killing him.

Behind them, a woman, bent nearly double with osteo-
porosis and leaning on a cane, made her way forward, helped
by two younger people. The bereft expression on her wrinkled face gave Chase a paroxysm of guilt. Here she was,
thinking horribly bad thoughts about a man who was someone's child, someone's son. The woman looked as if her
heart would break. The young woman and even younger
man, maybe a teenager, on either side of her looked sorrow-
ful, too, but nothing like the old, bent woman.

After shedding the animosity she'd been feeling, Chase
found room in her heart for pity for this family. Iversen
seemed to have been a successful businessman. Maybe he
had provided well for his relatives. Maybe they would miss

him. Maybe they would even have a hard time getting by without him.

The woman's progress was so slow it took a minute or two for her to reach the row at the back where Chase stood. It would take them forever to get to the front pews that were reserved for the family. Chase turned to watch the procession. The young woman wore black, but her dress was inappropriately short and tight for the solemn occasion. A neck tattoo peeked out of her low top. The teenaged boy wore slacks and a white shirt, but looked ill at ease in them. His expression was more glum than bereaved, Chase thought. He seemed angry. Maybe he was angry that Torvald was dead.

The service was mercifully short. A Lutheran minister gave a generic message about our fleeting time on earth and about not knowing when it would end, then everyone stood and recited the Twenty-Third Psalm, which was printed on the small cards they'd been given when they'd entered.

Chase turned hers over to find Torvald's birth and death dates. It also said he was survived by his grandmother, sister, and nephew. The sister's name was Elinda. That was the same name she'd seen in Gabe's book. The nephew was listed as Felix. Those must be the three who had followed the coffin. Torvald was predeceased by his parents and a brother who must have been Felix's father.

To Chase's dismay, the family stood at the rear to greet the attendees as they left. She had hoped to slip out and avoid them. Chase hated funerals. Could she leave without going past them?

No, the doorway was too narrow to avoid the line funneling past Torvald's relatives. The line moved fairly quickly, at least. When Chase came to the boy, she shook his hand and said, "So sorry." The young woman, Elinda, was next. Her young face was attractive, but she wore layers of slathered-on makeup, her eyes surrounded by thick, greasy black hollows.

"I saw your name in Gabe's visitation book," Chase said, taking her hand.

To her shock, Elinda's pretty face crumpled and she suppressed a few sobs.

"Oh, sorry. I didn't mean to upset you." Chase patted the hand she held.

"I'm gonna miss him so much." Her voice was thin through her tears.

Chase fished a tissue out of the packet in her purse and handed it to the woman, who swiped the mascara and eyeliner off her cheeks.

"Torvald must have been a good brother to you," Chase said, still holding one of Elinda's hands.

"Torvald?"

"You said you'll miss him."

Elinda sniffed. "Gabe. I'll miss Gabe." She drew her hand out of Chase's and turned to the next person in line.

Chase gave her condolences to Torvald's grandmother and fled.

Back in her apartment, she fixed more hot chocolate to ward off the chill she'd gotten from being out in the rainy weather, and from Torvald's odd family.

Elinda would miss Gabe? She had to be Hilda's floozy. Her clothing was tight enough and she had at least one tattoo. She might have known Gabe through her brother. Torvald was quite a bit older than Elinda. She must be his baby sister. Why would she want to hook up with Gabe, who was so much older than she was? He'd probably made her think he had tons of money. Maybe he'd thought he actually would have tons after he acquired the location of the Bar None and started doing more business. Chase thought about how strange people are.

As soon as she sat down to think about Torvald's family, and Elinda, and to sip her cocoa, her doorbell rang downstairs.

Reluctantly, she left the steaming cup on the counter and hurried down the steps. When she cracked the door open, she was shocked to see Doris standing in the cold rain. She was shocked that Doris would visit her, but even more shocked by the woman's appearance.

Doris usually wore quite a bit of makeup. What was left of it was streaming down her face in orange and black rivulets.

Chase threw the door open so she could get out of the rain. Doris stumbled inside and Chase caught the fumes. She realized Doris had had more than she should to drink. The woman stood just inside the door, swaying, not even wiping the rain from her face.

"Mrs. Naughtly," Chase said, "would you like to come in and sit down?"

Doris nodded, wordlessly. She looked about to cry. Although she may have been doing that already. It was hard to tell with the rain and makeup streaking her cheeks. Chase guided her to a stool at the kitchen work island, but Doris was so wobbly sitting there, they moved to the office and Chase pointed to her desk chair, complete with a back and arms. All Chase needed was for Doris to fall from the stool, conk her head on the floor, and sue the Bar None.

Doris took off her raincoat, handed it to Chase, and sank into the chair. There were hooks inside the back door, so Chase shook out the raincoat and ran to hang it there. She didn't want Doris messing with her computer or looking through her desk, but when Chase ran back, Doris was sitting motionless, hunched over with her hands between her knees. She looked frightened.

When a long minute passed without Doris speaking, Chase said, "Is there something I can help you with?"

The look Doris gave her was tragic. "Yes. No. How could you? I don't know." She shook her head and a few drops of rainwater flew to the floor. Her dyed blonde hair, usually stiffly sprayed, was soaked and hung in limp, dripping hanks. "They're all dead. I don't know what's going on."

"You mean . . . Gabe?"

"And Torvald. They're both dead. I don't understand it. Could it be my fault?"

"Your fault?" Had she killed both of them? "Why do you think that?"

"I quarreled with Gabe. Violently. Then he died the same day."

"You quarreled with Torvald, too?"

"Yes." The word was almost a cry. "It was just a fling, he said. Then he . . . insulted me. Then he was dead."

The wind picked up outside and flung rain against the back windows. Was everyone in Dinkytown having affairs?

Doris started coughing and Chase ran to get her a glass of water. Doris sipped it and that seemed to help her spasms.

"How would quarreling with them make you think you killed them?" Chase asked. "Did you, well, did you attack them? With knives?"

"No!" She looked at Chase with horror. "No, not me. But maybe . . ."

"Maybe who?"

Doris shook her head slowly enough that no more raindrops flew from her hair. "Ted. Ted knew I'd fought with Gabe. He saw me leave and even told me he'd hidden my jacket so the police wouldn't think I murdered him."

Chase had wondered if Ted had told his mother about that.

"And Torvald?"

"Ted may have known about that fight, too."

"Did Torvald attack you? Throw anything at you?"

"No, nothing like that. But I think Ted saw me leave his car."

"So you think that Ted . . . killed them?"

"No, not Ted! Well, maybe. Do you think he did?"

"Why are you telling me this? Shouldn't you talk to the police?"

"You seem to have the ear of the handsome detective. Can you find out if anyone knows anything about where Ted was when they were both murdered?"

"Mrs. Naughtly, have you talked to your son about this?"

Of course, if her son were a murderer, voicing her suspicions might seal his fate. Chase changed tactics.

"It would be better for you to talk to the police yourself. Lay out everything you know. Let them gather the evidence and find out what's going on."

Doris didn't answer. She took another sip of water. Her hands seemed steadier now. The storm outside had subsided and reverted back to being the gentle rain it had been for the past several hours of the evening.

"Don't you think that's best?" Chase urged.

"I can't throw suspicion onto my own son."

That would be one consideration, Chase thought. The other would be that, if her own son were out murdering people, it would be good to get him stopped.

"So you're afraid Ted might have actually killed his own father? And Torvald?"

Doris raised her head and frowned. "I'm so confused."

She wasn't the only one.

"I think both you and Ted should be very careful, just in case you become the targets of this killer. You're all connected in some way." They should be careful, that is, if they weren't murderers themselves. Chase had a hard time seeing

ultra-feminine Doris or shifty-thief Ted as murderers, but
what did she know? No one knew why either one of the
victims had been killed, let alone who had killed them.

Doris eventually left, a little more sober than when she
had arrived. The rain quit entirely and Doris was able to get
to her car without getting any wetter than she'd been when
she entered the back door of the shop.

Chase got ready for bed but lay awake for a short time
wondering about Elinda, the angry young nephew, Doris—
and Ted.

Chase was so rested by Wednesday morning, she made an
early trip by car to pick up some flour and sugar. She'd noticed
they were a little low and the regular delivery wouldn't come
for another few days. Anna was arriving as she returned.

As Anna and Chase walked together from their cars
toward the shop, Chase saw Vi waiting outside the door. The
weather had suddenly turned warm and sunshiny. Chase
knew this was an aberration and wouldn't be likely to last
this time of year. It was almost too warm to wear a sweater,
let alone a jacket. Chase shed hers as soon as she got inside.

"You're here early," Anna said to Vi, who followed Chase
through the door into the kitchen. Today Vi wore a lilac
sateen blouse with designer cloth-covered buttons. Her
brown eyes picked up a bit of purple tint from the fabric.

"My rattletrap car broke down. I got a ride here, but my
ride had to drop me off early."

"Oh my. I'm so sorry," said Anna, touching Vi's arm.
"Will you be able to get it fixed?"

Vi shrugged. "I haven't called anybody. I can get rides
for now."

"Do you want me to call a mechanic to look at it?"

"You don't need to do that. I don't want you to go to any
fuss. I'll be okay."

Vi didn't seem very concerned that she had no transportation. If it had been her BMW that broke down, Chase wondered if she would be more concerned. But, since the BMW had been repossessed, maybe she was putting on a show of not caring about this car. Or maybe she'd decided to actually not care about them anymore. Buying what she couldn't afford had gotten her into trouble. Or maybe she was being brave, or trying to take care of herself.

Chase ran upstairs to tend to Quincy. He complained loudly about his breakfast being late, but forgave his mistress when she dished out the homemade treat he liked so much. As Chase watched her pet daintily chomp his food, she wondered who Vi had gotten a ride from. Shaun? Had he merely been chauffeuring Vi last night and not tailing Chase, after all?

TWENTY-SIX

Downstairs, Chase got a call from Laci saying that she'd seen her doctor again, but wasn't cleared to work yet.

The morning flew by, with a steady stream of customers, although there weren't many at a time.

"You never told me exactly why Detective Olson decided to detain you," Anna said. As usual at this time of day, she was stirring a batch of batter. Chase had been getting a head start on the midmonth payroll and was taking an iced-tea break in the kitchen. It was almost lunchtime. She would spell Vi in the front pretty soon.

Chase hadn't told Anna about the evidence against her. It seemed like blaming poor old Hilda, like telling on her, but she decided she wanted Anna's opinion.

"You remember the older woman who lives across from Gabe Naughtly's condo?" Chase said. "The one who had Quincy last week?"

Anna nodded, concentrating on her bowl. She stuck it under the beaters and turned the mixer on.

Chase raised her voice to be heard over the whirring. "She told the detective that she saw me quite a bit before I said I was there."

"At the condo, you mean?"

"Yes. She said I was there after Doris and Torvald left, around four thirty, hours before I was really there. And she says that I had blood on my clothes."

"She's sure she saw you?"

"She said she saw 'that nice girl from the Bar None' leave the condo with blood on her clothing. Come into the office. I want to ask you something."

Anna switched off the mixer and followed Chase.

As soon as Chase closed the door and Anna sat in the desk chair, Vi called to them and knocked on the door.

"Can someone watch the front? I have an emergency."

So much for discussing Hilda with Anna. They both returned to the kitchen.

Vi clutched her tote bag to her chest and looked as worried as Chase had ever seen her. "Is there something we can do?"

"No. It's a family thing. I just found out. It won't take long. Maybe an hour. There aren't any customers right now."

Anna went to Vi, put her hand on Vi's sateen sleeve, and nodded. "It's nearly time for your lunch break. You can take it now. We'll be fine."

Vi scurried out the back door.

"I wonder where she's going," Chase said. "She doesn't have a car. That reminds me. I told you that Mike saw another person in the car with Shaun last night, but I didn't mention that I think it might have been Vi."

"That makes sense." Anna started pouring batter onto a baking pan. "They seem to have gotten to know each other. You said they were talking outside the other day."

Chase grimaced. "I don't think that's a good thing, but I guess it's lucky he's giving her transportation."

"We should have found out exactly where her car is. I could have someone go out and look at it. Do you think it's at her home?"

Chase recalled that Vi lived in an expensive part of town, near Lake Calhoun. "If it is, I'll bet it seems strange, that beat-up old car, in that neighborhood."

"One of us ought to get out front. I said she could leave, so I'll go." Anna untied her apron and draped it over a stool. Chase shook her head after Anna left, and hung it on the proper hook.

Mike called as soon as she returned to the office. Quincy jumped softly into her lap when she sat at the computer.

"I talked to Karla," he said.

"Who's that? Oh, your cleaning lady?"

"Yes. She calls her service Karla Kleening, both starting with the letter K."

"Cute. Or should I say, *kute* with a *K*?" Should she be worried about Karla with a *K*? She tossed Quincy off her lap and began to pace.

"She is kind of cute," he said. "She's short and round and has more energy than a Dalmatian puppy."

Maybe Mike liked round women. Chase wasn't round, not all over anyway. "Did she tell you anything interesting about finding Torvald?"

"I'm not sure. When she found him, she didn't touch anything, aside from trying to push the door open so she could get in. As soon as she realized he was probably dead, she backed up and called the police. She said she found a button in the corner, after the body was gone. Iversen's landlord asked her to clean up so he could re-rent the place."

"A button? I don't see what difference that would make."

"She said it matched a button she found about a week before that. She thinks it's from a woman's piece of clothing, probably a top. Too small and delicate for a man's shirt, she said."

"Is she taking it to the police?"

Mike hesitated. "Well, that's a problem. She says she swept it up and threw it out. Later, she realized that, because it was so much like the other one, maybe she should have kept it. But she didn't have the first one either."

"None of this sounds like it's going to help the police any."

"No, it doesn't."

Chase heard a beeping sound.

"That's my front door. I think my next appointment is here," Mike said. "I'll call you later."

Still fretting about Karla, Chase opened the office door to the kitchen. Then, remembering that they needed more paper bags in the front, she hoisted a box of them and set it on the kitchen counter.

After being shoved off the treat maker's lap, the cat stalked the room with his tail twitching. A box of comfy paper products stood in the corner with its top open. The cat jumped into the space, just barely big enough to contain him, and took a snooze. The box was left on the kitchen counter. Soon, the cat awoke and peered over the edge of the box.

The box seemed extra-heavy. Chase would carry it up front later. She paced the kitchen. She decided that as soon as Vi returned and Anna was back in the kitchen, she was going to sound her out about Hilda Bjorn. Could the old woman be malicious? Mistaken? Senile? She hadn't seemed senile. Maybe she could talk to the neighbor, Professor Fear, and find out more about her personality.

There was another thorn in her side at the moment, Karla the Kleener. She was growing more and more fond of Michael Ramos. But the thorn from Karla was a mere sliver compared to the stab that Hilda was delivering to her. How could the woman insist that Chase had run from Gabe's with blood on her clothes? And how could Chase clear herself of the charges? She didn't have any bloody clothing, but that didn't prove anything. She could have thrown her clothes away. As for the timing, how could she prove she wasn't there at 4:30?

She thought back to that day. She'd been so upset about Gabe coming into the shop and threatening her, and then even more upset about losing control and threatening him, she had taken a walk around the parking lot at about that very time, to cool off and calm herself down. It was a very short walk, not enough time to get to that condo and back. She would never mention that to Detective Olson. No one at the Bar None had said anything about that. Unless Anna had.

TWENTY-SEVEN

The kitchen closed in, stifling her. Maybe she would return to Hilda's and see if she was home. She grabbed her sweater from the hook and opened the rear door. She hesitated. She should tell Anna she was leaving. Turning around, she saw Quincy leap from the box on the counter. He darted between her legs and was gone before she could completely recover her balance.

"Anna!" she called, hoping Anna could hear her. "Quincy's out again. I'm going after him." She hoped Anna had heard. She followed Quincy, hoping he would stop at the trash bin. He wasn't there, but she spotted him rounding the building at the corner. Again.

He was heading the way he'd headed several other times, for the block of Gabe's condo and Hilda Bjorn's house.

Chase was tired of running after that cat. If he was so overweight, why could he run so fast? She knew where he was going, so she decided she wasn't going to rush. On her ambling way, she mused that Chase was certainly an apt nickname for her, since chasing was one of her main occupations. If only Quincy weren't so clever. She hadn't seen him get out of the office, but he must have smuggled himself out in the box of paper bags.

As she approached Hilda's place, Professor Fear rode to his own house from the other direction, pedaling his fat-tired blue bicycle. His hair was more windblown than the last time she'd seen him, most likely due to the bike. He didn't notice her at first.

"Hi, Professor Fear," she called. "Do you know if Ms. Bjorn is home?"

"She should be. I saw her this morning. She wasn't feeling well and was going to stay home all day." He carried his bike up his porch steps and chained it.

Chase called her thanks, but they were unacknowledged. The man merely straightened up from securing his bicycle and entered his home. Maybe she should bring Ms. Bjorn something. Tuna hot dish? Chicken soup? Would that help convince the woman that Chase was not a killer?

Quincy sat purring on Hilda Bjorn's wicker rocker. It still swayed from his jump onto its seat. Chase picked him up, trying to determine whether or not he was lighter after his jaunt. She couldn't tell.

She knocked on the front door, but didn't hear any movement inside. Since she knew Hilda was there, and was ill, she tried the doorknob. It wasn't locked. She pushed the door open a few inches and called, "Ms. Bjorn?" She repeated the name a few times, getting louder each time and nudging the door farther open with each repetition. She thought she heard a door close at the back the house.

She entered the living room, a small, snug room with afghans draped over the couch and both of the overstuffed chairs. One end of the room held a dining table and hutch. Ms. Bjorn must be in her bedroom, poor thing. Chase tried the first door leading off the hall that ran the length of the house. It was a bedroom, and probably Hilda's, but no one was in the room. The bedclothes were smoothed, but the bed wasn't made up. A coverlet and two pillow shams rested on an old-fashioned fainting couch under the window. Chase tried the bathroom off the bedroom, but it, too, was empty.

Reentering the hallway, she tried the next room, also a bedroom. The heavy red draperies were drawn and the room was dark. It was obviously the guest room and hadn't been occupied recently, from the evidence of a layer of dust on the wooden floor.

She left the room. Quincy wriggled out of her arms and ran toward the rear of the house. Chase ran after him, stopping short when she got to the end of the hallway.

Hilda lay on her kitchen floor, a small puddle of blood beside her. It brought back the vision of Gabe so vividly, Chase started to feel faint.

Chase clutched the doorjamb and gave a loud gasp. Hilda's eyes fluttered open.

"Oh my," the woman breathed, barely audible.

Chase knelt and took Hilda's hand. "It's okay, I'm here," she said. Hilda pulled her hand away and frowned.

Sitting back on her heels, Chase whipped her cell phone out of her pocket and dialed 911. Before the operator answered, Chase heard sirens. Puzzled, she completed the call anyway. The sirens probably weren't coming here. The woman at the call center, after finding out where Chase was, told her to stay put.

"Don't you want to know what the emergency is?" asked Chase, standing up and regarding Hilda, who didn't seem awake anymore. Something blue lay on the floor, in the shadow of the dark wood cabinets. "The woman here needs help right away. Hilda Bjorn. She's been sick, but—"

"Help is on the way. You need to stay right where you are. Don't move and don't touch anything."

Chase thought that was odd. "I should pick up my cat.

He might disturb something. There's blood." There was something else on the floor, near Hilda's head. Something small and round. It might have been a button.

Quincy was, in fact, ignoring everything else and sniffing poor Ms. Bjorn's feet. She was barefoot, wearing a gown and robe. She must have felt his whiskers because she twitched her foot. Quincy transferred his sniffing to the door that led to the backyard.

"I repeat," the voice on the line said, "don't move and don't touch anything."

"Can I hang up now?"

Two policemen came quietly into the kitchen, their guns drawn.

Chase flinched and dropped her phone.

"Don't move," one of the men said, the square-jawed one.

"No, I won't." Her voice was faint, just above a whisper. She didn't think she could have said it any louder at the moment. The barrel of the gun loomed, huge and deadly. She wished it weren't pointing at her. She raised her hands in the air, surrendering. "My cat," she said.

"Is that it?" the rounder-faced one asked, jerking his head toward the door and Quincy.

"*Him*. That's *him*."

The policemen exchanged a private look.

"Go get it," the lantern-jawed one said to her. "Then stand right there and don't move."

She walked to the back door, weak-kneed. Professor Fear's face, wearing an incredulous expression, peered in at her through the windowpane. She saw a policeman come up behind him and motion him off the back porch. After she picked Quincy up, she stole glances out the door. Professor Fear stood in the yard talking to the policeman, waving his hands toward the house.

Meanwhile, in the kitchen, one of the policemen knelt beside Hilda Bjorn until a pair of medics arrived. They scooped her onto a gurney and whisked her down the hall, seconds after entering the room.

Chase was relieved that Hilda's color was good and she didn't seem to be bleeding much.

The two policemen remaining in the kitchen huddled together across the room for a quiet conversation. One shook his head at everything the other one said.

"Is anyone there?" a familiar voice called from the front of the house.

It was Mike Ramos! Chase was so relieved to hear his voice she nearly dropped Quincy.

TWENTY-EIGHT

The square-jawed policeman raised his gun again, this time pointing it at the newcomer. Mike stopped in the doorway to Hilda's kitchen, his eyes wide.

"What's going on?" Mike asked.

"Who are you and what are you doing here?" The policeman sounded as suspicious of Mike as he had of Chase. She wondered if Mike's heart was hammering as fast as hers was.

"I'm Dr. Ramos. I live across the street. I was coming home for lunch and saw the commotion. Is Ms. Bjorn all right?"

"I think someone hit her on the head," Chase blurted.

The round-faced policeman silenced her with a glare. The other one was talking on a phone.

"I saw the ambulance take her away," said Mike. "Is she going to be okay?"

"Are you a medical doctor?" asked the policeman not on the phone.

"No, a veterinarian."

"Isn't that medical?" asked Chase.

"You be quiet." Another one of those stern glares. He went to talk to his partner again. After further hushed debate, he turned to Mike. "Would you be able to take this animal?"

"Take him where?" Mike and Chase both said together.

The policeman unhooked a set of handcuffs from his belt. "We're taking her in, but can't take the cat."

"You're what?" Mike said it, but Chase thought it at the same time.

There was no answer. Mike threw Chase a worried glance. "What did you do?"

"I found Ms. Bjorn on her floor and called nine one one."

"Quincy got out again, I gather."

Chase nodded. She wanted to ask him what he was doing here when he had told her an appointment was coming in his door and he needed to hang up on their conversation.

"I'm sure this will get cleared up in a hurry." Mike took Quincy from Chase, giving her a pat on the shoulder. It should have been reassuring, but she barely noticed, as the policeman, the round-faced one, grabbed her wrists and pulled them behind her to snap on the cuffs. They were cold and uncomfortable.

"Can I get my phone?" Chase asked. It lay on the floor where she had dropped it. It was unbroken, at least. The round-faced policeman picked it up and pocketed it.

"I'll take care of Quincy," Mike said, as he left. "Then I'll go to the station. Call me when you know what's going on."

Chase nodded again, unable to speak her thanks. As soon as Mike was gone, tears started spilling down her face. It was distressing that she wasn't able to wipe them with her hands secured behind her. The taller, square-jawed one took her elbow and guided her, not ungently, out of the kitchen and to the front room. He motioned her onto one of the soft chairs and she perched on the edge of the cushion, not able to sit back because of the awkward handcuffs.

After a few minutes she asked what they were waiting for. As she was speaking, a team of forensic people entered with cameras and bags of equipment. Oh yes, she thought, the CSI people. Detective Olson followed them. They all proceeded down the hallway, but Detective Olson soon returned.

He took a seat in the other easy chair and sat facing her. "What's going on?" he asked the uniformed policeman. He didn't seem like the monster he had been when he was grilling her.

"Suspect was found standing over the victim. Victim was on the floor, bleeding and unconscious, with a heavy piece of marble beside her."

The detective turned to Chase. "Again?"

"Not exactly. This wasn't a stabbing. And I didn't do it this time either."

The policeman, still standing, stirred a bit. He was frowning at Chase. She didn't think he believed her. He stood at attention, his hands clasped behind him, and swayed slightly.

"I know, you were chasing your cat," said the detective.

"Yes."

"No, not really. Chasing your cat again? I was joking."

"Quincy likes Ms. Bjorn. He's run away and come here before." She wished that policeman would stop swaying. And frowning.

"Tell me exactly what happened, Ms. Oliver." Detective Olson took out a notepad. The whole scenario was all too depressingly familiar, from the use of *Ms. Oliver* to the notepad. At least she was in a living room.

She related how Quincy must have gotten out of the office as she hung up from talking with Mike. She called him Dr. Ramos, making herself a mental note to ask Mike, when she picked Quincy up, why he was going home to lunch right after he'd told her his next appointment was at his office.

After she'd told Detective Olson the rest, which wasn't much—that she'd gone after Quincy, learned from Professor Fear that Ms. Bjorn had been ill today, and had entered her house to see if she could do anything for her—he wrote for another minute or so, then looked up.

"Why would you be concerned about the woman who is a witness against you?"

"She's . . . she's an old woman and she's sick and she's . . . wrong."

"Were you thinking of attempting to change her mind about what she saw?"

He could tell that? "No, of course not. That would be tampering, wouldn't it?"

Detective Olson narrowed his eyes in an unattractive way.

"Since I was here, because Quincy was here, I thought I'd peek in and see if she needed anything. Professor Fear said—"

"Yes, I heard you. He said she was sick." He still didn't seem convinced, but told the policeman to take the handcuffs off.

"My cell phone," Chase said.

Detective Olson retrieved it and handed it to her. "If I need anything further, I'll be in touch," he said.

Grateful, Chase stammered something and fled.

TWENTY-NINE

C hase approached Mike's condo with caution. She didn't want to interrupt anything between him and the red-haired dog owner, the one who had let her dog get hold of a chicken. Chase still thought that was irresponsible.

Mike's truck was at the curb, behind his Ford sedan. No other cars were parked nearby. The woman must not be there. Chase rang his doorbell. He answered the door alone. So far, so good. Quincy was curled up on his couch, asleep. Evidently, finding bodies, even those of people he'd known and napped on, didn't bother him overly much.

"Thanks, Mike. I'll take him."

"What's your hurry? Come on in." He stepped aside and motioned her inside. "I'll get you some iced tea or . . . coffee?"

"I'd better call Anna. She has no idea where I am."

"Are you doing all right without me?" Chase asked when Anna answered the office phone.

Anna said that Vi had returned and was in front, selling.

She said they'd both been worried about where Chase was until Anna noticed that the office door was open and Quincy was gone. "Where are you two?"

Chase told Anna about Quincy going to Hilda's and about finding the elderly woman on her floor, unconscious at first. "I think she was hit on the head. There was something chunky beside her on the floor."

"The poor woman. Will she be all right?"

"They took her away in an ambulance."

"Are you at the hospital?"

"No, I was . . . detained."

"Detained?"

"By the police. Just for a bit."

Chase heard Anna's intake of breath. "Do they think you did it?"

"I'm not sure. I don't think so. That is, I don't think Detective Olson thinks so, but the uniformed cops were ready to take me to the station. I was handcuffed until the detective showed up."

"That's awful." Chase heard beeping on Anna's end of the call. "That's the timer. I'm making caramel."

Chase knew timing was critical for that process. "I'll be back to the shop in a few minutes."

After she finished the call, Mike asked if she had to go right away.

"Maybe I could have a glass of iced tea," Chase said. She realized she was parched. Maybe extreme emotions did that to a person.

Mike disappeared into his kitchen and emerged in a few moments with a frosty glass of iced tea that Chase grabbed. She gulped down half of it, then realized what she was doing. "I've forgotten my manners. Thank you, Mike."

He grinned and her heart gave a little lurch. "Any time, Chase. By the way, I think Quincy is losing weight. He seems lighter."

That made her feel lighter, too. She was doing it right! Chase looked at the tabby, who still appeared sound asleep except for his ears, which were swiveled their way. Then they twitched and swiveled toward the front door. A second later, the doorbell rang.

When Mike opened the door, the redhead stood there, her hair standing up straight and a huge toothy smile on her face.

"Am I early?"

"At least he had the good grace to look embarrassed," said Chase.

The shop had closed at 6:00, half an hour ago, and Vi had taken off soon after that. Shaun Everly had pulled up in front and beeped his horn. Vi had slung her tote over the shoulder and gotten ready to run out as if a movie star were waiting for her.

Chase had stood in her way. "Are you sure you know what you're doing?"

"What do you mean?" Vi drew herself up to her full height, which was more than Chase's. She raised her perfect eyebrows just two hairs.

"Shaun can't be trusted."

"What do you mean? I'm not trusting him with anything. Torvald did and look where that got him."

"You think Shaun killed Torvald?"

Vi frowned. "I never thought of that. Torvald was mean enough to kill someone, but I don't think Shaun is. They just wanted your place."

"Shaun wanted it?"

"I think so."

"He turned on me and he can turn on you."

"*He* turned on *you*? That's not the way I heard it."

"Vi, I need to sit down with you and tell you the whole story."

"Yes, I'd like to hear your side. But right now I have to leave."

She had hurried out, jumped into Shaun's Porsche, and they had roared away.

"How lucky Dr. Ramos showed up to take Quincy," said Anna, now in the kitchen, cleaning up from the day's baking.

"I know. But he'd just told me, before Quincy got out and I went after him, that his next appointment was there, at his office. Then, a few minutes later, he was coming home for lunch and saw the cars at Hilda's house." Chase sprayed down the countertops with disinfectant and wiped them.

"Maybe it wasn't his appointment." Anna finished wiping the baking sheets dry and tucked them into the cabinet. "Maybe it was . . . I don't know, the mailman? And his appointment was a no-show."

"I suppose." Or maybe it was the redhead, who seemed to be everywhere lately. "I hope Hilda Bjorn will recover," Chase went on. "If she got hit in the head, I hope she's not brain damaged." She moved to the sink and started giving it the nightly scour.

"Are you going to visit her in the hospital?"

"I don't think I can do that. Detective Olson didn't seem to think I should have been in her house at all. He actually thought I was there to try to change her eyewitness account."

"Weren't you?"

"I was there to get Quincy!" She straightened, her scrubbing cloth dripping onto the floor.

"Don't get huffy, Charity. I can imagine you would have tried to talk to her about what she saw, once you were inside." Anna took the cloth from Chase, then swiped the floor with a paper towel.

Chase pulled out a stool. "Yes. You're right. I did think

it would be a chance to ask her exactly what she saw. She can't have seen me, but she must have seen someone."

"And that someone is the killer?"

"I'm not sure. But there's a discrepancy between what I'm saying and what she's saying, so that throws suspicion on me. If our stories matched, it would be much better."

"I thought eyewitness accounts have been shown to be unreliable."

"Tell that to Detective Olson."

"Meanwhile, you would do well, Charity, to stay away from Hilda Bjorn, I agree." Anna gave a last wipe of the stovetop. "So I suppose I should visit her."

"And get her to change her story?" Chase felt a slow smile starting.

"I didn't say that." But Anna was smiling, too.

THIRTY

Chase stopped her bicycle in the middle of the bridge, her favorite part of the early morning ride she had been doing all too seldom lately.

"Looks like it'll be warm again today," said Julie, stopping beside her.

"I'm so glad you could make it this morning. We haven't done this in ages."

"Too long," agreed Julie. "What with my trial and your troubles . . . Trial and troubles, sounds like a blues song, doesn't it?"

"What do you think of your chances right now?" The testimony for Julie's big trial was in its fifth day, having started last Friday.

"It's hard to tell. This jury is very good at keeping a straight face and not letting on what they're thinking. Better even than most of them are, I think."

"Have you been able to find out anything else about that restraining order Iversen took out?"

"I haven't had a chance to try, but I may be able to sneak a peek later this week. I did get a look at Hilda Bjorn's file. They've opened a new case on her attack, of course."

"Is my name the only one down for a suspect?"

"Well, so far, yes. But it's very early days for that. What I want to tell you is that she's doing well and they expect a full recovery. Did you know that she's eighty-seven years old?"

"I'm glad she'll be all right. But I wish she'd realize she's wrong about seeing me right at the time when the murder was committed. Someone needs to recover her memory."

"Grandma said she's going to see Hilda in the hospital tonight."

"Yes. I hope Anna can jog her recall. This will get Anna's mind off the trial, too."

"I think it would be better if something could get Bill Shandy's mind off it. He's so concerned for his rotten stepson."

"What's going on with his own son?"

"Rick? He's almost worse than Marvin!" Julie picked up a stone from the bridge and heaved it over the railing. They both watched it plummet and sink into the depths of the Mississippi. "The guy has just lost another job. He only keeps them a few months, according to Grandma. He's hitting his father up for money again. She says Bill feels so guilty because he has the money, but doesn't think he should keep handing it out to him. He knows he should make his son grow up and take responsibility."

"I agree. I might put it differently, though. He should *let* him grow up. Maybe the problem with all three of his kids is that he's given them too much."

"You could be right. Rick is the youngest and he's forty-two."

"And still asking his father for money?"

Julie nodded, staring at the swirling Mississippi below them. "At least every month."

A pair of mallards floated by. They didn't seem to have a care in the world.

"Still, a guy can't be responsible for what his grown children do," Chase said. "Poor Bill."

"Marvin's mother might be more to blame than Bill. Grandma says she was always urging Bill to never let her children be poor. Now that she's dead, he feels he should honor her wishes."

"But he can't stand behind a son, or a stepson, who's doing illegal things! Stealing from a charity organization that was formed to help children—that's pretty low."

"You don't have to tell me. I'm on the prosecution's side."

"Do you have the proof to convict him?"

"Oh yes. But don't tell Grandma. I'm trying to keep as much of this from her as I can."

"It's a deal," Chase said.

"And I'm still nervous about getting you that info after your questioning. You haven't mentioned that to anyone, have you?"

"Of course not! I'll never do that."

"I know. It just gives me the willies. I hope you're completely out of this mess soon."

"You and me both."

When Chase returned to her apartment to change clothes for work, Quincy was acting strange. He didn't rise from his bed to greet her, but sat licking one of his forepaws. She went to the bedroom to change, but he didn't follow her like he usually did.

"Hey, big guy," she said, coming into the kitchen, her shorts changed for slacks, but still wearing her T-shirt. "How about your morning din din?" She scooped out the dry diet food and topped it with her concoction. When she set it on the floor, Quincy stared for a minute, then got up and limped across the floor to his dish much more slowly than usual. Chase wondered if she should worry. When he finally got there, Chase saw that he had left tracks on the gray tile kitchen floor. Wondering what on earth he'd stepped in, she grabbed a paper towel to wipe the floor. The towel, however, showed bright red. She almost dropped it. Yes, she should worry! Quincy was bleeding!

It seemed to be his right front paw, so she grasped his leg to try to see if the bottom of his foot was cut. He snatched it away and hissed! Oh dear. Something must be very sore, his paw or his leg or something.

She heard Anna come in the back door and rushed downstairs to tell her that poor Quincy was bleeding.

"Poor baby!" Anna cried. "Can I try to look at him?"

"Sure, you can try. He won't let me touch his leg."

Anna trotted up the stairs. Chase was a little miffed. Why did Anna think Quincy would let her handle him when he wouldn't let his owner, his favorite person, do it?

She followed Anna up the stairs and came into her living room to find Quincy sitting in Anna's lap. He was on a dishtowel she had put over her jeans. Chase bit her words back when she realized that it was one of her good dishtowels, one of a set that she'd gotten on a trip to Amish country to see her friend Charlotte Bessette, who owned a wonderful cheese shop in the town of Providence, Ohio.

Not only had her cat abandoned her, he was managing to get bloodstains all over her nice linen dish towel.

"Look, Charity." Anna lifted his front leg from the paw. "His dewclaw is bleeding."

Chase realized she had grabbed his leg exactly on his dewclaw. No wonder he'd been irritated. "Why is it bleeding? Should I call Mike?"

"Dr. Ramos? Yes, I think so. Something's wrong. Maybe it's infected."

"The vet sees him all the time. How could it get infected that fast?"

Anna gave her a stern look. "I'm not a veterinarian. How should I know?"

Quincy curled up in Anna's lap with his tail over his nose. "It doesn't seem to be hurting him," Chase said. "I'll go later. Right now we need to get the shop opened."

It was obvious Anna thought Chase was doing the wrong thing by waiting, but she didn't say a word, just gently set Quincy in his bed and swept past her on the way to the kitchen.

Chase finished dressing, ran a brush through her hair, and went to work. Once she and Anna got to working, and established their habitual rhythm, the day seemed brighter.

"Have you decided what you're going to say to Hilda Bjorn when you see her tonight? Julie said you were visiting her in the hospital."

"I am going to. I haven't decided exactly. But I do want to see how definite she is about who she saw and when she saw them. I won't single you out, but I'll ask her about everyone she saw. Maybe that will jar something loose."

"We should keep in mind that she was viciously attacked. I suppose you'll be safe enough in the hospital, but if someone thinks you're getting information from her, do you think you'll be in danger?"

"Who's going to know I'm there?"

"I don't know. But someone knew she was giving evidence to the police."

"Unless her attack has nothing to do with the murders. That's another thing I'll try to find out, what goes on in her life and if she's in danger from elsewhere."

"That's a good idea. I hadn't thought of that." Her mind had held one track lately: the murders and the whys and wherefores connected with them. Hilda probably had a family somewhere, possibly relatives with feuds and factions. Maybe someone was in her will and wanted to inherit soon.

Chase's mind turned to the dead men, Gabe and Torvald. Their connection was that they were working together to obtain her shop. In other words, *she* was the link between them. But how did Hilda Bjorn fit in? Could Anna find out?

THIRTY-ONE

W hen Vi set her big tote bag on the counter and got a sandwich out of an insulated carrier for her lunch, Chase took the stool next to her.

"Are you still getting rides from Shaun Everly?"

Vi, who had just bitten off a mouthful of ham and swiss on rye bread, nodded. She finished her bite and said, "Not much longer, though. I found someone who will fix my Hyundai in exchange for some of my old clothes."

"That sounds lucky! So you found a female auto mechanic?"

"I did." Vi sounded proud. "She lives in Shaun's apartment building."

Which, Chase knew, was also where Laci lived.

"Are you doing all right with your finances now?"

Vi shrugged. "I guess so. I'm not out of money."

Chase studied the young woman for a moment. The more she got to know her, the more enigmatic she seemed. Vi was the last person Chase would expect to do business by bartering. She did know that Vi had very little money smarts. After all, she'd gotten herself into enough trouble with her overdue bills that she had felt compelled to dip into the Bar None till. "You be sure and let me or Anna know if you get into any more trouble with your finances." Chase certainly didn't want that to happen again!

"Sure." Vi seemed unconcerned.

"Which clothes are you giving up?" Chase had never seen Vi wear anything that looked as if it should be given away. That mechanic might be getting a heck of a good deal.

"Oh, they're some that I'm not wearing." She waved her hand to indicate how inconsequential those clothes were.

"Say, I'll bet you might know the answer to a question I have."

Vi crumpled her sandwich bag and stuffed it into the insulated lunch carrier, then stuffed that inside her tote. "Okay."

"How did Shaun and Torvald know each other?"

"Did they?"

Chase remembered, at that moment, that Vi had denied knowing Torvald Iversen herself, after Chase had seen them arguing in the parking lot. "Yes. And you knew Torvald, too. I saw you talking to him one day outside." Could Torvald have been the potential source of her money that had fallen through? He'd been a financer, but who would finance Vi? And why?

"Who?" Vi asked, her smooth face the picture of innocence.

"Tall, thin guy, usually wore a blazer."

Vi raised her impeccable eyebrows and blinked. "Oh, is *that* who that was? The creep was trying to pick me up."

To Chase's ear, her statement rang false.

Chase crated Quincy, without too much difficulty, right after she closed the shop, and drove him to Mike's veterinary office in Minnetonka Mills. She'd called and described Quincy's distress and Mike had said he'd work her in at the end of his day. She got there at 6:30 on the dot. Since it was after regular hours, his outside door was locked, but he opened it as soon as she knocked. His receptionist had gone for the day, so Mike led the way into the first examining room himself.

"I appreciate you doing this," Chase said.

"No problem."

They were being so formal. It was as if the redhead were standing in the corner of the room, listening to them. At least, that's how Chase felt.

Mike lifted Quincy's paw, gingerly, not touching the dewclaw, which was still seeping a bit.

"Ouch. You have an ingrown toenail, buddy." He turned to Chase, his lips pursed ruefully. "Sorry I didn't notice this before."

"I guess you were concentrating on the size of his tummy." Even to herself, Chase sounded cold and distant.

"Are you all right?"

"Mm–hmm."

Mike turned to face her directly. "Are you mad at me?"

Chase couldn't look him in the eye. "Why should I be?"

"Beats me. Are you free for dinner this weekend?"

"I'm not sure."

"How about lunch, then?"

"You don't have plans?"

"Nope. I have the whole weekend free. All day Saturday and Sunday. But you're open on Saturday and—"

"Dr. Ramos?" A short, round woman in her late forties, or possibly early fifties, poked her head into the room. "Is there anything else? You want me to wait and do this room?"

Mike gave her a friendly smile. "No, Karla, I'll wipe it down myself. You'd better get home. Thanks."

That was Karla? Cute Karla? She *was* cute. She wore her

graying hair in a thick braid that wound around the top of her head and her elbows were as dimpled as her cheeks.

"Nighty night, then." Karla closed the door. Chase felt some of the stiffness go out of the room, and out of herself. That nice, older woman was no romantic threat.

"I could do dinner on Saturday," she said.

"Good. We need to talk."

Did that sound ominous? Promising? Both?

Anna called Chase a little before 8:00 that night. "I got in to see Hilda. I had to say I was her cousin."

"How did it go?" Chase asked.

"Not as well as I would have liked. The poor woman is sedated up to her eyeballs. She was very nice and very polite, and very vague. She doesn't seem to remember anything right now."

"Oh great. Wait, that could help. If she loses her memory of that day, I'm off the hook."

"I suppose." Anna sounded doubtful. "One problem was that she didn't know who I was. I tried to explain that I worked at Bar None, but she grew agitated every time I said the name of our shop."

Chase told Anna how Mike had clipped Quincy's dewclaw, then clipped the other one as a precaution.

"He refused to charge me anything."

"I'll have to remember to start dating a vet if I get another pet."

Anna and her husband had owned a series of miniature dachshunds. The two elderly dogs they'd owned when he'd died had passed away within two years. Anna hadn't had the heart to get another pet since then.

Well, if Anna thought she and Mike were dating, and if she was going to dinner on Saturday, maybe she should shove the redhead out of her mind. If only she could.

THIRTY-TWO

Anna had sounded pleased when Chase told her that she and Mike Ramos were going to dinner on Saturday. Chase had noticed this matchmaking tendency in Anna before, but it hadn't come up lately. Julie was much too busy with her job in the state attorney's office to see anyone and Chase had needed time to recover from her ordeal when she first came back home to Minneapolis.

Before they hung up, Anna had said that she and Bill Shandy were going out Saturday, too. Chase didn't consider that she herself tended toward matchmaking, but she would be more than pleased if those two worked out. Bill deserved a chance at happiness and Anna was beginning to get over losing her mate, enough so that she was ready to start seeing Bill—and to tell Chase and Julie that she was doing it. Even if it did bother Julie because her trial was so closely connected.

Chase shook herself. What was she doing, daydreaming

about romances when she was a suspect in two murders? Three, if Hilda Bjorn didn't pull through.

Chase was filling in at the sales counter while Vi went out to lunch on Friday. Business was sporadic, as it often was, coming in waves and lulls. During one of the lulls, Chase, humming "Wouldn't It Be Loverly" from *My Fair Lady*, turned from restocking the pink shelves with preboxed treats to find Torvald's sister, Elinda, regarding her from just inside the front door. She was dressed, again, in tight-fitted clothing, a short black skirt and a purple blouse that strained to contain her bosom, with a miniature black purse over her shoulder.

"Hi," Chase said. "Can I help you? Would you like some dessert bars?"

"No, I don't think so. I wanted to see the place Gabe and Torvald were so crazy about getting." And Shaun? Chase could see more tattoos now. One snaked up her left arm and another wound around her right ankle.

Chase waved her arm around the shop with a smile. "This is it."

"He died for this?" Elinda's sneer dismissed Chase's shop as something not worth dying for.

Chase's smile died. "Excuse me? How do you figure that?"

"He wanted to buy you out." She stated that as if it explained everything.

"I don't think I'm following you. Yes, he wanted to buy my shop. However, I never gave him the impression—*we* never gave him the impression that we would sell it. This property has been in Anna's family for a long time."

"Who's Anna?"

"She's the other owner."

"Which one of you killed him?"

Chase stomped her foot. "Neither of us killed him! Torvald killed him!"

Elinda took a step back, blinking. "You're crazy."

Anna, no doubt responding to Chase's foot stomp, poked her head through the kitchen doors. "Everything all right?"

"Are you the one who killed Gabe?" Elinda asked Anna.

"Oh, sure." Anna blinked. "I ran over there and stuck a knife in him, just for the heck of it. I had no reason to, and didn't have time to do it, but somehow, that's what happened." Anna looked at Chase. "Who is *this*?"

"She's Torvald's sister and Gabe's mistress."

"Oh!" Anna was struck by enlightenment. "She's Hilda's floozy."

Elinda looked confused. "Huh?"

"Tell me," Chase said. "Exactly what time were you at Gabe's the day he died?"

"I wasn't there that day."

"You certainly were," Anna said. "The older woman across the street saw you enter and exit."

"Ted saw you, too," Chase added. "Gabe's son."

"Ted?" Elinda asked. "A guy named Ted was going with Krystal, but not for long. Are you telling me he was Gabe's son? I never even knew Gabe had a son. For some reason, Gabe never introduced me to any of his family."

"Just answer the question," said Anna. "What time were you there?"

"Was he dead when you got there?" Chase asked.

"No! He wasn't dead! I didn't kill him! He called me to come over and I got there about, I don't know, around three thirty, I think."

Chase nodded. "That fits. That's when Ted says she was there, soon after Gabe got home from our shop. Before Doris got there." If Elinda had killed Gabe, Doris may have walked in, seen him dead, and fled, just as she'd said she had. He couldn't have thrown tomato sauce on Doris if he was dead when she visited, though.

"I don't have to stand for this. I have places to be."

"Dressed like that?" Anna said.

"I'll have you know this is just like what I wear for work. Krystal and I both work at Cooter's Sports Bar. She's my roommate. We'd feel overdressed if we wore jeans, after working there."

Something clicked into place for Chase. "Krystal. She dated Ted, you said?"

"She was with Ted Naughtly when Laci passed out." Anna nodded.

"Ted Naughtly?" Elinda said. "So he *is* Gabe's son?"

"He is," Chase said.

"He's been spying on me?"

Anna narrowed her eyes at the young woman. "Did you come back to Gabe's condo after Doris left?"

"That bitch was there? No. Gabe said he was too busy to see me that day. I'll bet it was because he was seeing her. We kinda had a spat. I wasn't going to talk to him again until he called me." Elinda whipped a tissue out of her tiny purse and dabbed at her eyes. "And now he's dead. I wish I hadn't gone away." She stopped dabbing her eyes. "He saw *her* after he sent *me* away? Is that what you're saying?"

Anna nodded. Elinda stormed out of the shop. Could Elinda be crossed off as a suspect? If only the police would cross off Chase.

Somehow, Chase made it through the rest of the hours of operation on Friday. The words *murder suspect* kept echoing in her mind throughout the day, preventing her from thinking about anything else, even driving all the show tunes out of her head.

After the shop closed, she and Anna went through the

cleaning up motions mechanically, without any conversation beyond what was needed to do the job. Anna seemed to have something on her mind, too. Chase was too unnerved by the visit from Elinda and too distracted to rouse herself to be concerned about Anna.

Later, upstairs, relaxing with a glass of wine that didn't do much toward easing her fears, she chided herself for not being more concerned about Anna. She lifted her cell phone, which seemed to weigh five pounds, and called Anna, but didn't get an answer. She tried Julie with the same result, then settled for a warm, purring cat in her lap until the phone rang.

"Detective Olson here. I need you to come to the station." He sounded crisp and official.

"Now? It's late and I've had a glass of wine. I shouldn't drive." She didn't really think that one glass would impair her coordination, but it sounded like a good excuse to her. She certainly didn't want to go to the station and be held all night again.

"I'll come to your place. I have a few more questions."

"What about?" It could be about Gabe, or Torvald, or Hilda. Any of the cases she was a prime suspect in.

"I'll tell you when I get there."

The connection went dead. At least she wouldn't have to go to the station. Chase paced the floor of her apartment until she heard the doorbell. Just outside the rear door to the shop were two doorbells, one for her apartment and one for the shop. The shop bell tinkled like an old-fashioned brass bell, but the apartment doorbell chimed, so she could easily tell the difference. The chimes, usually pleasant, sounded dull tonight to her ear. Chase trudged down the stairs to let Detective Olson in and led him up to her apartment.

"Where do you want to talk?" he asked.

"In here, I guess." Chase walked into her living room and sat on the couch. Detective Olson took the stuffed chair, kneeing the hassock aside.

He was in a cotton shirt, without his jacket. The day had been warm, but now the air was cooling off. His blue shirt sleeves were rolled up and cuffed, revealing strong forearms with soft brown hairs curling over the edges of the cuffs. His shirt was a shade or two lighter than his eyes. He pulled out a notepad.

It occurred to Chase that the man was a guest, although uninvited, in her home. She remembered her manners. "Would you like something to drink?" Anna would be appalled if she didn't offer.

"What do you have?"

She didn't want to offer wine to an officer of the law, even though her mostly empty glass was on the table beside him.

"I could make coffee or tea."

"Just a glass of water, please."

She had to admit that this was nicer than being interrogated in the station. She felt a degree of control over the situation in her own home. That control might be all in her mind, but she felt it nonetheless.

After she set a glass of ice water at his elbow, she returned to the couch while Detective Niles Olson drained half the glass.

Quincy sauntered in from the bedroom, where he had, no doubt, been under the bed until he'd decided to check out the newcomer. He sniffed the man's leather shoes, then made his decision. He rubbed his side against the detective's pant leg.

"Quince, you'll get hair on him." Chase jumped up to get her cat, but Detective Olson waved her away.

"That's fine. It'll mingle with the dog hairs from my golden retriever."

"How do you manage a dog with the hours you must keep?"

"I have a neighbor who looks in on her from time to time. It's very handy. Now, I'd like to know a bit more about you finding Hilda Bjorn."

"There's nothing more to tell. I've told you everything a thousand times."

"Try this. Lean your head back and close your eyes."

She laid her head against the leather back of the couch. If this was going to be another semi–hypnotism session, that might be good. Maybe she would remember something crucial, something that would get her off the hook. She felt herself beginning to relax already.

"You're walking into the house. What do you see?"

"I see her living room." Chase detailed going from room to room, thinking the house was empty. Lulled by his smooth voice, she got more and more relaxed and comfortable. It was, again, almost like being hypnotized, being right there at the scene. Then she got to the kitchen in the rear of the house. She shuddered, recalling Hilda on the floor, thinking she was dead.

"Exactly what do you see?" Was he trying to find some way to clear her? It almost seemed like it.

"I see her. At first I think she's dead. But she isn't. I'm glad she's not bleeding too much. I see something blue. I also see a button by her head."

"A button? What does it look like?"

"It's . . . it's purple." Chase's eyes opened and her hand flew to her mouth. It was Vi's button. Or was it Laci's? She couldn't tell if it was cloth-covered or not.

"You recognize it?"

"No, no, I don't. It's only a . . . purple button."

Mike had said there was a button at Torvald's when Karla found him.

"Ms. Bjorn had another button just like it clutched in her hand. Tell me if you know where it came from."

She couldn't. Besides, she didn't want Detective Olson to think Vi or Laci had attacked the old woman. He asked a few more times, trying to trip her up, she felt. Maybe trying to get her to tell him more, but she had no more to tell him.

"Has Doris Naughtly talked to you?" She remembered that she had urged the woman to voice her fears about her son to the authorities.

"I've talked to her. Several times. What do you mean?"

"She came here that rainy night—Tuesday, I think."

"You think she has more information for me? She's holding out?"

"Not that so much as she's afraid her son might have motive to kill the two men. I don't know what either one of them would have to do with Hilda Bjorn."

"Maybe I'll give Doris Naughtly another call. And her son, too."

"Elinda, Torvald's sister, came to see me today, here at the shop."

That got his attention. "What did she want?"

"I'm not sure. She was Gabe's mistress. Did you know that?"

Detective Olson gave her a look that said, *Come on now.* "Yes, we know that."

"Have you ruled her out?"

He stood and left.

Later, Chase remembered that Elinda had been wearing a purple top. Had her blouse had purple buttons? Maybe.

For the rest of the evening, Chase vegetated, putting all her interviews with the detective out of her mind as much as she could, aided by a TV showing of *Oklahoma!*, and sipping a little more wine. She might have had one or two glasses too many, judging by the headache on Saturday morning.

Saturday, the shop was blessedly busy, keeping her from thinking about what had happened the night before. Although she did keep her glance on Vi's blouse buttons a few times, thinking of Laci's pastel buttons, too. Her head ached all day.

Once again, Anna was distracted. But this time, Chase

thought she might know what was on her mind. She had mentioned she was seeing Bill that night. Bill was lucky to have someone who cared about him the way Anna did. She hoped he appreciated her.

After work, Chase's spirits lifted as she changed clothes and primped for her dinner with Mike. Karla, even though she was, as advertised, cute, was much too old for Mike. Chase had worked herself into a fret for nothing over Karla. The redhead, on the other hand, was obviously not a bit too old for him, and prone to hugging.

THIRTY-THREE

Mike picked her up at her place and drove to the restaurant Anna used to take her to when she was much younger, Lord Fletcher's on Lake Minnetonka. They made small talk on the way, Chase saying that she thought Quincy was going to be able to lose quite a bit of weight with her homemade Kitty Patties, Mike telling her a hilarious story about a dog owner who thought the dog's dewclaws were tumors and should be removed.

Underlying the pleasant banter was the tension, for Chase, of knowing that, sometime during the evening, she would confront him about what had happened on Wednesday. Mike held the car door for her and they strolled through the parking lot in the soft twilight to the bright lights of the restaurant.

It was set up for the boat crowd, with a dock where boaters could moor their crafts and jump out and eat in bathing suits in the summertime. Now, with autumn upon them, the

boaters were outnumbered by diners wearing considerably
more clothing.

They were shown to indoor seats overlooking the water
of the West Arm Bay of Lake Minnetonka. Mike ordered a
half carafe of chardonnay and they sipped as the sun set in
a spectacular array of golds and bronzes over the barely
rippling water, calmed for dusk.

After a platter of selected artisan cheeses and charcuterie,
and a second glass of wine, Chase felt brave enough to carry
out her intended interrogation.

"So, tell me something."

Mike gave her a sharp look. Something in her tone had
alerted him that her question might not be casual. "Okay,"
he said. "Tell you what?"

"When we were on the phone, your next appointment
was just showing up, you said."

"This was on Wednesday?"

"Yes, the day I found Hilda Bjorn unconscious on her
kitchen floor."

"I remember. I hung up because I heard the front door
open."

Chase had heard the noise over the phone. "You said your
next appointment was there."

Mike nodded and took another sip of wine. Or was it a
gulp? Did he have a guilty conscience? Was he actually
meeting the redhead at his office?

"So, if you had an appointment, how did you get to Hilda's house so quickly? You were there right after I got to
her place."

"My next appointment didn't show up. The front door
was the postman delivering my mail."

Just as Anna had said. Chase let out a breath she hadn't
known she was holding. No redheaded assignation. At least
not that day, at that time.

"I left to come home for lunch soon after we hung up and I saw the commotion right away. Somehow, every time there's commotion on my street, you're involved. I guess that's why I decided to check out what was going on." He grinned. "Sure enough, there you were, in the thick of it. You and Quincy."

The waiter arrived to take their entrée orders. After Mike ordered king crab legs for them to split, with Caesar salads to start, Chase gave him a big smile. "You know, I'm very glad you did show up. I don't know what to do with Quincy every time I get arrested."

Mike frowned. "Do the police seriously suspect you had anything to do with that poor woman's attack?"

"I'm not sure. Sometimes the detective acts like he does, and sometimes he acts like he doesn't. But he keeps questioning me."

"I don't like that one bit."

"I don't either!" She toyed with her wineglass as another thought occurred. "I don't understand how the police got there just seconds after I dialed nine one one at Hilda's house."

"When I got there, I heard Hilda's neighbor, the guy who rides the bike—"

"Professor Fear?"

"Yes, that's him. He was talking to a policeman in front of the house. He said he'd called when he saw a suspicious person run out the back door."

"The attacker! And not me either."

Later, after Mike had dropped her off—without a good night kiss again—Chase wondered if she should have pursued her question further. She was satisfied that his reason for being in the vicinity when she found Hilda was innocent, but what about the woman he'd hugged on his front porch? Was that innocent?

Sunday started off slowly. The shop had only a half-dozen customers before noon. Vi wandered into the kitchen between the trickles to chat with Chase and Anna. Anna had quit baking for the day since there was enough stock if this lack of volume kept up. Chase was caught up in the office, so the three of them sipped iced teas at the island counter.

"Are you still hanging around with Shaun?" Anna asked.

Chase was glad Anna brought that up, because she wanted to—but, at the same time, didn't want to. The less she said about Mr. Everly, the better.

"He's been very good to me." Did she sound defensive? "We get along well together."

"That's nice." Anna had a way of making it sound not . . . nice.

Vi grimaced. "I am sorry I ever introduced him to Mr. Iversen, though."

Chase choked on her tea. "You . . . introduced them to each other?" Vi must have forgotten she'd told Chase she didn't know Mr. Iversen.

"I wish I hadn't. Shaun was stringing Iversen along, just like Gabe did. And now I don't know . . . well, I wonder if he had anything to do with what happened to Iversen."

"What do you mean, 'stringing him along'?" Chase asked. "How was Shaun doing that?"

"He was pretending he had a lot of money to invest in buying your shop. Heck, Shaun's always bragging to me about how much money he has, but I don't believe him. He'd take me to nicer places if he was rolling in dough."

"And Gabe?" Anna said. "He was stringing Iversen along, too? The same way?"

"Sure. Gabe told him he could go halves with Iversen's investor to buy this place." Vi swept her arm around the room. "Make me laugh! Gabe didn't have anything. His wife is the one with the money. She was leaving him high and dry."

"How do you know all this?" Chase said.

"Torvald told me all about Gabe. He was getting fed up with him and had discovered he wouldn't be able to hold up his end of their bargain. That was just before Gabe got killed."

Chase was back to thinking that Torvald must have murdered Gabe, not that she'd ever been very far from that thought. "What about Shaun?"

"Shaun hasn't told me he doesn't have the money. But I've heard him telling Iversen how wealthy he is, how wealthy his father is, his uncle, his whole family. If they were all so loaded, I'd like to know why I don't get better jewelry from him. Look at this." Vi stretched out her right hand to display a ring with a bright blue stone.

"It's pretty," said Anna, leaning forward to see it better.

"It's tiny." Vi regarded her hand solemnly. "And it's crystal, cheap."

It *was* small, and probably hadn't cost much, Chase thought. But it was one more piece of jewelry than Shaun had ever bought her.

"It doesn't matter that much. I think he's two-timing me, anyway."

"Maybe he doesn't want to move too fast," Anna said. "Some men like to take things slow."

"He's quick enough to tell lies about me to everyone he sees," said Chase. "Be careful with him, Vi. He's a snake."

"Don't worry, I don't believe half of what he says. I can take care of myself."

"I'm sure you can, dear." Anna patted the hand that bore the cheap, tiny-stoned ring. "I believe I heard the front door."

"Finally." Vi jumped off the stool and went to the front to sell dessert bars.

"I'm bored," Anna said. "I think I'll try out a new recipe." She rummaged in the cupboards, clanging her metal bowls and equipment onto the granite counter and pulling out bins of flour and sugar. Then she went through the cupboards again, ending up on her knees.

"What are you looking for?" asked Chase.

"My little blue marble rolling pin, my favorite one."

"You were using it the other day, weren't you? On Wednesday? It couldn't be too far back."

"You'd think so."

Chase joined her, taking everything out of the cupboards methodically and putting it away.

Anna sat back on her heels. "It's not here."

Chase had to agree. "Did you take it home?"

Anna shook her head. "Did you take it upstairs?"

"Could Quincy have done something with it?"

"It's awfully heavy for him. It weighs at least five pounds."

"He weighs a lot more than that."

"Yes, I know. And I'm not slipping him treats anymore, if that's what you were going to say. I do think that, if you'd listened to me and trained him to walking on a leash, like Sophie Winston, the Domestic Diva, suggests in her column, 'The Good Life,' he wouldn't be having these weight problems now."

Not that again. Anna hadn't brought up "The Good Life" column for a while now, but she'd harped on it when Chase wrote her from Chicago that she had acquired a kitten from the shelter not too far from her apartment. Julie had met Sophie when she'd spent a summer in Alexandria, Virginia, between law-school semesters. Anna had been so thrilled that her granddaughter knew a genuine celebrity that she'd faithfully followed the column ever since.

It was nearly time for Vi to take her lunch, so Chase went to relieve her. She was startled to see Vi and Elinda, facing off in front of the sales counter. Torvald's nephew, the one listed as Felix on the card at Torvald's funeral, stood behind his aunt, looking embarrassed.

"You said you'd pay him." Elinda jerked a thumb over her shoulder at her nephew.

Vi flinched when she saw Chase enter the room. "What are you talking about?"

"You know what I'm talking about."

"Excuse me." Vi turned to Chase. "Would you please wait on these customers? I need to take a little break."

"I just came in to relieve you for lunch, so go ahead," Chase said. As Vi left the room, Chase asked Elinda, "Is there a problem?"

"Yes, there is." As she had the last time she visited the store, she stalked out. Felix threw Chase an apologetic look and followed her.

When Vi returned from lunch, Chase tried to ask her what was going on between her and the Iversens, but she avoided answering.

"I have no idea what that woman is talking about. I think she has me confused with someone else."

Chase concluded that several people seemed to be confused lately. She was certainly one of them. The afternoon continued as slowly as the morning had.

After a couple more hours, Vi wandered into the kitchen. "This is the slowest day we've had since I started here."

"Did you sell some product just now?" Chase asked.

"Of course."

That made Chase smile.

"Can I leave early?"

She sounded a bit whiny. Chase would rather she have stayed, but couldn't think why she should with business so slow. "Do you want to leave now? I can cover for the rest of the afternoon."

"Sure. I have my own car back, so I don't have to call for a ride."

Chase was glad she wouldn't have a chance of confronting Shaun. Maybe Vi would see less of him since she wasn't dependent on him for rides anymore. She followed Vi to the parking lot with a bag of trash. Vi climbed into her gray Hyundai, giving the rust spots a sad look, and drove off with a rattle of her tailpipe.

When Chase returned to the kitchen, Anna had abandoned her search and picked up her purse and car keys.

"I'm too low on shortening to bake anything anyway. I'll run out and get some."

While Anna was gone, Chase held the fort in the front. Perversely, as soon as she was alone in the shop, an influx of customers flooded the showroom and everyone seemed to want to buy dozens and dozens of treats. She scurried to keep up with the orders, wishing Vi hadn't left. It was inconvenient and annoying.

THIRTY-FOUR

B y the time Anna returned from shopping, the crowd
had thinned and there were only three customers browsing the shelves and display case. Chase was worn out from
the influx that had arrived when she was alone, though. She
stuck her head through the double doors and beckoned Anna
to the front.

"Could you take over for just a bit?" Chase whispered.
"I have to sit down a minute." Her wrenched back, which
had been feeling much better, was giving her twinges of
pain once again.

"Was I gone that long?"

Now that Anna mentioned it, she *had* been gone longer
than normal for a trip to the grocery store. It had been a
couple of hours.

Anna looked sheepish. "I stopped in to see Bill. Sorry."

"Tell me all about it later." Chase fled to the office, where
she could put her feet up on the desk. Her headache from
yesterday was returning, and she hadn't had that much wine

at dinner with Mike. Maybe she'd give it up entirely for a while. She rubbed her temples, which made it worse.

After telling Anna she would be upstairs, she went to her apartment for some aspirin. Quincy, whom she'd left upstairs today, greeted her with a loud meow. She stooped to stroke his soft back. By the time she reached the medicine cabinet, the headache was blinding. Her back felt worse, too. She downed a few pills, then started downstairs.

The treat maker was in the apartment at an odd time of day. The cat went on high alert with the departure from normal daily routine. When no treats materialized, he started to head for his bed, then stopped and listened. She was going out again. The middle of the day stretched so long between the two feedings. The human wasn't being as careful as usual lately. The butterscotch tabby was able to slip out of the apartment and down the steps. Thwarted by a closed back door, he scurried through the kitchen and was able to push through the swinging doors, then dart out the front with a trio of departing customers.

"Not again!" Chase ran down the stairs, tripping at the bottom in her haste. She caught herself against the wall, feeling the awkward position in her aching back, and went after Quincy.

She spied the tip of his tail. He had run into the salesroom! That was surely some sort of health code violation. She hurried to get him out of there as soon as she could. But when she reached the front of the shop, she didn't see him.

"Did you see Quincy come in here?" she asked Anna, who was bent over in the far corner, restocking a low shelf.

"Is he loose *again*?" She straightened, an alarmed look in her bright blue eyes.

"I saw him push through the swinging door. He has to be in here."

"Lady, are you looking for a striped cat?" An elderly man wearing an argyle vest and thick glasses pointed to the front door. "He left out that way."

"How could he?" Chase said. She had been surprised he got through the swinging double doors, but surely he couldn't work a doorknob. She went to the front window, followed by the man.

"Went out with those people." He gestured through the glass to a group of three women strolling toward the corner.

"Just what I need."

"Go," Anna said. "I'll stay here. You go get him."

Chase did, but couldn't locate Quincy outside. He wasn't visible on the sidewalk, on either side of the street, or even in the street. She went around to the back and checked near the trash bin, but he wasn't there either, unless he was crouched under it where she couldn't see him. Sighing and groaning, she knelt on the pavement and managed to peer underneath the bin. No cat.

She went all the way to Hilda Bjorn's house, but he had vanished.

As she crossed the street to check around Gabe's empty condo, Anna came running up the street.

"I warmed some of your special treats for him." She waved a plastic bag as she approached. "Maybe we can lure him out if he's hiding."

"Why would he hide from me?"

"Maybe he's upset by his latest vet visit and the ingrown dewclaw. Or something might have scared him out here after he got outside."

"That could be, I guess. He's not used to being out."

"He ought to be, by now."

"No kidding." Chase took the bag from Anna and opened it. The aroma of fresh meat rose from the warm Kitty Patties. "Oh, Quincy," she called. "Num nums!"

Anna opened the other baggie and they split up, covering both sides of the street on the way back to the shop, stopping and peering into bushes and under cars.

No Quincy.

Chase saw the "Closed" sign in the front door.

"I flipped it before I left," said Anna. "It was nearly closing time and no one was there."

Chase glanced at her watch. "It's past time now. It's after seven."

The sun was fast approaching the horizon over the trees and buildings across the street.

"What if we don't find him?" Chase struggled to keep the tremor out of her voice.

"We'll find him, dear. Cats sometimes take off for a while, but they always come home."

"Always? Unless they get run over. Or trapped somewhere and die of thirst. Or attacked by dogs. Or—" Her voice was rising, getting screechy. She was waving her arms like a wild woman, but she couldn't stop.

"You can't talk like that. You can't think like that." Anna grabbed Chase's shoulder and spun her around to face the woman who was, after all, her surrogate grandmother.

Chase grew still on the outside, but was still quaking on the inside. "He's never been out all night before. He doesn't know how to take care of himself on the streets." Her voice betrayed her, cracking and squeaky.

Anna frowned. "Do I have to slap you silly? Stop this right now." She gave Chase's shoulder a shake, not a gentle one, and let go of her. "Let's go over every place again."

The treats were cooling by then and Chase wasn't sure Quincy would be able to smell them. Especially if he was trapped somewhere, dying of thirst. "Will it do any good? I've been everywhere twice, up the street and back."

Anna tapped her foot. "He must have gone somewhere else. Where could it be?"

Chase took her cell phone from her pocket. "I'm calling Mike. He might have some ideas."

He didn't.

Chase stuck her cell into her pocket. "He just says that this happens sometimes."

"Exactly what I said."

"And Mike said that wherever Quincy is, he's probably all right and will come home when he's ready."

"Exactly what I said."

"All right, but neither of you are making me feel any better."

Chase texted Julie as she trudged back to the shop. Julie returned the message saying that she'd call later.

Just before Chase crawled into bed, Julie rang.

"Did you find Quincy yet?" she said. She sounded tired.

"Is the trial going on today? Sunday?" Chase asked.

"No, but we met in the office most of the day. I'm beginning to wonder if I'm cut out for this kind of litigation. Grandma said Quincy ran away again."

"He's still gone. We looked in the places he usually goes. I don't know where else to look."

"I sure wish I could be there with you, at least. And wish I could help look for him, too."

"I don't think it would do any good."

"He'll come back. You know cats do that."

"Mike and Anna both told me that. But this is Quincy. My babykins."

"He's still a cat. I don't think he's even used up one of his lives yet, has he?"

Chase had to chuckle at that. "No, he's led a sheltered life. I worry that he doesn't have any experience being out on the streets."

"The mean streets of Dinkytown?"

Her spirits lifted after the phone call until she started fretting again five minutes later.

Chase lay awake most of the night, dozing for short periods, getting up often to run downstairs to see if Quincy was clawing at the door, trying to get in. In the morning, she was a wreck. Anna came over to keep her company Monday, the day the shop was closed. She kept Chase supplied with hot chamomile tea. The warm spell was gone. Near-freezing temperatures were expected overnight.

Chase lurched through the day, running to the rear door every fifteen minutes until Anna commanded her to stop.

"We'll hear him if he's there. His meow is loud enough to hear in the next county, you know."

Chase pictured him barely able to stand, let alone meow, lying outside the door, but she started checking only every half hour to appease Anna.

Another sleepless night and another awful day passed the same way. At least the shop was closed Mondays and Tuesdays.

Mike came over Tuesday night with a thermos of hot chocolate. The weather was taking a turn for the worse, getting colder and blustery.

She cried in his arms most of the time he was there. After he left, she didn't feel any better. For two hours, she sat in front of her television, not seeing anything but the weather report. Colder and windier. She shivered. Her poor kitty! Where was he?!

Dragging every step of the way to her bedroom, she took off her clothes and pulled on a flannel nightgown. She stopped with one arm in the sleeve. She'd heard something! A meow! A loud meow!

She thrust her other arm through the flannel and grabbed her robe, stepped into her fuzzy slippers, and tore down the stairs. She threw open the door and took her breath in sharply.

Quincy lay on the cement, almost exactly as she had pictured him. Limp and lifeless.

THIRTY-FIVE

Chase scooped up her cat. He drooped in her arms. He was alive, though, and warm. She felt his little heart beating through his rib cage and he swiveled his right ear an eighth of an inch.

She inspected him closely. His left ear was torn and his inner eyelids were covering most of both his beautiful amber eyes. He was a poor, sick ghost of himself. She mounted the steps carefully, trying not to jostle her poor kitty. Cradling him in one arm, she retrieved her cell from her nightstand and called Mike.

A sleepy voice answered in a croak. "Chase? Do you know what time it is?"

She glanced at her alarm clock. "Oh. No, I didn't. It's past one. Sorry. Mike, Quincy is home."

"That's great." He didn't sound very happy about it. Was the redhead in his bed?

"He's not well. His ear has a chunk taken out of it and his third eyelid is showing."

"Oh, that's not good." Now he sounded awake and alert. "I'd better take a look. Can you bring him to the condo?"

"So you're alone?"

"Of course. It's the middle of the night."

"I'll be there in five minutes."

She laid the injured animal gently on her bed and threw on the clothes she had just taken off, jeans and a sweater. She pulled on her dirty socks and tied her sneakers, then rummaged around for something to wrap Quincy in.

He hadn't moved a muscle since she'd put him on the bed. Her heart hammered against her rib cage. She got a clean bath towel and cradled him in it, stepped carefully down the stairs, and put him in the front passenger seat. He didn't stir.

She could easily have walked to Mike's condo, but didn't want to carry Quincy in the cold, exposing him to the elements. The wind whipped her hair as she rounded the car to get into the driver's seat. A plastic bag flew by her windshield as she turned on the lights and the engine. The trees were swaying in the stiff breeze when she got out at Mike's and carried Quincy up the sidewalk.

Mike must have been waiting for her at his front door. He ran out and took the cat from her. Chase followed Mike inside where he put Quincy on his kitchen counter and unwrapped him from the bath towel.

Aside from a couple of *Hm*s and other grunts, he said nothing as he poked and prodded, using his veterinary instruments to take Quincy's temperature and listen to his insides. Chase held her breath while he did his examination.

Finally, he straightened. Giving Quincy a soft pat, he wrapped him up again.

"He's been in a fight. I guess you could tell that."

"That's how his ear got torn?"

"Seems that way. It's just nicked a little, you know, not torn."

"Did he lose the fight?"

Mike smiled. "I haven't seen the other guy, but I'd guess that yes, he lost. His nictitating membrane is up, as you noticed."

"His what?"

"His third eyelid. It's a sign of stress, or maybe infection."

"It looks horrible."

"It's not necessarily always a sign of sickness. Cats sometimes show it when they're relaxed and content. Lots of animals have them, mammals and birds."

"They do?"

Mike nodded, stroking Quincy absently. "Humans are one of the few mammals who don't. But its appearance along with the other symptoms is not a good sign. He's also dehydrated, so I should put him on IVs for at least a few hours. I'll include some antibiotics."

Chase cringed. Quincy with tubes in his little legs? Yuck. "Okay. You can do that tonight?"

"I should." Mike paused to think, a hand on his chin. "But I'll have to take him in to my clinic. You could take him to the twenty-four-hour hospital, but maybe we can do it this way instead. I have the tubing and meds at the practice, so I'll take him there to get him started, then we can bring him back here for the rest of the night. He might perk up by morning."

Chase breathed out a sigh of pent-up worry. Someone was going to take care of him. "He'll be all right?"

"Oh sure. This is a minor setback, especially if we treat him right away."

She felt her knees grow weak and her ears start ringing. The room grew dim.

She felt a breeze on her face. Opening her eyes, she found herself lying on Mike's couch. He was standing over her, fanning her.

"I'm not licensed to treat people, Chase."

"What happened?"

"You fainted." He gave her an odd smile. "You also mumbled something about 'the redhead.'"

"I did?"

Mike nodded.

Chase couldn't look at him. What had she said? She must have babbled in her coma, or her faint, or whatever. It wasn't sleep.

"Were you referring to Jasmine?"

Jasmine? "I don't know if I was or not. Who is she?"

"She's the widow of my best friend from college. He died two months ago and she's having a hard time."

"Is she the dog owner who let her dog eat a chicken?"

"She didn't *let* him eat it."

He sounded testy. She should drop the subject. Then she remembered where she was and what was happening.

"Quincy!" She sat up. "How long was I out? We have to get Quincy to your place."

"Yes, we do. You were only out for a couple of minutes. Do you want to stay here?"

Mike frowned and cupped his chin in his fist. "On second thought, maybe I should run in and get the equipment, bring it back, and do the operation here."

"Operation?"

"Sorry, wrong word. Procedure. Get him started on fluids and antibiotics. It'll be easy since he's a shorthair."

"Sounds good." She sank back into the couch.

Visions of dogs on IVs and redheads with spiky hair danced in her head as she lay with Quincy tucked in beside her, still wrapped in the beach towel.

So *Jasmine* was the widow of his college friend. It didn't mean she wasn't something more.

THIRTY-SIX

Wednesday morning she had to open the shop. Technically, she didn't *have* to, because Anna would have done it for her, but she felt the need to do something. She hadn't accomplished anything for the last two days, except worry about Quincy. The shop would at least give her something else to occupy her mind.

She put him on soft towels in his crate and set it in the corner of the kitchen where she could keep an eye on him. Mike had sedated him so that the IV would stay in place until he was fully hydrated and until he had had enough antibiotics. The vet had promised to come by at noon to check on him.

What a relief if was, not having to put him into the emergency vet hospital! Not to mention how nice it was not to have to pay the extra expense of boarding him there. There were definite advantages to dating a vet when you owned a cat, as Anna, The All Wise, had noted.

Chase hoped a health inspector wouldn't come by today

when they had a furry animal in the kitchen. That would not be good. But she couldn't leave him in the office. She just couldn't. She turned her eyes aside and pretended not to notice when Anna slipped a bit of crumbled topping into his crate. Quincy gave it a lethargic sniff and a halfhearted lick, but he was too dopey to actually eat it.

The shop was bustling and kept both women busy. At about ten o'clock, Chase ran to answer the phone in the office. It was Laci Carlson.

"How are you? Are you feeling any better?"

"Yes, much." She sounded bright and chipper. "The doctor told me yesterday that I could go back to work! Isn't that wonderful?"

She had picked the right day. Vi was slammed, almost overwhelmed, in the front. "Yes, it is. Can you come in today?"

"I'm all dressed. I'll be there in ten minutes."

She made it in five.

Vi frowned at Laci. "You again?" was her greeting.

"Vi," Chase said, pulling her aside and huddling near the swinging doors with both of them. "You will work with Laci. Laci, you will work with Violet. We need both of you. I don't need you quarreling. One of you work behind the counter and the other cover the floor. Stay away from each other. I don't want to hear any bickering."

"I'll take the floor." Vi flounced away and Laci took her position at the cash register, looking relieved to not have to be near Vi.

Chase felt like a junior high school principal, lecturing these two grown women. Well, barely grown, but out of high school anyway, and old enough to act responsibly on the job. How could she have forgotten how awful it was to have them working together? Chase would have to do something. She and Anna couldn't keep employing both of them. She realized Anna was right about that. They could work separate days, but there were times when two people were needed in front. She shoved that worry down below her concern for Quincy, and for herself.

When she reentered the kitchen, Anna was standing in the middle of the room, fuming.

"I really need to find my blue marble rolling pin."

The office phone trilled again and Chase went to get it. This time it was Detective Olson.

"I may need your help," he said, not sounding as unfriendly as he sometimes did. "The last time we spoke, you mentioned, very briefly, that you saw something blue by Ms. Bjorn's head."

"Yes, I remember. There was a button and . . . something blue." And suddenly, she got a clear mental picture of it. Something blue. Blue marble.

"Do you recall what it was?"

She stiffened and hesitated a split second before she told the lie. "No, I didn't get that good a look at it. Just something . . . blue." She knew he wanted her to tell him she had recognized it, Anna's favorite rolling pin. He couldn't know that it was from the Bar None, though. Could he?

"You're sure?"

"I'm sure," she told him and hung up.

Slowly, she trudged into the kitchen. Anna still stood with her hands on her hips, fuming.

"Anna, I saw something next to Hilda Bjorn after she was attacked. It was blue."

"Blue? How big was it?"

"About eight inches long. It looked very much like your missing rolling pin."

Anna's mouth dropped open. "No, that can't be right." She shook her head. "How would it get there?"

"I have no idea. But if it is yours, if it came from our kitchen . . ." A cold weight settled into Chase's stomach. "If it's from our kitchen, they'll think I did it."

Anna's mouth stayed open. "No. No, you did not do that. I know you wouldn't bash in an old woman's head."

The cold in her stomach crawled up her spine. It sounded to her like Anna was trying to convince herself. Did she think Chase could attack someone with a piece of heavy marble?

"You know what's crazy?" said Anna. "I can't even find my *green* marble rolling pin. Someone is stealing rolling pins."

Loud voices sounded from the front. Laci and Vi again.

Feeling so weary she could barely walk, Chase made her way to the front to referee.

"You're doing this on purpose to make me lose my temper!" Vi shouted at the cringing Laci.

Both of them were behind the counter. There were a half-dozen customers in the shop, all standing motionless, watching the scene.

Vi grabbed Laci's hair. "The twenties go on *top* of the checks!" She tugged and Laci's intricate updo came unraveled, shedding bobby pins. "You're a complete idiot!" She shook Laci's head, still holding on to her hair.

Laci flushed crimson and grabbed the front of Vi's pastel blue satin blouse. "I am not an idiot!" Laci shouted and ripped Vi's blouse open. Buttons flew to the floor.

"Quit that!" Chase roused herself and jumped between them, too late. The customers had all fled. Chase grabbed Vi and pried her fingers out of Laci's hair. By then Anna had arrived and pinned Laci's arms to her sides. Laci struggled against Anna, her face growing redder and redder. Vi panted from exertion.

"That's enough." Chase kept her grip tight as Vi tried to shake herself loose. "You're both fired."

Vi and Laci both grew still.

Vi recovered first. "Fired? How can you fire me?"

"Easy," said Chase. "I can't take this anymore. You've driven all the customers away. We can't afford that."

"I'm your best salesperson. You can't run this place without me." Vi held her blouse together and pouted.

"Watch me," said Chase. "Get your purse and go. Now."

Anna was trying to catch her eye, but Chase angled her sightline away to avoid looking at her.

"Laci, you, too," Chase said.

Vi snatched her purse from under the counter and stalked out, holding her head high in defiance. She looked regal, even with a ripped blouse, leaving in disgrace.

Laci, however, began to tremble. Tears coursed down her cheeks from her huge sky-blue eyes.

"Oh, sweetie," Anna said and folded the girl in her arms. Laci stood and sobbed for a good three minutes while Chase watched helplessly. Anna was falling for Laci's drama and undermining Chase, darn her, when Anna had wanted to get rid of Laci all along.

They had always worked as a team. They *needed* to work that way. If they were going to pull against each other, fight each other, the partnership just wouldn't work.

Chase threw up her hands and stalked to the kitchen, leaving Anna consoling Laci. Chase poured herself the last cup from the coffeemaker and sat on a stool. It wasn't noon yet and she had almost single-handedly consumed an entire pot of coffee. No wonder her hand shook when she lifted the cup.

No, it wasn't all caffeine. Part of her shakiness was anger and adrenaline. She could count on one hand the physical confrontations she'd been involved with over the course of her thirty-two years. It would be fine with her if she went another thirty-two years without another one. Or more.

Her mind strayed to her poor pet. She knelt on the floor and stroked him gently, avoiding the leg with the IV. He was dopey, but he lifted his elegant head and gave her a hoarse purr. She hoped he knew she was doing all this for his benefit. Would a cat know that, though? Was anyone harboring good feelings toward her at the moment?

A tear strayed down her cheek. She was taking care of Quincy. Anna was taking care of Laci. But who was taking care of Chase Oliver?

THIRTY-SEVEN

A nna stole up behind Chase so quietly, she didn't hear a thing.

"I sent Laci home," Anna said.

"Well, that's good, since I just fired her."

"Charity, darling, we have to talk about these things before you go off on a cockamamie spree."

"Me? I was cockamamie? Did you see what they were doing? They were attacking each other. All the customers left. This is no way to run a business."

Anna stuck two cups of water into the microwave to make tea for them. "You're right. We need to hire someone else, or two someones. I'll put ads in the paper and online as soon as I finish this." The timer dinged and she dunked bags of Earl Grey into the hot water. She sat beside Chase for moment, sipping, then sprang up. "No, I'll do it now."

She disappeared into the office to use the company computer. Chase swiped at the lone tear on her face, grateful that no more were following it. She hated people who wallowed in self-pity. This wasn't like her, and she was determined not to give in to her incipient feelings of depression.

Ticking off the points on her fingers, she counted her blessings. She'd read once that it was an antidote to depression.

One: Quincy was home and would recover.

Two: Anna and Julie were her good friends, her beloved family, and they were loyal and true. Almost all the time.

Three: A handsome man had taken her out to dinner. (At this point, Detective Niles Olson's deep blue eyes intruded, but she shut them out.)

Four: Four? She pondered. She was healthy and half owned a business that was doing nicely.

Five: Surely she could think of one more.

"There, that's done." Anna bustled into the kitchen. "Now I have to finish the batch I was baking." She picked up the icing tube and squeezed vanilla drizzle on the latest batch.

Chase felt the stabbing pain in her back, a dull pounding in her head, and another ache deep inside. She must have winced because Anna noticed.

"You don't look well, dear." Anna switched off the mixer and started the oven preheating. "Would you like to go upstairs and have a nap?"

"How can I? Someone needs to be out front."

"Why don't we close for the rest of the day? You've had too much piled onto your thin shoulders. We own the place, right? We can close up if we want to." She squeezed Chase's hand. "There should be some advantage to owning your own business."

"Oh, Anna!" Chase wailed. She buried her face in Anna's aproned chest and sobbed.

Chase lifted her head when she heard the back doorbell. Anna went to let in Mike Ramos.

"Hi," he boomed, full of joviality. "I've come to see my

favorite . . ." His face grew solemn when he saw Chase. "Is this not a good time?"

"No, it's a good time." Chase sniffed.

Anna handed her a tissue.

"I must look awful," Chase said.

"Well, you look . . ."

"We're having a bad day," Anna said. "We just had to fire both of our employees."

Chase was glad Anna said "we" fired them. It made her feel more like a teammate.

Anna went into the office and left Chase to tell Mike about the fight between Vi and Laci.

"I don't see that you had a choice," he said after she'd related the details of the incident. "But I'm sorry you're going through that."

If she hadn't just cried herself out on Anna's bosom, she might have considered doing it on Mike's broad chest. But she found herself regaining her composure. "I guess you should look at Quincy."

Mike gave Quincy a going-over and pronounced him on the mend.

"I've taken out the IV, and the anesthetic should begin to wear off soon."

As he left, he promised to call her the next day and arrange a date.

He actually used the word *date*, Chase noted. So, they were dating. That was official. She called to Anna that she was going upstairs now for a lie-down.

An hour later, Chase came downstairs, feeling more refreshed than she would have anticipated. Anna had flipped the sign on the door to "Closed" and was still baking. She gestured to a small heap on the counter. "I picked those things up, from the floor and the top of the display case."

A half-dozen bobby pins lay in a pile with two satin-covered buttons.

"The debris from the knock-down, drag-out," Chase said. She fingered one of the blue buttons. "You know, I wonder how many people sew designer buttons onto their blouses."

"Vi does, often." Anna was taking hot, loaded baking pans from the oven. She'd made several batches, four at a time in the large oven, while Chase had been napping. The kitchen was filled with the mouthwatering aromas.

"Yes, but do you notice other people doing it much?"

Anna closed the door and switched off the oven. "Not too much. It's an old-fashioned effect, isn't it?"

"I wonder . . ."

"Yes? You know, I think they're used on wedding dresses, mostly, aren't they?"

"I wonder how easy they are to get." Chase went to the office computer and did a couple of searches. "That's what I thought," she mumbled to herself.

She returned to the kitchen and picked up her cell phone to call Detective Olson. It rang in her hand. After almost dropping it, she answered the call from Julie.

"How's the trial going?" Chase asked.

"It should wrap up by the end of the week. I asked Jay to look up a record for you. Guess who Torvald took out the restraining order against?"

"Gabe Naughtly?"

"No. Violet Peters."

THIRTY-EIGHT

"**S**peak of the devil," Chase said, carrying her phone into the office to sit in the chair there. It was easier on her poor back than the stools in the kitchen.

"Vi is the devil?" Julie asked. "Look, I have to go, but maybe we can get together tomorrow night. If the jury goes into deliberations, I'll be freer than I have been since this trial started."

"That'll be great. We need to get some more bike rides in before it starts to snow. How does it look for your team?"

"It's hard to tell. Everyone on the jury has such a good poker face. I think we'll convict, but don't quote me. Poor Grandma. She's not talking to me about this."

"She's seeing, Bill, though. I'm sure that's helping him, and probably her, too."

"Hey, wouldn't it be nice if they got together?"

"They aren't together now?"

"You know what I mean. Maybe . . . move in together . . . get married?"

"Now, that would be fun!"

"Don't you dare tell her I said anything about this. Now I *really* have to go."

"My lips are sealed." Chase smiled for the first time that day as they ended the conversation.

After she hung up with Julie, she completed the interrupted call to Detective Niles Olson, he of the incredibly dark blue eyes.

Keep your mind on what you're doing, not on how good looking the cop is, she told herself, waiting for him to pick up.

"Olson, homicide." He sounded brusk, in a hurry.

"Oh yes, this is Chase. Chase Oliver." Why was she dithering like a teenager? Maybe because she could picture those blue eyes, hard and full of ice. "I had a thought that, well, might help."

"Go on." Yes, he was in a hurry.

"About the button I saw on the floor. It's cloth-covered?"

"Yes. It is." He sounded like, *So what?*

"Not many people use those."

"We'll take that into consideration." He paused for a breath or two. When he continued, his voice had softened. "Yes, we know Violet Peters often wears that type of clothing. However, I can't get a search warrant on a button."

"You can't?"

He blew air into his phone. "I tried, if you really want to know. The judge wasn't buying it."

"Oh. I thought it was evidence."

"It is, but it's not enough. Just because no one else you know wears those buttons, doesn't mean that she's the only person who does."

"Oh."

"We're watching her, though. She's on our radar. Can you tell me why she stormed out of your place earlier today?"

He *was* watching her. "She and Laci got into a fight and I fired both of them."

"Really? They fought each other?"

"Yes, it was awful. Vi pulled Laci's hair and it came all undone and Laci grabbed Vi's blouse and ripped some buttons off."

"Are the buttons still there? You have them?"

"Sure."

"Would you mind if someone came by and picked up those buttons?"

"Of course not. If it'll help solve the murder. How will they help, though? They're not the same color, or from the same blouse, I'm sure."

"I'm not at liberty to say, but it could help. How many do you have?"

"Only two."

"That's enough. I'll be there in ten."

Chase felt a thrill inside as she cut the connection. She had evidence. She was helping solve the case.

Wait a minute. Did this mean that Vi was the killer? Why on earth would she go around killing those men, and attacking an old woman? It didn't make sense.

But . . . Torvald had taken out a restraining order. That meant, she thought, that he must have been afraid of Vi. Were there other reasons to take out restraining orders? Chase had never been afraid of Vi. How could Torvald Iversen be?

Anna wandered into the office. "Who were you talking to?"

"Detective Olson. He's coming in a few minutes to pick up the buttons Laci tore off Vi's blouse."

Frown lines sprouted on Anna's forehead. "Vi's buttons? What on earth?"

"Anna, could Vi have killed those men?"

"I hope not. That would mean we've been employing a murderess. But what I came in to tell you is that I think I should visit Hilda Bjorn in the hospital again, since we're closed."

"Is she still there?"

"I went by her house Tuesday and that neighbor of hers, Professor Fear, told me she's still there and is expected to be for another week."

"That's an awfully long time. She's been there a week already."

"She's not young, Charity. Older people take longer to recover."

"And the attack was pretty horrible, from what I could tell. I thought she was dead when I first saw her." Chase pictured the scene once more, shivered, then shook her head to get it out of her mind.

"Are you feeling better?" Anna asked.

"You know, I think I am. My headache is gone and my back is feeling much better."

"It will probably be around five when I get back from seeing Hilda. If you're hungry then, do you want to go somewhere for an early supper?"

Chase accepted as the chimes on the front door sounded.

Detective Olson walked into the kitchen. "When your sign says closed, maybe you should lock the door," he said.

"We're terrible about locking doors, Detective," Anna said. "But you're right. We should do that."

He saw the things on the island counter and bent to examine them.

"Do you want Laci's bobby pins, too?" Chase asked.

He cocked his head in thought. "Wouldn't hurt. Maybe I will." He opened a paper bag and swept the items into it. Would Laci's DNA be on them? Was she a suspect, too?

"Let's hope nothing comes of this," Anna said.

"Why do you say that, Mrs. Larson?"

"Laci and Vi are ours. They're like family."

Chase didn't have the same opinion anymore, but she kept her thoughts to herself. Neither Vi nor Laci would fit into her family, she was sure.

After Detective Olson left, Anna asked Chase if she wanted to come with her to the hospital.

"I think I'd better keep an eye on Quincy, especially if we're going out for a bit later."

"Good idea."

Anna put some of the bars she had baked earlier into a bag, in case Hilda would be able to eat them. She shrugged into her turquoise blanket jacket and left.

"It's you and me, little fella," Chase said, stooping to give Quincy a rub between his ears. He closed his eyes and his purr was almost up to full volume. He must have been feeling better.

THIRTY-NINE

"I'm so glad I brought along the dessert bars when I went to see Hilda Bjorn," Anna said, taking a spoonful of minestrone at the Italian restaurant next door to the Bar None.

It had been the easiest place to meet for their early supper, although it wasn't all that early by the time Anna showed up. Chase had finished off half a basket of breadsticks before she came. They ordered, getting the half-price bottle of wine that was the special that night, and Anna said she had great news after their orders arrived.

"You loosened her tongue? Or her memory?" Chase asked.

"Both! We started talking about the Bar None and she told me how much she liked the Raspberry Chiffon Bars she got when you had given her the free dozen."

"A lot of good that did me! My goodwill gesture is mainly what makes me the best suspect for Detective Olson." Chase refilled her wineglass. At this rate she was going to drink most of it. Anna's half glassful sat untouched while she worked on her soup and the last breadstick in the basket.

"No, no, listen. She went on and on about 'that nice girl' who sold the bars to her. I pinned her down. She meant the girl behind the counter, the one who rang her up."

"You mean the 'nice girl' that she saw go into Gabe's at just the right time to kill him isn't me?" Chase twirled her fork in the middle of her salad.

"It seems that it's Violet."

Chase dropped her fork with a clang and almost let out a whoop of astonishment in the restaurant. She restrained herself, since that behavior would have clashed with the linen tablecloths and muted lighting. She leaned over the table, putting her head close to Anna's. "What about her saying she saw the one with the cat?"

"I asked her about that. She said she meant the shop with the cat. Not the girl with the cat."

"We have to let Detective Olson know this." Chase's voice was an urgent whisper. "I think you'll have to tell him, since Hilda talked to you. Get out your cell phone."

Anna looked around at the nicely dressed dinner crowd. "I don't think I should do it here."

"All right. Let's finish eating and go outside to do it."

"I'm parked behind the Bar None. Walk with me after we pay."

They finished the rest of the meal in record time and skipped dessert, even though Chase had looked forward to it for hours. This was much more important.

On the sidewalk in front of the restaurant, Anna realized that her cell phone was in her car.

"Let's go!" Chase said. She fairly skipped through the shop and out the back beside Anna, to get to where Anna had parked behind the Bar None.

It seemed that Anna took forever to unlock her car and find her phone, which had fallen onto the floor under the passenger seat. When Anna straightened, holding the phone, she said, "I don't know Detective Olson's number. Do you?"

Chase grabbed her own phone from her purse. "Yes, I have it."

She dictated the number as Anna pressed the buttons.

"Well?" Chase's body was humming with nervous energy.

"It's ringing. Oh, it's going to voice mail."

Chase deflated. "How could he? Call again."

"There's no point. I'll call later." She stuck the phone into her purse. The trees at the edge of the lot filtered the dim light from the streetlamp to send shadows scurrying along the pavement.

"I want to be off the hook," Chase said, whining slightly. "I want the detective to know it's Violet Peters he should have at the top of his suspect list, at least for Gabe Naughtly's murder. I didn't tell you yet that Julie says Torvald Iversen took out a restraining order against her, so she probably killed him, too."

"And I guess she's the logical person to have filched my blue marble rolling pin."

Chase snapped her fingers. "Sure. She was in the shop and left through the kitchen shortly before I went and found Hilda. I'll bet Vi wanted to do away with Hilda before she told someone it was her, not me, Hilda saw the day Gabe was murdered."

A darker shadow moved across the ground between them. Chase looked around. Too late.

Violet Peters had a thin, wiry arm around Anna's neck and the blade of a knife pressed against her throat.

Chase felt her eyes grow wide and her mouth drop open.

"Don't make a sound." Vi's whisper was guttural, grating.

Chase closed her mouth, but felt her eyes still ready to pop. Blood whooshed through her eardrums and pounded inside her head.

"Both of you, into the car."

"Vi," Chase said, breathing hard. "Don't do this. This isn't the way to—"

"Be quiet. You know what I've done. I heard *her* telling you." At the stressed word, the point pressed harder into Anna's neck.

"We haven't told anyone. The detective didn't answer his phone. What you're doing won't do you any—"

"I *said*, get into the car."

"Yes, yes, you did. We will." Chase tried the door and pretended to be unable to open it. "It's locked."

"Well, unlock it." Vi sounded like she was trying to reason with an imbecile.

Chase felt like an imbecile. Why on earth had they discussed this in such a public place? Anna should have called from inside the shop. That would have made so much more sense and would have been so much safer.

"I need her purse. The car keys." Chase gestured to the bag on Anna's shoulder. Vi ripped it off and threw it to Chase with more force than necessary. Chase figured all three of them were producing enormous amounts of adrenaline at the moment. She'd better be careful she didn't set off a murderous rage in Vi.

Chase fiddled inside the purse for a moment, then fished out the car keys. "Got 'em." She held them up.

Vi seemed to growl at her. Where was the sleek, sophisticated, attractive Violet? This woman's face was a distorted mask of raw hatred.

Shaking less than she'd anticipated, Chase clicked the driver's door.

"Unlock the rear doors."

Chase reached down to the inside of the front door and complied.

"In," said Vi to Chase. "You drive." Vi opened the rear

door, shoved Anna inside, then, quick as a flash, was in the
seat beside her with the knife point at her throat again.

"Where do you want me to drive?" Chase asked.

"Let's go out to Lake Minnetonka. It'll be nice and dark."

That's when Chase's hands started to shake.

FORTY

Chase couldn't decide if she should try to perform heroics or not. At the moment, she didn't think she would be able to, with the attention it took for her to drive Anna's unfamiliar car. However, the picture of a shiny, razor-sharp blade pressed into the soft flesh of Anna's neck was clear in her mind.

"Get on Interstate Thirty-Five," Vi growled from the backseat and, a minute later, "take Three Ninety-Four."

Chase swerved onto the ramps and around the curves and headed west. "Where, exactly, are we going?"

They were heading toward the lake, but Lake Minnetonka could more properly be called a bunch of connected bays. Saying they were going to Lake Minnetonka was like saying they were going to Canada. It was a vague destination.

"Gray's Bay Dam," came the terse answer.

That was bad. There was a fishing area there, and a park. The place would be deserted now, and dark. The sun had set at around seven. The dam wasn't high, but high enough that a couple of disabled bodies could easily be rolled into the water.

Chase tried to get that latest picture out of her mind and think clearly. She had to find out exactly what Vi's plan was. The route was straight for several miles until they would need to turn off onto Bushaway Road. There was time.

"We're going to Gray's Bay, you say. Violet, are you still holding the knife on Anna back there?"

"What do you think?"

"I think we'll be at the Gray's Bay Dam in about fifteen minutes. What are you going to do with me and Anna when we get there to keep us from telling the police what we know about you and the murders?"

"What's the matter with you? Just be quiet and drive."

They had crossed Interstate 494 on Interstate 394, which had devolved into Wayzata Boulevard, pronounced "Y-zetta" by the locals. "We're already on Wayzata Boulevard. I think that, since you admitted to us that you killed those men, and attacked Hilda Bjorn, you think you might have to get rid of us. Is that what you're thinking?"

"Why are you talking so loud?"

"If Hilda had died, everything would have been okay, wouldn't it?"

"Everything *is* going to be okay."

"Not for me and Anna! You're going to kill us with that knife."

Vi reached one thin arm to the front and snatched Anna's purse off the passenger seat.

Chase's heart sank. In the rearview mirror she saw Vi hold up Anna's phone, which she had just fished out of the purse.

"You called someone! Anna's phone was on!"

Which meant that, now, it wasn't on. When Chase had

gotten the keys from Anna's purse, she had redialed Detective Olson's number and left the connection open. Had he answered the call? Had he heard anything? Had the connection been good enough for him to understand what she was saying?

The turn onto Bushaway Road came way too soon. There wasn't another soul on the dark road, which was lined with tangled undergrowth and thick trees at that point. Chase slowed the car to a roll, but Vi noticed and told her to speed up.

The trees thinned out, then were missing entirely when they reached the dam, but the people were missing, too, and there was no lighting.

"Keep going, keep going. Slow now."

Chase eyed the frail wire fencing on either side of the paving. The fences stood a few feet from the two-lane road, leaving virtually no shoulder. They couldn't stop on the dam.

"Go past the fence. There, turn there."

Chase turned left onto the turnout to a small fishing area. Her mind, which should have been working a million miles an hour, was stuck on idle. As she got out of the car, her gears started to turn. What was Vi going to do with them?

"How did you get messed up with Gabe and Torvald anyway?" Chase said. "I heard you talking to someone named Felix. Torvald's nephew? Have you known him long?"

Vi backed out of the car, dragging Anna with her, the knife never more than an inch from Anna's precious neck.

If Vi forced them into the water, they could swim to shore. Especially if she did it from here, a small parking lot that led to a gentle slope with access to the water for fishing.

The black water made ominous sucking sounds against the shore. A gust of cold air blew Chase's straight hair off her neck. She realized the nape of her neck was sweaty, even in the frigid evening air.

"Stand against the car." Vi gave Anna a rough shove, pinning her to the car with the knife.

Then Chase saw Vi shrug her oversize handbag off her shoulder and extract Anna's second-favorite rolling pin, a green marble one two inches longer than the short blue one.

She was going to bash them over the head with it! The same way she'd tried to kill Hilda.

Please, please, Niles. Please have heard what I said on the way out here. Please be on the way.

A car went by on the road above, slowing slightly, but not stopping. Stray rays from the headlights filtered down to glint off Vi's knife.

Chase concentrated on not looking at the car. Vi didn't give it a glance either. Had it been a police car? Or Detective Olson in a plain car?

Please, please, please.

"Which one first?" Vi seemed to be mumbling to herself.

"Me," Chase said. "Me first." She couldn't bear it if Vi hit Anna on the head with that heavy piece of rock.

At last, Chase felt her mind speed up. A plan formed. Would it work? If it didn't, nothing would matter, so it had to.

First, some distraction.

"Vi, if Anna and I are both gone, would you mind taking care of Quincy?"

"Have you lost your mind? You're thinking about your cat right now?"

"I don't want him to suffer."

"And you think I'd be a good person to look after him? I'm not crazy about animals. Touching those rats was horrible."

"You put the rats in the kitchen?"

"Yes. Torvald and Gabe hired me to do it. I had help from that kid."

"Felix? Torvald's nephew?" Chase knew now that he was the young man she'd seen arguing in the parking lot with Vi that one time.

"Yes!" Vi shouted. "I know Felix! His mother is a friend of my mother. We played together as kids. He's the one who thought his uncle and Gabe could help me out with the money. So I cut him in for a share if he'd handle those rats."

"Elinda said you never paid him."

"How could I? No one paid me. I asked them over and over. Gabe had loaned me rent money and said he'd cancel my debt if I did that for him."

"Gabe loaned you money?" How could he? "I didn't think Gabe had any money."

"He had enough for three months' worth of my rent. But then he said there was interest or something and he needed me to pay him more. I was losing everything! My dad would have a cow if I got evicted."

Vi seemed to be reliving her ordeal, the prospect of being penniless. Her agitation was increasing. Maybe Chase should try to calm her down.

"I can see how you would feel," Chase said.

"I went to Gabe's a million times, then I asked Torvald a million more times. I got so mad at Gabe, I just grabbed that knife and stabbed him. You just don't realize how easy it is to kill someone with a sharp knife. I didn't exactly mean to kill Gabe. I was sorry right away. He might have been easier to get money from than Torvald. That guy was impossible. He's the one who insisted I carry through with the rat plan after Gabe died on me. Then he wouldn't pay me either."

"Why?" This squeak came from Anna, in spite of the blade at her neck. "How could they want to put the rats in the shop?"

"How do you think?" In the darkness, Chase could hear the sneer in Vi's voice. "You know they wanted you to sell to them. Since you wouldn't budge, they were desperate about trying to drive you out of business. Gabe even told me I could be the manager of his donut shop when he got your place. Then, after I kept after him about the money, he took that back. I think Torvald told him to. Those two were liars and cheats. They promised me everything and took it all back. They both deserved to die. Torvald was working on Shaun then, but he didn't have the money either."

"They called the health inspector, too, I suppose," Anna said.

"You need to be quiet, old woman."

"Old woman?"

"I said, be quiet." Vi's words were soft but menacing. She had the green rolling pin in one hand, the other held the knife, still digging into Anna's neck as Vi held her pinned against the car with her body.

"Torvald had me sign this stupid piece of paper." Vi sounded a bit calmer, but not a lot. "He called it a note. He said, 'Here, just sign this little note.' Like a note is less that a whole letter, right? It should be something informal. But no, he tells me later it's a binding, official, legal contract. He said he could put me in jail for not paying it!"

The girl was clueless. She had no idea what a note was. Chase looked at Vi, whose hands were full. How was Vi going to bash one of them without the other one tackling her?

Anna started to speak again. "I don't think he could have—"

"I told you to be quiet!"

Vi threw the rolling pin to the ground, reached into her bag, and pulled out a spool of twine.

Oh. She was going to bind them. Vi tossed the twine to Chase. "Tie her up," she commanded. "Wrists first." She flicked a piece of twine off the spool and returned the knife to Anna's neck before Chase saw that she'd missed a chance.

She wouldn't miss the next one. Now, tying Anna, she'd be close enough to Vi to try to get the knife away from her.

Chase took the length of twine and bent close to Anna's wrists. She lunged into Vi to throw her off Anna.

Anna's cry pierced Chase's heart.

FORTY-ONE

A thin stream of blood, dark in the low light, trickled from the knife point down Anna's throat.

Chase drew back. She'd been too clumsy. She hadn't knocked Vi over at all, had only caused her to drive the sharp point a fraction of an inch deeper.

Another car cruised past on the road above them, slowing as the last one had. It had come from the other direction. Could Chase hope that the police had arrived and were searching for her, up and down the dam?

"I'll do it," Chase said. "I'll tie her up."

"Never mind." Vi drew an ugly black pistol from her own purse. It looked too heavy for her delicate hand, but she didn't have any trouble holding and aiming it. "I was hoping I wouldn't have to do this. It's so noisy." She discarded the knife, dropped it onto the ground next to the rolling pin, and stepped back. Vi made sure to stay out of reach as she trained the gun on Anna. "Get next to her," she said to Chase. "Both of you, against the car."

Chase crowded next to Anna and grasped her hand. It was cold and shook with tremors.

What could Chase do to appease Vi at this point? It was too late to agree to sell to a couple of dead men. Or to offer her job back. Vi would never believe that Chase and Anna would keep quiet if she let them go, or give her time to get away and disappear.

"Start walking." Vi jerked the gun up and down. "To the water." She stood aside to let them pass.

The knife and the heavy rolling pin lay between them, forgotten by Vi after she'd switched to the pistol.

Chase motioned for Anna to go first. When Anna was a few feet from her, Chase pretended to stumble, stooped to catch herself, grabbed the rolling pin, and heaved it at Vi.

Her aim was good. She hit Vi on the side of the head and this time Vi went down. She clutched her head with both hands.

Anna swooped and grabbed the gun from the ground.

"I guess you ladies are doing all right," said a male voice behind them.

Chase turned to see Detective Olson, his own gun drawn, flanked by several uniformed policemen, all aiming at Violet Peters.

"You heard?" Chase asked.

"I heard every word. It was very clever of you to guide us here. Ms. Bjorn was reinterviewed an hour ago and she told us that the woman she'd seen at Gabe's condo was 'that other nice girl'—not the owner, the other one, she said.

"The lab has already checked out the buttons. Ms. Peters ordered them, always from the same place, so they're quite distinctive. And she must not sew them on very securely, because they apparently tend to fall off easily. We found at least one at each crime scene."

Vi was helped to her feet, then handcuffed. The hot glares she was throwing the policemen, and one policewoman, were almost enough to melt their metal badges.

"They said they'd pay me," Vi muttered, to no one in particular. "They never paid me for anything. It was hard putting those rats there. After all the risk I took, they acted like they didn't have to do anything for me. They owed me. They owed me money and a job. They both cheated me!"

Julie, Anna, and Chase sat on Chase's balcony, each wrapped in a thick woolen blanket. The old-fashioned globe streetlamps glowed, casting golden pools on the sidewalk below them, where shoppers, wrapped in heavy jackets, hurried through the chilly night. The three women sipped goblets of dark red wine and nibbled Anna's latest creation, dessert bars that tasted like donuts. She hadn't decided what to call them yet and Julie said she hadn't decided if she liked them. To help make up her mind, she reached for a third one from the copper tray on the low table next to her.

Quincy nestled in Chase's lap, purring so loudly that some of the pedestrians below glanced up when they passed by.

Anna ran her hands over the smoothness of the new blue marble rolling pin Julie had surprised her with tonight. She laid it on the table next to her with a smile.

"What do you think of Inger?" Chase asked. She had hired the young woman while Anna was in Woodstone, Connecticut, for a rest and recuperation, visiting her old friend Alice Slocum. Alice was the secretary for the police department there and had a friend named Gigi who furnished them with delicious meals from her Gourmet Delite catering service.

"She seems capable. I'm sure she'll do well."

"I feel bad about it, but I asked Niles how to run a background check on her. She checks out fine."

"Niles? You're on a first-name basis now?" Julie smiled. "What happened to Mike? Is he Dr. Ramos now?"

Chase hesitated. "Nooo, not exactly."

"You're stringing both of them along?"

"Not stringing along! I'm just not dating either one exclusively."

"It doesn't hurt to take your time," said Anna, "or to keep your options open."

"At least neither one of them is anything like Shaun Everly."

"Is he still around?" Julie asked. "I never got to meet the cad."

"No, he's gone back to Chicago. I found the deposit slip, finally. I sent a note to his uncle, accompanied by a copy of the evidence that he was the one stealing from the restaurant, not me. His uncle is bringing charges. Last I heard, he was in jail and no one had posted bail for him. Detective Olson has a friend on the force there and he said he'd keep me updated. I can't wait to find out the outcome of the trial."

"Sometimes the justice system does dispense justice," Anna said.

Julie nodded in agreement. "You were talking about keeping your options open, Grandma," she said. The light from inside Chase's apartment caught Julie's mischievous smile as she turned her head toward Anna. "Is Bill Shandy still on the fence?"

"I thought you'd never ask." Anna reached into her pocket and fumbled under the blanket for moment. When she brought her left hand up, a brilliant diamond winked in the light on the ring finger.

Quincy raised his head as a shard of reflected light from the ring ran across his face. He gave the ring a glance, then, seeming content, lowered his head and resumed purring.

RECIPES

HULA BARS

Oven: 375
Yield: 36 small dessert bar squares
or 18 dessert bars

Crust:
- ½ cup melted margarine
- ½ cup brown sugar, firmly packed
- 1 cup all-purpose flour
- ½ teaspoon vanilla extract
- ½ teaspoon coconut extract

Filling:
- 2 eggs
- 1 cup brown sugar, firmly packed
- 2 tablespoons all-purpose flour
- ½ teaspoon baking powder

½ teaspoon vanilla extract
½ teaspoon coconut extract
¼ teaspoon salt
1⅓ cups (1 package) walnut chips
½ cup dried pineapple
½ cup coconut, lightly packed

Topping:
¼ cup powdered sugar

Preheat oven to 375 degrees F (190 degrees C).

Spray Pam on sides and bottom of 8x8 baking pan.

Melt the margarine. You can use a glass measuring cup and the microwave.

In a smallish to medium bowl, stir together brown sugar and flour. Stir in the margarine and extracts. Press into the bottom of the prepared pan.

When the oven is preheated, bake the crust for 15 minutes.

While the crust bakes, prepare the filling. In a medium bowl, beat the eggs until frothy.

In a small bowl, stir together the brown sugar, flour, baking powder, extracts, and salt. Stir this into the eggs.

Mix in the walnuts, pineapple, and coconut. Spoon this over the crust and return the pan to the oven.

Bake 20–25 more minutes, or until a toothpick comes out clean. Cool on a rack. Cut into 36 bite-size squares or 18 bars. Put them on a preparation plate and dust with powdered sugar. Transfer to serving plate or storage container.

KITTY PATTIES

Yield: 8 small patties

½ pound ground beef
½ pound ground turkey
4 tablespoons low-salt chicken stock
½ cup oatmeal or 1 instant packet
4 eggs

Mix meat and broth, then add oatmeal and egg. Make into 8 small patties.

Broil 1 or 2 at a time, leaving them fairly rare.

Allow to cool, then serve.

You can keep some in the refrigerator for 3 days at the most, but only if the meat is very fresh.

Freeze the other patties until ready to use, up to 4 months.

Janet Cantrell is the Agatha Award–nominated author of the Fat Cat Mysteries. She and her husband live in Tennessee.

OUT OF CIRCULATION
- A Cat in the Stacks Mystery -

Small-town librarian Charlie Harris and his Maine
coon cat, Diesel, are famous all over Athena, Mississippi, for their charming Southern manners and
sleuthing skills. When a tiff between Athena's richest
ladies ends with one of them dead, it's up to Charlie
and his feline friend to set the record straight before
his own life is stamped out.

**"James should soon be on everyone's
favorite list of authors."**
—Leann Sweeney, author of the Cats in Trouble Mysteries

FROM *NEW YORK TIMES* BESTSELLING AUTHOR

Miranda James

- The Cat in the Stacks Mysteries -

MURDER PAST DUE
CLASSIFIED AS MURDER
FILE M FOR MURDER
OUT OF CIRCULATION

Praise for the Cat in the Stacks Mysteries

"Courtly librarian Charlie Harris
and his Maine coon cat, Diesel,
are an endearing detective duo.
Warm, charming, and Southern as the tastiest grits."
—Carolyn Hart, author of the Bailey Ruth Mysteries

"An intelligent amateur sleuth with a lovable sidekick."
—*Lesa's Book Critiques*

facebook.com/TheCrimeSceneBooks
penguin.com